Stephen's Light

Stephen's Light

by E. M. ALMEDINGEN

Martha Edith Almedingen

HOLT, RINEHART AND WINSTON
New York   Chicago   San Francisco

CONTENTS

19518

PREFATORY NOTE

THE city in *Stephen's Light* is a composite picture of a late mediaeval town. Its beginnings may be found in my earlier book *The Inmost Heart,* though here, in *Stephen's Light,* an archbishop occupies the palace once owned by the duchess, and the Island, the monks having gone, now belongs to the ladies of an abbey. The landscape of hill and lake, street and square, palace and cathedral is indeed the same, not so the climate informing it, because the story belongs not to the twelfth but to the late fifteenth century when a renascence made itself felt not only in the field of arts and humanities but also in a burgher's kitchen equipment and a weaver's demand for an increased wage.

In what concerns the present occupants of the Island, the framework of their charter is borrowed from what is extant of the records of the Stefankloster in Augsburg, founded in A.D. 968. That charter incorporated a clause about the candidates having to produce proofs of six generations of nobility. Strictly speaking, the Augsburg ladies were not nuns though the head had the right to style herself "abbess." It was a voluntary foundation for daughters of noble houses, who might (though there is no evidence that they did) return to the world and marry. The house had considerable possessions in Augsburg and elsewhere. The ladies retained the enjoyment of their income and lived under a modified Benedictine rule. One Anna von Harrsh-Almedingen, who died in 1488, was abbess there.

Alice Chester of Bristol is an historical person; the builder's account for the house she had built in Bristol has recently come to light. Apart from her, the other characters are imaginary, and the Abbey of Our Lady and St. Matthias, the Apostle, is fictitious, though the picture of the daily life of the ladies is drawn from contemporary records. Documents of the Hanseatic League dating back to the fifteenth century show that there were women like Sabina who played an active part in commerce.

E. M. ALMEDINGEN.

PART I

"Whose Heart in My Heart?"

"JESU, MARY, but such things can't be allowed to happen!"

Her mother's shrill voice reached Sabina in the herb garden. She raised her head and looked towards the house. The servant girl, her thin roughened hands deep in the purple scatter of betony, spoke in a tautened voice:

"Ah, dear, whatever could have happened?"

And she got up hurriedly, clumsily, when Sabina's grey-sleeved arm shot out.

"It wouldn't concern you," she spoke harshly. "There's the clary for you to gather." She glanced at the basket on the ground. "How badly you've picked the mint, Helga! My mother will be angry. She likes her herbs tidy."

The maid mumbled an apology, and Sabina watched her move on to a patch further down where, with the pear trees in the background, clary, fennel and other herbs rioted together. Rue they must not forget, and a handful of smallage to mix with the parsley, everything to be pounded together with a little ginger and two dozen eggs. Two dozen eggs which must be broken—broken, thought Sabina. Of course, you had to break the eggs to make the arboulastre. But what was it that should not be allowed to happen?

"Mind you pick the smallage carefully, Helga."

Between her and the house the mossy path gleamed under the sunlight, but she must not go back to the house until she had finished gathering the herbs. Yet Sabina stood idly, a sprig of mint crushed between her fingers. They were in May, she remembered, with things growing and spreading in the garden, and the chickweed and goose grass invading the little patch where marigolds would soon be in bloom. She moved past the clumps of gooseberries, to a small clearing where she could see a corner of the yard, and there was old Bruno's mule, his nose buried in a sack of corn. Bruno must have brought them a message from the Lady. Did they want a bolt of black serge for new habits, or what? Surely, Bruno could have brought no message to make her mother raise her voice in distress.

Here was Helga, the basket full, and Sabina took it from her. They would have an arboulastre for supper after the new French receipt Richard had brought, but he would not be there to eat it. He was on the Island, he had gone to see the Lady on some business or other. . . .

"Now go and get two dozen eggs and be careful over that step in the dairy. You'll be beaten if you break the eggs again." The words were harsh, not so the look that accompanied them, and the girl ran, her tawny hair shining, her bare legs grass-stained. She would run into the kitchens, Sabina thought, and see old Bruno and hear . . . What would the girl hear? Here Sabina saw the back door open. Her mother came out, the coif awry, wisps of pale hair about her forehead, a fat, red-cheeked woman who looked at her daughter and the pear trees with clouded eyes.

"Oh Sabina . . . Sabina . . ."

Now she knew that a disaster had happened. She had been wrong in feeling happy. She remembered a fearful, un-May-like storm of the night before, and it was easy to imagine the guesthouse on the Island struck by lightning. She took a few steps forward. Her mother seemed to be standing very far away and the sunlit path looked as dark as a tunnel.

"Richard?" Sabina's dry lips moved at last. "Is it Richard, Madam?"

Her mother neither moved nor spoke.

Within a splintered instant Sabina remembered that her wedding-day was but a fortnight distant. Scented rushes would be spread on all the floors of the house, and she would wear her new white kirtle embroidered with silver vine leaves. At least, she had thought she would wear it. She steeled herself for another effort:

"Dead? Is he dead, Madam?"

"I wish he were," her mother cried. "Jesu, Mary, that such a calamity should have happened to us! He has run away with Dame Adela."

Sabina heard the words very clearly, and there came such a drought into her mind that she knew she could not cry. She stared at the red-winged butterfly vanishing in a cloud of pear blossom. She was aware of the sense of bruised herbs all about her. She saw her mother's old-fashioned, long-pointed toes peep from under the hem of ample brown skirts. The moss-embroidered path glinted with a mocking intensity. All of it Sabina perceived, dully aware that she must seek refuge in small, inconsequential things

if but to forget the ghastly drought in her mind. Anna spoke
again:

"Stop crushing the herbs, child, and come in."

[2]

Now it was afternoon. Sunlight flung its pale-gold loz-
enges on the bare floorboards. Crumbs were scattered all
over the long narrow table, and someone, in passing, must
have twitched at the cloth because it lay, a cream-coloured
tumble, on the floor. No servants were called in to clear
away the trenchers and beakers. People must have eaten
and drunk at that table, but Sabina could not tell. She sat
in a corner, her shoulders pressed against the hard wain-
scot, her eyes bent. The place was full of voices, and they
seemed to reach her from a great distance, and that was
absurd, the room being far from spacious. It was also
strange that they should all be angry with her for having
said:

"But it's happened. It's done. It can't be undone."

"Hold your tongue," her father had then shouted at her,
and now Sabina wished she might leave the room, but she
had no strength to move: she felt as limp as a willow switch
soaked too long in the water.

It seemed to matter little that Richard had committed an
enormity by running away with a nun from the Island.
They acknowledged it for a grave trespass but they knew
that other people would deal with it. It mattered greatly
that Conrad was in disgrace. For a rich mercer's only child
to be jilted by a mere foreigner was something that brushed

against the honour of the city. Richard, though in the employ
of the Hansa and with roots of his own at Lübeck, came
from Troyes. They supposed him to be the subject of the
French king, whose war with England was indeed over, but
whoever heard of any redress being obtained from that
king? It was difficult enough to see justice done in the
courts of the Empire, and what chance would Conrad have
in a foreign country? Moreover, that handsome young villain was known to have had a lawyer's training. Here a
pause fell, and then old Canon Hugo from the cathedral
stared at the horn cup between his thin blue-veined hands
and murmured:

"I wish, Master Conrad, you had never sent that young
man to the Ladies' Island."

Conrad's well-fleshed face went as crimson as the gown
he wore.

"I did it to oblige the ladies. They wanted to save on
attorney's fees. So off I sent him—with three bolts of best
violet cloth for their Lenten hangings—as a gift, of course."

Excited murmurs rippled up and down the room. The
men leant forward, the women sucked in their lips and gave
a tug or two to their wimples.

"What was it all about?" came the choral question.

"A great to-do over Dame Melburga's dowry," Conrad
replied and paused with the air of a man reluctant to say
more, but they urged him on, and Sabina knew they now
wanted to hear about Dame Melburga's dowry. The disaster was differently coloured for each of them, she felt. There
was her mother bewailing the disgrace and fussing over the
complications woven into the cancelling of the marriage-
feast. There was her father angrily aware that the lowest

scum in the city would be busily and happily prattling about the affair for weeks to come. And there were the kindred and the acquaintance most concerned with the dishonour meted out to the city. But nobody, not even her mother, thought that it mattered because two young people had kissed and loved, and hoped for a heaven of their own. Here Sabina drew a sharp breath. Of such things she must not think at all because they hurt beyond wounding.

"Well," Conrad began, "Dame Melburga comes from Brunswick, and the young scoundrel has friends there. Her father killed a cousin in a brawl, and the Duke has outlawed him. All his estates being forfeit, Dame Melburga's annual rents have ceased, and by all accounts her father has taken service under the Swedish king. So the Lady called the chapter together, and that day it blew fit to fell a tree, and she told me that the roof of the chapter-house had not been mended since the great gale last winter. Twice, if not three times, did she mention that roof to me. Ah, but the Lady is clever." Here Conrad paused to enable everybody to agree with him.

"So there was a lot of shuffling about before the ladies could settle down—what with the pigeons' droppings all over the floor, and the wind and the rain coming in through the roof, and the benches being moved this way and that way. Then Dame Lucia produced the evidences of Dame Melburga's dowry, and that started an argument because the papers had been found in a walnut coffer, and the Lady said that all the evidences should be kept together in a chest in the treasuress's office, and someone remembered that the key of the chest had been borrowed and never returned, and they argued so much that they came to the real matter with their minds full of the Lady's homily about the untidiness in the house. In the end the ladies heard all about the fishing and hunting rights commuted to so many vats of wine, firkins of herrings, bolts of black cloth, and some of that cranberry preserve they make in Brunswick, and they all agreed it was a matter for the courts, and the Lady knew of nobody likely to be of use to them in Brunswick until that young man turned up on the Island fully ten days ago. Yes, I did send him because she had asked for help, and I knew he was at home in legal matters."

"We have able lawyers in the city who might have handled the matter for the Lady," grumbled Hugo the mercer. "Cheese-paring, I call it."

"And what business had they to let the young man into the cloisters?"

"Always trying to make a dime go as far as a ducat!"

"Dame Adela was neither treasuress nor chambress. He should never have met her at all. How did he contrive it? Gossip. Doesn't the Lady say anything about it in her letter?"

"No, she doesn't." Conrad stared at the parchment on the table and read aloud:

"Since it was on your recommendation that one Richard of Troyes, in the employ of the Hansa, had gained admittance to our Island, we hold you responsible for the grevious outrage by him committed. Dame Adela was so steadfast in her religious profession that none but the evil one could have enticed her away from the enclosure . . ." and the barbed phrases continued weaving one threat after another: the Lady would write to the Archbishop, the king of France, the Emperor and, finally, to the Pope. Dame

Adela's father was of English birth; some of her dowry came as a revenue from certain mills and saltings in Essex, and the Prioress of St. Helen's in London was a dear friend of the Lady. The letter ended with a sharply worded claim for damages all the more alarming for being unspecified.

Conrad came to the end and swept the wine-stained parchment off the table.

"Let her write to the Pope," he said hoarsely. "Would such a thing have happened if she kept her house in order?"

"And never another Christmas offering will they get from us," cried Anna. "Not even a rotten fig shall we send them! Enticing Dame Adela from the enclosure indeed! what business had the Lady to allow a stranger into the cloister? She should have discussed the matter with him in the parlour, with a senior lady present. But is there any seemliness left in those places today? And now what am I to do with the mutton hams and the gingerbread and roast apples for the paupers' dole at the feast? There'll be no feast now but the poor will come just the same, and how could we refuse a promised dole? And what is going to happen to the marriage-contract? Good parchment does not grow on currant bushes!"

From Dame Melburga and the cranberry preserve of Brunswick, from Dame Adela and the mills and saltings in Essex, they turned their attention to the pauper dole and the marriage-contract.

"Master Albert will see to it for you."

"Yes, and wheedle a fat fee, too! Ah those lawyers! Always battening on people's misfortunes!"

Here, Sabina ceased to listen. Suddenly and sharply she remembered Dame Adela's cherry-coloured mouth and cool grey eyes, the grace of high breeding in every bone and muscle. There was something she had once heard about Dame Adela, some furtive whispers among the ladies that it was not very wholesome for anyone to see visions in such perilous, heresy-stained days as theirs were. Had Dame Adela ever seen a vision? Sabina could not tell but she knew that Dame Adela's father was a distant kinsman to the English king. Yet she had chosen to elope with a man who, whatever his brilliant promise, had neither birth nor property. Here Sabina clenched her small fists together. She must stop thinking, and she must say something lest the chill in her heart and the darkness in her mind were to overwhelm her utterly. So she said:

"But it's done. It's happened. It can't be undone."

They stared at her.

"It's all your own fault. You'd have held the man if you'd any wits about you."

"Think of the disgrace!"

"Now it'll be the Island for you, or else the Carmelites up the hill."

"But what are we to do with the paupers' dole?" Anna wanted to know again, and Conrad turned on her.

"It's your doing," he thundered. "You would have the girl sent to the Island to learn her letters. Well, she's learned them finely. What man wants a clerk for a wife? Richard must have got scared of the wench—"

"Dame Adela couldn't be illiterate," Anna was quick to point out but Conrad's anger at once silenced her. Now, under the dark raftered ceiling, anger moved in thick waves, slurring the speech and sharpening the gesture until old Canon Bruno spoke conciliatingly:

"Now, now. . . . The girl's right. It's all sad enough and it can't be undone, and these are grim enough days for us all. Peasants in constant revolt up and down the Empire, and much heresy, too. And here, in our city, these weavers dissatisfied with their wages, and what with the printing of books and the infidel Turk having come so near . . ." the old man went on in the querulous manner of those who are eager to condemn the present because of yesterday's vanished grace. "It would be best to give your daughter to God, Conrad."

But Sabina rose, curtseyed, and looked at her father.

"Sir, we should be given time to think about it. Can I be certain that I am called to such a life? I know there are some ladies on the Island who should never have gone there—" she broke off, blushed her deepest, wildest crimson, moved to the door and closed it on the heightened bourdon of angry voices.

"Called to such a life? What's the matter with the girl?"

"Learnt her letters, has she? Yes, and a few other things as well!"

"I heard that the Dominicans at Nüremberg have lost two lawsuits running, gossip. Why, they'll be glad to have Sabina's dowry."

"Send her to the Carmelites. They'll beat the nonsense out of her!"

"Ah, her dowry! Two dozen shifts of the finest Louvain linen we were giving with her."

"The Carmelites will need none of those shifts."

"Take a stick to her, Conrad, and never trust a foreigner again."

"You're right, gossip. There was a fellow from Antwerp

who cheated me over twenty bolts of Brabant cloth. He said that the colour was all the fashion. I should have known better. Nobody wears yellow today."

"The young man's a fool as well as a scoundrel. You should see Sabina's dowry chests, and he won't get as much as a horn spoon with a runaway nun."

Sabina heard none of it. The narrow spiral stairway behind her, she reached her room, its two irregular windows set between the high gables. The maids had not done their day's business. The lid of a chest stood upright, and a string of finely carved jasper beads ran down the length of crimson petticoat half-pulled out of the chest. Sabina stared at the petticoat and then crouched low on the cradled floorboards. Presently, the sun set over her bowed head and the crumpled grey skirts here and there darkened by her tears. Shouting and bustling went on below, but Sabina heard none of it. She was conscious of nothing except that every moment brought a small separate death to her.

[3]

"Now then, girls, get you to your jobs! There's all the milk to skim and saffron to pound, and those skillets to clean, and the dear Lord knows what else besides! Now then, stop the chatter and get on with the work."

The huge cave-like kitchen smelt of new bread, smoke, spices and onions together. Beyond, stretched a warren of closets and cubbyholes, all within Hilda's small kingdom, and now, her minions set to work, she smoothed the stained drab kirtle, pushed the limp coif off her forehead, and paused, the gnarled fingers of her left hand fumbling with cherrywood beads polished by many years' use rather than by a craftsman's cunning. In her youth, Hilda used to mutter her Paters and Aves, now the words had gone from her memory, yet some comfort remained in the mere feel of the beads.

Presently they vanished in her pouch, and she waddled toward the crazily perched ladder. She must be alone for a bit, she said to herself, even though the day's work was by no means finished. There were the eggs to whip for the arboulastre and the green goose to be stuffed. Still, there was ample time for it all. The guests were still in the parlour, the mistress would not want an early supper that evening, and Sabina had gone upstairs. She would not knock at the door, Hilda thought, slowly climbing the ladder. She could always wait on the landing until she was wanted.

She reached the top and paused, trying not to pant too loudly. What a day! So much trouble falling on Stephen's Light just as though the great bell of St. Agnes' had rung right within the house—as it would ring awkward to arm and muster whenever some trouble threatened the city. Today neither Emperor nor Duke, nor yet the Turk menaced the place, but Hilda found it easy to imagine the troubled, ascending sounds ringing under the roof. Her young mistress's world was broken, and Hilda must wait outside on the landing until she was wanted.

"Oh St. Pirim," she muttered under her breath, "St. Ursula, and all the rest of you, saints of God, singing and playing on your harps and dancing on the golden floor. You've got what you wanted, and it can't matter much to you that the world's got into a mess. All the same, trouble's the spice of life, and I'm afraid I'd get bored with that golden floor—not that I'm ever likely to see it. Someone'll be sure to say, 'Ah Hilda, and what about those silver hairpins and the buckle and the embroidered veil?' Well, I can't remember it all, but never have I been light-fingered with her belongings, and that might count for something—not that I care much either way. Ah my poor little chick. . . . My poor little chick. . . .''

She waited, but no sound came from behind the door, and Hilda decided she would dare and knock once she got her inward peace back again. All the shouting and the bustling in the house had, as it were, turned her into a mean, crotchety woman, scolding and cuffing the maids, leering at the men, secreting a jug of the finest Rhenish in a place where her mistress would never find it. Now, outside Sabina's door, Hilda longed for a different, sweeter climate. She leant against the railing and kept very still. God, the Lady Mary and St. Boniface, she folded the three names into her thought. They inhabited the heaven, its pure golden floor never in need of the scrubbing brush, and they had a special place there, too, far away from the saints' singing. All was quiet where they were, the kind of quiet she sometimes felt to be in the deeps of the well in the yard. Yes, thought Hilda, quiet was a blessed thing: quietly was He born and quietly did He come even to such as she.

In a few moments she knocked, lifted the knobbly hasp, and walked in.

Sabina sat by the coffer, the string of jasper beads dangling from her hand. The crimson coverlet off the bed lay on the floor in the middle of the room, and the stuff bulged here and there. Hilda glanced at it but asked no questions.

"Your hair needs brushing, sweetheart. Let me do it for you."

Sabina asked in a leaden voice:

"Have the guests gone?"

"Not all of them."

"Anyone staying to supper?"

"Now don't you look so wild, my pretty! Who would be asked to supper this evening? Here, bend your head just a little."

"I think," Sabina said slowly, "that I am going mad. . . ."

"If you were," Hilda stooped to pick up the comb from the chest, "you wouldn't know anything about it."

"Wouldn't I?" Sabina leapt to her feet and pulled the crimson coverlet off the floor. There, tumbled, gashed from waist to hem, lay the white damask kirtle embroidered with tiny silver vine leaves.

"There," Sabina's voice shook. "Look at it! The stuff was so strong that I couldn't tear it with my fingers. I took a knife to it. Look at it!"

Hilda, the ivory comb held in readiness, looked at the floor. She made no comment beyond saying:

"Well, that damask might do for girdles. Now, then, my chick, let me finish your hair. There, that looks better! Put a fresh coif on, my pet. And you're as sane as I am. Any heart may get broken but it's foolish to throw the pieces away. You keep them, my sweet, and in God's good time they may come together again."

"And what do you know of that?"

Hilda put away the comb, stooped and tossed the crimson coverlet over the ruined wedding-kirtle.

"What do I know of it? Well may you ask, my darling, seeing that I have hardly a tooth left in my head. But I was eighteen once, and the fellow swore he loved me. A shepherd he was in a great lord's service round by Augsburg. It was his way with the reed that bewitched me, and his eyes were so blue that I felt drowned in them. Then he went off to fight somewhere—I can't remember. It was long before the Turk's day, my pet. He may have been killed. I never knew. But it was good at the time. It came and it went."

"Suppose," Sabina's voice fell to a tautened whisper, "suppose they were to catch him—"

"He's clever enough to get off with a fine."

"But—but she—"

"Ah, that's a differently made fishing-net. She'd get her deserts all right. I have heard folks say that runaway nuns may be buried alive or burned, but I am not sure. It all seems such a muddle, my darling. By all we hear, those holy ladies may do anything they please in their cloisters, but let one of them get out, and everybody's hand is against her. Say what you like, my chick, that girl must have had pluck."

"Stop," Sabina shouted, and Hilda bit her lip. She knew she had made a mistake but she was not going to unsay the words she had spoken. She closed the lid of a coffer and tidied away some odds and ends of finery. Her eyes fell on a cobweb above the door lintel when Sabina said in a much calmer voice:

"There's talk about me becoming a nun."

Hilda brushed away the cobweb.

"Didn't you hear what I said?"

"It isn't for me to speak of such matters."

"Why do you dislike the ladies? You thought my father was wrong to send me to the Island, didn't you?"

"The master knew best."

"What have you got against them? They've never done you any wrong. Why, Dame Elizabeth sent you such a pretty cross made of boxwood after I'd told her how well you looked after me."

"I've still got it," admitted Hilda.

"Well, then, why must you make a face sour enough to make the milk turn?"

"You listen to me, my pet. My father was a good carpenter, and he taught me that every tool has its proper use. You can't rivet two pieces of wood with a plane, and you don't polish timber with a gauge. And that's how I see the matter. God can't truly be served by hours of mouthed psalms and prayers, your hands fondling a lapdog and your mind set on lechery and gluttony. Did the Lady Mary mince about Nazareth in embroidered shoes, rings on her hands and scent all over her veil? And I reckon that she's a woman who served her God to the uttermost. But you'd better forget what I've said. Some pious folks might tell you that it smacks of heresy—not that I care much. Now then, all set and tidy you are. Why, what's the matter?"

"Leave me," Sabina said through her tears.

Hilda went, her heart heavy. Once again she must have said the wrong thing. That was always her misfortune—to mean well with all her heart and to fail in her speech. She supposed she should have remembered that Sabina knew the ladies on the Island and loved them, but she, Hilda, had no use for them, and not an honest man in the city but shared her opinion that the religious folks had fallen very low. Ah well, once again she must leave it all to God and the Lady Mary, she thought, climbing down the ladder, but it was sad that such trouble should have come to Stephen's Light, and she would have been wiser to stay below in the kitchens. The eggs to whip and the goose to stuff —that was her business.

[4]

Stephen's Light stood in its own spacious grounds, the cobbled forecourt separated by a high wall from the narrow street. Conrad's grandfather had built it but the name was of much older lineage than the house. Pious folk in the city would have it that the house stood on the same spot where —generations back—the city's greatest sinner, about to commit a heinous crime, had seen a great light breaking right over his head and so moving him that forthwith the sinner vanished in the saint—in less time, as it were, than it takes to stone a cherry. The legend was pleasing. It remained no more than a legend for the great majority. There was neither shrine nor relic of any such saint in the city, and hagiography, however fabled in detail, must needs have a grain of truth for its beginning. The city, proud of its cathedral and devoted to its genuine shrines, liked to sift fable from fact, and most people remembered well that a hovel had once stood there, owned by one Stephen, a candlemaker, who got expelled from his gild and came to a sorry end for mixing cheap tallow with honest wax and selling his wares at exorbitant prices. They duly hanged him in the square for this and other trespasses, and the hovel was burnt down. Later, it was easy to imagine lights and sounds round about the spot, and Conrad's grandfather, in between buying and selling cloth, helped to extend the haunted area by carefully detailed stories of his own invention. In the end, he was able to purchase the land for less than the price of one bolt of Brabant cloth. He was a burgher of such importance that the sordid story of a common felon was soon elbowed out by wholly different themes. Fantastic rumours of fabulous wealth gradually spread all over the city.

He cared nothing for rumours. He was busily building.

Wars might rage, weird flames be seen across evening skies, ships laden with rare cargoes founder on the world's seven seas, murder and brigandage fret the face of the Empire, and the great bell of St. Agnes' ring awkward to arm and muster because of apprentices rising against their masters, but Conrad's grandfather, having once begun to build, could not stop. Stephen's Light grew up and up, spread right, spread left, the great flagged court in front was walled off the street, the grounds behind—a modest enough patch at the time of the purchase—now sloped right down to the meadows held by the monks of St. Eugene, and the city acknowledged itself to be proud of the house.

Its foundations were of pale stone quarried in the north of Italy and brought over at great expense. Half-way up, the stone gave way to stout timber felled in the Black Forest. The great gabled porch, facing the forecourt, was carved all over with mermaids, fishes and curiously plumaged birds, all painted green, silver, blue and crimson. The teasingly irregular windows came to be glazed some time before the Archbishop thought that he could afford the luxury in his own palace up the hill. In brief, by Conrad's time, Stephen's Light stood for an honourable landmark. In hostelries, at the market, by the great West door of the cathedral, people might be heard saying weightily:

"Why, surely, the Emperor must be in the right about Burgundy. I heard them say so at Stephen's Light."

Or else:

"Now, neighbour, mind you have a good key fitted to your salt cupboard. They say at Stephen's Light that the tax is almost certain to rise."

From France and the Low Countries, from Italy and England, men rode to Stephen's Light to sell stuffs, and women of the city came to buy them. The women, clutching the embroidered pouches at their girdles, stopped outside the wide, low-ledged window to the left of the porch, there to choose, to haggle, and to purchase. The men, their horses left in a hunchback's care, went in through the porch to a big square room at the back where, in the scent of spiced wine and dried verbena, they discussed business, political news, and any other matter that caught at them during their wanderings across Europe and beyond.

Some people in the city thought that Conrad's gold was kept in the vault below that particular room. Others alleged that it was at Augsburg in the care of a great banking house, but nobody knew for certain, and it seemed enough to be proud of Stephen's Light where the floor rushes never stank, the leather curtains were never warped, and the hearths hardly smoked no matter how madly the wind might ride, and where the orchard had a strip fenced off for the pigstyes. Conrad's grandfather used to follow Noah's custom in the matter of pigs and poultry, but Conrad never

allowed them under his roof, and the air in the house remained pure enough except when the kitchen folk burnt
the fat, or forgot that the fish bought on Monday could not
keep fresh till Saturday, and then Anna scolded and had
sweet herbs scattered all over the passages.

They were all proud of Conrad. They could not say they
were proud of Anna. They took her for granted. Tall and
portly, she was as good as bread and as dull as unseasoned
cabbage soup. Pious practices, needlework and the unceas-
ing duties in the stillroom and the dairy, were her pattern.
She loved her husband, food, clothes and Sabina, in that
order. Yet she had a quality of her own. She said little to
strangers and never gossiped outside the house, but her
presence was felt under that roof, and people cleared the
way for her as, accompanied by a maid and a serving-man,
Anna went to mass or to market. For all her dullness, she
was one of the veins in the heart of Stephen's Light.

Sabina, for all the reticence developed by upbringing and
custom, knew that. There was a heart beating at Stephen's
Light. The rhythm seldom, if ever, found expression in
caresses. You rose from your bed to fill the hours with
clearly appointed purposes. You went to sleep once all
those purposes were accomplished. But at Stephen's Light,
the most prosaic purpose seemed informed with a peculiar
quality. Water tasted pure and bread sweet under that roof.
To Sabina, all of it came early and without words.

Often enough she would escape into the orchard. Past a
clump of gnarled pear trees, where white violets grew in
March and April, she slipped through a gate into the
monks' meadows and there felt the wind from the lake
brush against her face. She ran down and down until the

landscape lay before her—the thickly wooded scarf of the
hills to the north, the great sheet of the lake and, midway,
as though flung on its blue breast, the grey-white buildings
on the Ladies' Island leapt into gold and rose when the sun
happened to slant across them.

Such was Sabina's world and, once she turned away from
the lake, she would see the irregular clusters of green roofs
and red roofs climbing on and on as though they were in a
hurry to get closer to the great twin towers of the cathedral,
which, as Sabina had been told, was one of the loveliest in
the whole of Christendom. She knew it and stayed unmoved
by the knowledge: such proud heritage seemed too vast and
remote for her to encompass. Stephen's Light offered no
grandeur of soaring pillars—but it was a home, a heart-
beat and a promise. The most secret matter of her life was
woven into its stone and timber. Early enough she learnt
that a bridegroom would one day be chosen for her from
among her father's wide acquaintance. But no bridegroom
could ever rob her of the place: she was an only child, and
all the delights of Stephen's Light were hers inalienably.

There, you stumbled on unexpected steps and came on
corners which breathed with enchantment. Stone and wood,
angle and line, all satisfied deeply. Ornamentation went no
further than the richly carved porch, and the very bareness
of the interior pleased Sabina. Conrad never grudged costly
stuffs for his wife's gowns and veils, but he refused to drape
either wall or window or floor. Travellers' stories made
Anna long for rare tapestries, for benches and trestles
made important and easeful by coverlets of embroidered
silk and branched velvet.

"No," Conrad said. "This is an honest burgher's home,

not a prince's palace or a shameful den in the Painted Street. I'll have no silly fripperies under my roof."

Sabina agreed with him. The beauty of the rooms was to her increased by their severity. But Anna must needs have that small hunger satisfied in some other fashion. She had a secret hoard of unimportant coins saved from the market money, and she made occasional furtive purchases, haggling with a pedlar in a corner of the yard, and later hiding her spoils in a special coffer on the little landing right under the gables: a piece of pale Italian silk with a deep golden fringe, a length of nacarat velvet, a square of some bright blue stuff worked all over with tiny silver stars, all put away in the oaken coffer, once a part of Anna's bridal portion when she left Mainz to marry Conrad.

"All of it is to be yours when you marry," she whispered to Sabina, her fat face flushed deep pink from bending, and Sabina thanked her politely though she did not think that the gaily coloured hoard could invite the least stir of rapture. The most gorgeous stuffs faded, got torn or stained, were worn out and cast aside. The house was different.

She loved it passionately. She loved the great room at the back with its thick-legged oak table, its high-backed benches, and the small stone statue of St. Sturm in a corner. That room was to her forbidden, and once Conrad cuffed her soundly for hiding behind a bench. An unlucky sneeze betrayed her, a spare old man in a lavender gown and a bright red liripipe shook his head at her, and Conrad threatened:

"I'll whip you hard next time you do such a thing. What will the Archbishop's grace think of such behaviour?"

Sabina, greatly daring, looked up. The old man smiled

at her, and she returned the smile, but Conrad would not relent, and the great room remained forbidden. Yet its windows faced the orchard, and most men were in the habit of talking fit to deafen anyone. Sabina discovered soon enough that she could crouch outside, right under the windows, none remarking her. So she came to hear about a strange new law which required all merchants sending their stuff to England to include four bow staves with every ton of merchandise.

"I've written to Riga and to Lübeck," Conrad was shouting. "We shall fight against such a law. Let the Wool Staple in England see to it! Why should we be expected to help the English in their trouble? Their quarrel with France is none of our concern. By the Lord's Cross, gossips, what with tolls, taxes, brigandage and piracy, there's no life for an honest merchant today! We may all end in gobbling raw herrings in some wretched hovel or other!"

Sabina had never heard of Riga or Lübeck. She did not know where England was, but Conrad's allusion to herrings eaten in a hovel smote at her with a flail. She knew well enough what hovels were like; there were many more than could be counted both inside and outside the city walls, filthy, mean shacks they were, and men and women who came in and out looked hardly human to her, and their children ran about almost naked throughout the four seasons of the year. That day Sabina was troubled. She dared not ask questions of Hilda or Hugo, still less of the maids. She walked round and round the house, pressing her hot palms against the smooth cool stone. In the evening, her tear-stained cheeks betrayed her to Anna.

"Is your stomach upset?"

Sabina shook her head, and suddenly her fears tumbled out in a clumsily worded spate.

"You foolish child! Who could have told you such nonsense? Did you meet some saucy apprentice on your way to mass this morning?"

"No, Madam."

"Who was it then? Surely, you could not have invented such a story! For people like us to live in a hovel! Oh Sabina!"

"I heard my father say so, Madam."

"What? Have you been eavesdropping again?"

"No, Madam," Sabina went on, unashamed of her fib; "he spoke so loudly that I heard him in the forecourt."

"Ah well, that's just his way of talking. Remember, nobody knows what is going to happen—but there's always God's providence. Of course, your father has many things to worry about . . ." here Anna paused as though she were searching for apt and convincing words but, none coming to her, she ended rather haltingly by repeating: "Nobody knows what is going to happen, but there's always God's providence."

Anna never knew how greatly she comforted Sabina by confirming her faith in the continuous surprise that life was to her. Nothing should ever be allowed to assail the security of Stephen's Light but, that apart, the salt of life lay in the unforeseeable. Sabina, crouching under the parlour windows, heard much about wars and wonders in foreign lands. Wars were dull and stupid, she thought, because someone always got beaten in the end, and to be beaten was surely folly. But stories of wonders flecked her mind's landscape with pinpoints of exciting light. A duke was so wicked that the very earth refused his body, and a woman in an abbey a day's journey from the city was so saintly that her prayers had brought the sap back to a withered beech. And all the stories came as grist to Sabina's mill until the morning when she heard a portly fat merchant from Chambéry tell Conrad that some brigands had robbed him on the way to Augsburg. The man added with a sigh:

"And all of it my own fault entirely. I was warned not to start on that particular day. The man knew a disaster would happen. I do wish I had listened to him."

Sabina scrambled to her feet, reached up to the broad window-sill, and shouted at the fat little man in a black jerkin and dull red hose:

"The man was a liar! Nobody know's what's going to happen," and she added as a prudent afterthought, "my mother said so."

Sabina was about eleven then. The misplaced prudence did not save her from a whipping, and she was locked up in an attic with a bowl of sour milk for the day's provender. Sabina wrenched open the casement, poured the milk down on the Frenchman's head just as he was about to cross the forecourt, and then dropped the bowl on the floor and watched the mad bustle below. Bluish-white runnels streaking the black jerkin, the little man screamed and swore in three languages, and Conrad shouted for servants to fetch cloths and hot water. Sabina moved away from the window, the whipping entirely forgotten.

Later, her parents came up. Their faces folded in gravity, they spoke of the evil one, but Sabina retorted that if she had the devil in her, she would be unable to say her prayers, and then and there she knelt on the sharp jagged shards and mumbled her Paternoster. Conrad looked uncomfortable, Anna's eyes were moist, and Hilda hurried to put ointment on the bony knees cut by the broken bowl. Sabina's triumph was heightened by a supper of roast goose with almond sauce.

The taste of the goose still upon her tongue, she felt happy. They might—and they did sometimes—use her roughly, cuff her and whip her. None the less, she mattered. Stephen's Light was her kingdom, and she loved it with a greedy, dumb adoration. Let its walls stay bare the better to set off her mother's scarlet kirtle and her father's green gown.

"Mine. . . . All mine," Sabina whispered to the cradled floorboards, the stubborn window hasps, the treacherous steep stairways.

There were other merchants' daughters leading their unremarked little lives up and down in the city, and a few among them were Sabina's playmates, sharing a doll and a ball, apples and gingerbread. There was the splendour of the Archbishop's castellated palace on the hill, the great cathedral, and always the pure magic of the lake. More immediately, there was the keen delight Sabina's amber beads afforded her, the pleasure in a new crimson hood and the small lute Conrad had brought from the Regensburg fair. Still, the hood would wear out, the beads and the lute might be broken or mislaid. Stephen's Light stood in fair weather and in foul, all of it a deeply satisfying unity—the house, the garden, the forecourt, the orchard and the slate-roofed warehouses where sunlight added glory to bolts of cloth, velvet and damask.

And on the very day when the sense of the place seemed

like wine in her veins, Sabina heard that she was going to the Ladies' Island to get her schooling, she alone of all the burghers' daughters to be thus honoured. She had indeed wondered if she might be taught her letters by someone like old Canon Albert at the cathedral, who taught the alphabet and the use of the abacus for a flagon of wine, a bag of spices, or a parcel of candles, but Canon Albert's limited services did not answer Conrad's purpose. A daughter of Stephen's Light was surely entitled to the best. The Island, he believed, could alone provide it.

Sabina had been to the Island before—for some great festivals, when she would walk behind her mother and listen to the reed-thin singing of the ladies in procession. All such occasions left behind them a jumbled sense of much bustling and giggling, the smell of hot wax, mulled wine and sweat-stained wimples, the taste of sugared almonds in Sabina's mouth and the ladies' moist kisses on her cheeks. In the late afternoon, with the great bells hushed and the important relic restored to its sanctuary, Sabina would dip her sticky fingers in the cool water of a trough, run across the smoothly grassed garth to her forbidden, tiptoe under an archway and steal a few moments of zealously unshared delight in the great northwest window where the story of St. Michael was worked out in the rare Flemish glaze, *"jeaune d'argent"* it was called, an incredible, delicate marriage of silver and gold.

Still later, at the jetty, slippery with lichen and weed, her mother and a few ladies, all flushed with too much spiced food and wine, would loiter, their shrill chatter fretting the air until it was time for the broad-bottomed barge to put out for the mainland. Far behind them, the bells from the great tower would ring farewell to the day's pious gaieties, and Sabina, her thoughts divided between the north-west window and the stuffed sturgeon, always fell asleep on the ride back to the city gates and the calm of Stephen's Light.

So she went to the Island, her mood prepared for a festival, and it shocked her not to find a single trace of it on her arrival. There were hardly any kisses and almond paste did not appear at dinner. For her snug, shuttered-in bed at Stephen's Light, with its warmly quilted coverlet of embroidered blue say, Sabina had a rough pallet on the floor, for honey-bread coarse lumpy gruel, and even baked apples tasted odd because they must be eaten on the same platter where—but a few minutes before—a piece of pickled fish had lain. In church, her small stool faced south, and she could not contemplate St. Michael's window. Soon enough, however, Sabina knew that she had no wish to contemplate it any longer: far too many discoveries came tumbling across her landscape.

She was on the Island for what schooling the ladies could give her. They were there to spend an entire and specially dedicated life, but soon enough Sabina learned that it was possible to intone *"Laudate Dominum, Omnes gentes . . ."* your left hand fondling a small, delicate lapdog and your right hand fumbling in the pouch for a comfit. It was equally possible to sit in the stall and to sleep. Yet such privileges belonged to the ladies alone. The very first time Sabina began munching a piece of bread, Dame Elizabeth's rod swished across her shoulders. It was obvious that you had to be a habited lady to indulge yourself in the least particular. Little by little, Sabina ceased to weep and to rebel.

Reading and writing were taught by Dame Elizabeth. For needlework, the little girls went to Dame Augusta. A piece of linen, rejected by the sacrist, was given to Sabina and a few simple stitches were explained, and she was left alone with her bone needle and a scatter of brightly coloured threads. She smudged the linen with charcoal in her hurry to get down to the blissful business of colour. The needle threaded with bright crimson, her mouth wide open, her brown eyes starry with pleasure, Sabina stitched away, the whole world forgotten, until Dame Augusta's dusty skirts rustled behind her.

"You'll unpick all of it at once. Six colours," she counted, a yellow thumb dabbing accusingly at the piece of linen. "Didn't I explain clearly? One colour for God's majesty, three for the Blessed Trinity, five for the holy wounds, seven for the gifts of the Holy Spirit, and nine for the angelic orders. And you go and put six colours together! Didn't I explain that even numbers are not pleasing to God by reason of the Unity being within the Trinity?"

"But, Madam, didn't Noah have the animals two by two in the ark?" Sabina ventured, and got her ears boxed twice for the temerity.

There she was, a tiny inconsequential cog in a vast machine which went on creaking month after month and year after year, part of her nation's flesh and blood, part of the society into which she was born. Once she had imagined that the ladies were separated from the common world by far more than the lake. The ladies, for all Sabina knew them to giggle and gossip and drink wine in loud gulps, had once seemed separate and exalted beings, vowed to the service of God, the Holy Lady and St. Matthias the Apostle. Yet a mere few months among them taught Sabina enough about the gulf between a true dedication and the ladies' daily use. She still supposed that their dedication was something of a matter to engage the attention of heaven, and she would picture it as a piece of virgin parchment spread on the golden floor.

Choir duties apart, the ladies' daily life was as ordinary a business as that led by anyone in the city—the only difference being that the city folk toiled all day and the ladies cut their labours to an elegant minimum.

Soon enough Sabina discovered that Dame Augusta hated Dame Elizabeth for her literary accomplishments, that Dame Cosima's gluttony had given birth to a mordant proverb, that Dame Lucia had been appointed treasuress because of her royal descent, that Dame Dorothea and Dame Hildegard had once bartered a pair of valuable gold pins to acquire two exceptionally bred lapdogs, and that Dame Blanche—for all her high antecedents—was always given uncongenial jobs because of the poor dowry she had brought. Sabina learned that all of them avoided Dame Hedwig so as not to be bored by the story of her latest vision and, finally that all of them, the ladies, the servants, the kitchen folk and the farm labourers, were afraid of and exasperated by the abbess, whose will was like a windmill in full tilt, whose whims and moods were as numerous as weeds in an ill-kept garden, and whose main preference was rooted in an unbridled passion for the past—always at the expense of the day's immediate needs.

The orchards sloped almost to the lip of the lake and one autumn afternoon, gathering walnuts, Sabina heard the scraping of oars in the rowlocks, and at once she slipped behind a generously boughed tree. Three or four ladies were coming up the path. They seemed in no hurry. They stopped. Sabina listened greedily.

"And how could I stop her, Madam?" Dame Lucia was saying plaintively. "I had the money and the list in my pouch, and I knew Dame Augusta badly needs new cloth for the hose, but the Lady would go to Master Herbert's, and now our library is enriched by yet another manuscript, and Dame Augusta may use the scullions' sacking for the hose. And your novices, Madam," she turned to Dame Elizabeth, "will be set to make endless copies. The Lady said to Master Herbert: 'I always come to your shop because you will not keep any printed books. They are a pollution to the mind and to the eye.' And the old sinner bowed! We all know of the shelves in his inner room—all crammed with volumes from Venice and Mainz, but the Lady'll never be invited into that room. Now why, may I ask, should we suffer from such a craze? Never a printed book to be seen in this house, and the money needed for household gear wasted on useless manuscripts! Of course, the man's a cheat. Being no scholar, how can the Lady tell what a manuscript is really worth?"

"What's this one about?" asked Dame Elizabeth.

"A sadly ragged parchment it looked to me, and he'd the impudence to say that it came from Monte Cassino as though they could ever have produced such rubbish! It looks a bad copy from some small house where they must have skimped on parchment, some boring hotch-potch of quotations in sixty-two chapters. The first is on charity and the second on patience. The novices will need a lot of that! I should say they'd be in their dotage by the time they've made ten copies."

"But, Madam, what happened to the rest of the money?"

"Need you ask? Of course, the Lady must call at the Golden Grape. I believe we've bought enough parchment, paper and powdered cuttlefish shell to satisfy a chancery's wants for a year. Now we shan't be able to hear ourselves speak for the scratching of quills—and all for the pleasure of the Lady who knows as much Latin as old Bruno's mule. Don't we all remember her *'In principia erunt Verbum'*— heard all the more clearly because she does enunciate perfectly? Well, I'll excuse myself from Vespers today. To go shopping with the Lady is like five Good Fridays rolled into one."

"Still," said someone, "manuscripts don't cost as much as stained glass, Madam."

"Ah indeed," sighed Dame Lucia. "That legacy left to Dame Johanna, and coming just when we needed a new roof for the chapter-house, but there! The Lady must needs invite that scoundrel from Antwerp!"

"Yet I suppose," said Dame Elizabeth, "that the northwest window is beautiful."

"It may well be," snapped Dame Lucia, "but I for one would have preferred not to get rain water and pigeondroppings all over my shoulders every time we sit in chapter."

They moved on towards the lodge gates, and Sabina picked up her basket. Maud, one of the three other girls on the Island, crept out from her own refuge.

"So you've heard it, too," she whispered to Sabina. "I suppose they'll go on quarrelling for weeks about that old manuscript. And there is the spice bill—still unpaid—not that it matters much, of course!"

Sabina stared.

"Dear Saints! If my father carried on in such a way, I'm afraid he'd come to grief."

"Ah yes," said Maud, "but he's a merchant, and it's all different. Lady Isabella knows everything will be all right. Of course, they do owe money—but it's almost impossible for lay people to sue a religious house. I've heard my father say so."

"And why should it be impossible?"

"Well, I suppose it would be rather like taking up cudgels against God."

"Then they should have no debts at all," Sabina said hotly. "When I was very little, a maid took me to the market, and I saw a small painted box, and I hadn't the money to buy it. But I took the box, and the maid told the man to come to Stephen's Light, and my father paid him and beat me for having carried away the box when I had no money. He says that honest folk always pay for what they buy."

"Oh of course," Maud said politely and pointed at the basket in Sabina's hand. "Shall we take the walnuts to Dame Anna?" she suggested, and they went up the path, the poison of an unfriendly silence between them because a burgher's child had ideas a prince's daughter could not understand.

"I hate them all here," thought Sabina savagely.

She did not, however, hate anyone for long. Many things

annoyed her, many more things jarred on her, but it was all new, and she must needs observe the new scene avidly, breathlessly. There came countless diversions from the day's routine such as furtive visits to the abbess's kitchens where dishes, never to be seen in the frater, were prepared by four fat cooks and an army of scullions, where, standing in the scent of wine, rose-water and cinnamon, Sabina could watch the whirls of almond paste, dyed green and violet, brushed over a big cake baked for Lady Isabella's dinner. Rarely enough, and always at a distance, the girls would catch a glimpse of the tall, portly woman, her great jewelled cross burning bright against the black scapular. That, however, happened seldom. Her kingdom being spacious, Lady Isabella preferred her privacies, which included a chapel. Having spent a large legacy on a stained-glass window for the church, she rarely looked at it.

Sabina failed to make an intimate friend either among the ladies or the other girls. But Dame Elizabeth at once satisfied and perplexed her. Dame Elizabeth could be severe, cold, ironic and gentle by turn, but Sabina felt drawn towards her for a reason she could not understand. She had often helped to distribute the paupers' dole outside her father's gate, chunks of maslin and pieces of salted cod, apples and bowls of unsweetened corn mush, and she had noticed the dumb pleading in the people's eyes whenever the food came to an end and the cook bluntly said there was no more to be had that day. Those people wore tatters, their faces and arms were covered with repulsive sores, and Sabina must hold a bunch of lavender to her nose when she came near them. Dame Elizabeth's veil and habit had not a darn on them, her skin reminded you of magnolia petals, her breath was sweet, and a drift of musk always came from her hands and her clothes. Yet the narrow, heavily lidded eyes were informed by something oddly akin to that hungry pleading Sabina had seen in the eyes of the poor. Sabina could not understand it at all. It seemed as though Dame Elizabeth had once longed for a carnation and been given a thistle instead.

Towards the very end of Sabina's stay on the Island, Dame Elizabeth said almost casually:

"There's a half-English novice among us. Her name is Adela, and I believe that she and I are going to be great friends."

"I am so glad, Madam," Sabina said sincerely, remembering that Dame Elizabeth's habitual reticence had won her no friends in the house.

"Thank you," and the elder woman added unexpectedly: "I rather hope to learn much from her, Sabina. She seems to stand so close to God."

Sabina's brown eyes flew wide. It was such an odd thing to hear from a nun just as though no other lady on the Island were standing close to God. Sabina waited but Dame Elizabeth wiped the quill in silence. The lesson was over, Sabina must go and occupy herself with the day's appointed stitchery, but her thoughts were still engaged with Dame Elizabeth's cryptic remarks. The hemming went crookedly, a skein of precious silver thread got mislaid, and Dame Augusta's rod came down on Sabina's shoulders more than once.

"This for negligence and that for stupidity," said Dame Augusta, adding a third stroke for good measure, and Sabina thought:

"She, at any rate, stands very far from God—and it is all very odd indeed."

A day or two before Sabina's departure, Dame Elizabeth drew her apart.

"I believe I was right about that novice, Sabina. You will understand that it is important for this house"—she blushed slightly as though hesitating about the end of the sentence. "Yes, it is important indeed to have someone with a gift of prayer."

Again she stopped, and Sabina waited politely. She almost wondered if her teacher were turning into another Dame Hedwig, whose fabled and muddled visions of angels' feet and roses falling from heaven no longer excited anyone on the Island, but it was obvious that Dame Elizabeth had no such stories to tell. Indeed, it seemed as though she regretted having said the little she had said, and all secretly Sabina considered it a piece of nonsense. She had seen Adela many a time. She was slim. She looked proud. She wore a shimmering silk veil and bangles on her delicately boned wrists. Her high origins had enabled her to come to the Island, and Sabina thought that the girl was stamped in the same mould as all the others until, on the very morning of her going back home, Sabina opened the small northeast door of the church and there, not in her stall, but in the middle of the choir, kneeling, her face upraised towards the altar, was Adela. Her face reflected a rapture beyond Sabina's comprehension. Hot and uncomfortable, she tripped away. She duly promised her prayers and a visit to Dame Elizabeth but the manner of her leave-taking was hurried and awkward. She had once imagined the matter of the ladies' dedication to be in the keeping of angels but Dame

Elizabeth's words and Dame Adela's upturned face hinted otherwise. Sabina felt so ill at ease that she must needs occupy her mind with Dame Hedwig's absurd visions and Dame Anna's capacity for consuming no fewer than eight pigeon pies at a meal. That, at any rate, was a familiar climate. It slightly shocked her but it could not bewilder her.

Adela looking as though she were holding an intimate conversation with the Creator of heaven and earth . . . Ah no. . . . Sabina preferred to forget it.

But now, with her heart's joy wrecked, she found herself remembering it.

[5]

It should never have happened in the spring with all the greening things rioting about in the garden and a secret trembling in the sky.

Sabina had always known that one day a suitable bridegroom would be chosen for her. He would take her and Stephen's Light together, and in the matter of choice her father's voice came first and last. To girls like her, marriage was primarily a contract, certainly not a business of whispers under the moonlight, drooping roses and the playing on a lute. Of course, it was a hallowed business but the legal aspect was so closely interwoven with the sacramental tissue as to appear at one with it.

One morning Sabina was helping Anna to hem a pale green kirtle she would wear on a pilgrimage to the well of the Lady of the Apple Trees, about half a day's journey from the city. Suddenly she heard voices and steps in her father's room, and one voice in particular arrested her— so vigorous, colourful and merry it rang. The pale cloth slid off her knees down to the floor.

"No," said Anna, "you must first finish the hem. And Hilda is much too busy to take you out walking this afternoon. Besides, I'll have no idleness, girl. Once the kirtle is finished, you will begin taking all the coverlets out for an airing."

"Yes, Madam."

Sabina stooped for the kirtle, re-threaded the needle, and stitched away. But the stranger's voice continued to compel her. She blushed deeply as though her face were bending over a hot cauldron. She said to herself that she was a fool to feel so troubled by a stranger's voice. Of course, the man had come to see her father on business and she might never meet him at all. Here, quite inconsequentially, Sabina thought of old Mother Gunta by the lake shore who, so they said, saw your fate in the burnt feathers of a black cockerel, and who could give shape and purpose to the future by a careful study of ashes from a may-tree fire. Were such things quite lawful? Sabina could not tell, but she knew that old Mother Gunta's wild-eyed daughter had been indicted and burnt for witchery. Sabina shivered a little.

Here she heard her father's voice lustily calling for wine, and a servant hurried along the passage. Anna stitched away. The cool room suddenly became a close dungeon. Sabina, compelling her hand to do the work, breathed hungrily. There came the sound of a window flung open, and the voices rang nearer and clearer. She heard her father's deep-throated laughter.

"Well, Richard, it's certainly good to see you. Master Albert will join us after dinner and everything will be settled. But you'd no business to go on such a voyage before coming here. You're a bad sailor, to begin with, and there are always pirates. Well, what do you think about the Turks?"

"I didn't like them at all, sir. Their business ways certainly aren't ours, and you find a man with four, five, and even six wives. And, of course, being infidels, they pay no homage to Our Lady. As to their women, why, I never met one of them face to face. . . ."

Here the door opened. Hilda came in and began mumbling a tiresome story about a vat of wine gone sour, a young pig stricken by sickness, and the goose pie for supper. Anna got up heavily and left the room. The needle jabbed Sabina's thumb. Master Albert was expected at Stephen's Light after dinner, her father had said. The lawyer's visit was more than a hint: it was an affirmation. Her eyes burning, her hands idle, Sabina sat and listened to the merry young voice speaking about the launching of several ships in Venice, the lilac gardens at Teheran, the rare fruits at a place whose name she did not know.

"Oh sir, it was good to travel so far East. I almost regret I had not gone to China."

"But he'll never go to China now," thought Sabina. "He's come to Stephen's Light, and Master Albert is expected. But I am a fool to get excited over a beautiful voice. He may well be a hunchback, with a mole on his nose, two chins, and a wart on his forehead—just like the bridegroom they got for Bertha."

The needle jabbed her forefinger. She brushed her hand

against her red sleeve and looked up to see Anna standing in the doorway, her fat face flushed, her smile honeyed.

"Go and fetch the filberts from the storeroom. We've got an important guest for dinner. Oh child, there's a blood-stain on your sleeve. Go and get tidy at once. And oh dear, you've never finished the hemming!"

"But there may be no pilgrimage," thought Sabina. Upstairs, she snatched at the round steel mirror. Her eyes were informed by a strange light and her cheeks looked crimson.

"Fool!" she stamped her foot. "It would serve me well if the man had five warts on his face!"

She changed her clothes, went downstairs, curtseyed to a pair of very slim legs in bright green hose, and sat down, her eyes bent because no girl might stare at a man unless she lodged somewhere along the Painted Street.

She forced herself to swallow the food she could not see. The room was filled with the young man's voice. Listening, Sabina imagined herself astride a palfrey, treading inlaid stone pavements under hot alien skies, fingering rare stuffs. Her eyes remained decorously lowered. Under the heavy blue kirtle her knees trembled.

"The wine, Sabina," said Conrad.

She rose, moved to the dresser and, all unseeingly, felt for the great silver flagon. Her fingers betrayed her. The flagon fell, the wine staining the kirtle and the fresh rushes at her feet. Truly, she was a sinner: one garment unfinished, another ruined, and her father's wine wantonly wasted. She stood there, dumbly conscious that she must do something and not knowing what it should be. The young man rose, moved towards her, stooped for the flagon,

and she heard his laughter above her parents' strident re-
bukes.

"My very best Rhenish, too!"

"But the flagon was so heavy, sir. Please allow me."

All at once Sabina forgot the rigorous exigencies of custom. She looked down. He, kneeling at her feet, a napkin in
his lean brown hands, looked up. The burning brown eyes
met the merry dark blue eyes. Something was asked and
answered within an instant. His youth, his beauty, his obvious delight in the business of living, Sabina was conscious
of all those and more than those. Here, her mother sent her
out of the room.

Upstairs, Sabina slipped into her Easter clothes, all pale
blue and silver, and hurried back, missing a step here and
there, and found Anna sucking a goose bone and a servant
sweeping up the wine-stained rushes.

"Oh—where is my father, Madam?"

"He's gone into the counting-house." Anna wiped her
mouth, waited for the servant to go, and scolded: "What
a poor beginning you've made, girl! Spilling your father's
best wine and then standing there like a frightened owlet!
However, it doesn't much matter seeing that things are being settled."

"Settled, Madam?"

"Yes, Master Albert has come to witness the signatures.
Your father is very pleased with the marriage-contract.
Master Richard is in the service of the Hansa for all he
comes from Troyes. Indeed, it's an excellent arrangement
all round. He knows all about your father's trade and something of the law as well, and there won't be so many fees to

pay with him about the place, and the Council are willing
to have him made a proper burgher—all on account of
your dowry, girl." Anna plunged her hand into a dish of
nuts and added, "He's coming to supper tomorrow evening
and you'll be able to talk to him a little—so long as you
keep all the proprieties in your mind." She cracked a filbert
with her still fine teeth and smiled reminiscently. "Things
have certainly changed since my young days, child. Why,
the very first time I saw your father was by the high altar at
St. Catherine's in Mainz, and of course I dared not look at
him."

Anna paused and pushed a dish of plum preserve towards Sabina.

"Eat some fruit now," she commanded. "It's good for
the bowels. Well, your father has certainly done well by
you, girl, and it won't matter much how often you see Master Richard so long as Hilda is in the room to observe proprieties. Not that there will be much time for idleness, I can
tell you—what with the bridal chests and the marriage-
feast, we'll have our hands full indeed. And that'll be a
marriage-feast for the city to remember long after your
children are dead, Sabina. Now, aren't you pleased?"

Pleased? It seemed a poor and pallid word for Sabina to
echo, and she did not echo it. She bent her head over the
plum preserve and said in a shaking voice:

"You and my father have always been good to me,
Madam."

"Yes, and you should have made a better beginning of
it," Anna reminded her again.

A better beginning? Sabina dared not tell her mother,

indeed, she dared tell nobody that the poor and clumsy beginning had been a threshold of glory for her.

Custom did not sanction, nor Sabina's scant leisure allow, many meetings with Richard. The marriage-contract, the feast and the dowry became the all-absorbing themes at Stephen's Light, where she and Richard would live once they were made man and wife. He had no permanent roots at Troyes and his employ by the Hansa would end with his marriage.

But even those brief, hurriedly snatched moments meant wealth to Sabina. Day by day, she was learning Richard. How much he had seen, how much he knew, how deeply he loved the sheer business of living! He had been to the city before, she heard, always on short, flying visits, just enough time for customer and market, a night at an inn, good sup and a rested horse at dawn to take him north or south, east or west, and every business venture of his was coloured with gaiety, zest and daring—wholly unlike the staid pattern followed by other merchants in the city. Sabina supposed it was all due to the French blood in Richard, but she was not certain, and she did not particularly wish to be certain. It was enough to have him just as he was: courteous, delicate in manner and speech, happy to be alive and, certainly, happy in Conrad's acceptance of his wooing. Deep in her own happiness, Sabina wondered if something between them had not begun in God's own thought, and sometimes she wished that Richard had been a clerk like Abélard, so that one day another Peter the Venerable might write to her, "At the day of His coming, His grace will restore him to you."

So Dame Elizabeth had once read aloud to Sabina. However, Richard was no clerk and she, Sabina, was no Heloïse and, in the place of a half-witted uncle, she had her most practical parents, and her marriage-feast certainly promised to be a nine days' wonder.

It pleased her to find Richard ready to share in all her various enthusiasms. Stephen's Light, she discovered, meant to him just what it meant to her: a warmly informed home. The city, he told her, was certainly a jewel in the Empire. It was true that Lübeck had a far better water supply and even a drainage system, but what could compare with the natural beauty of a place set between a queenly river and no less regal lake, a place, moreover, distinguished by its cathedral, its fair, its paved square, and its renowned inns? Their names rippled off Richard's tongue—the Golden Lion, the Three Falcons, the Black Eagle, the Twelve Apostles—

"Stop, stop," laughed Sabina. "Why, you know the place much better than I do. I've been to the fair, of course, and always to mass at St. Agnes' and sometimes at St. Martin's, you know that very old church with the pink marble altar that some say was brought from Italy long ago. I know nothing about the inns. Ah yes, there's the Ladies' Island. My father had me get my schooling there."

"Were you happy among them?"

"Well, yes, in a way."

"Did they try to make you stay on?"

"I'm a merchant's daughter," said Sabina primly, "and they're all great ladies." Here she added loyally: "But they were good to me. At least, Dame Elizabeth was. She even taught me a little Latin and she tried hard to make me fond of poetry."

"Goodness! You know some Latin! You must be learned indeed!"

Sabina blushed and shook her head. They were sitting together by an open window, with the pear blossom carpeting the mossy path outside. An orange and red butterfly beat against the panes. In the well of the room, Hilda's shoulders were bent over the spinning-wheel. Neither Richard nor Sabina heard the droning. She sat, her palms flat against the cool stone of the window-sill, her fair hair free except for a red velvet snood, her lips slightly apart, and Richard leant forward.

Her father's staid guests had kissed her according to custom, closed lips brushing against closed lips, but Richard's kisses swept over her like the hot July wind over the ripening corn. They touched her with fire, they enlarged her inner landscape, they enskied her. She drew her breath at last, burningly aware of Richard's hand upon her clenched fingers when the door opened, Hilda stopped spinning, and Sabina leapt to her feet and snatched at an apple to hide her bliss and her confusion.

It was Master Albert, the plump, wall-eyed lawyer, come in search of Conrad. Hilda left the room, and the portly, black-gowned man stood rubbing his fat white hands. He was at home in all legal matters but of conversation he had none, with the sole exception of a story about his journey to Paris made in his youth.

"I hear you've been to the East," Master Albert bowed to Richard. "I fear that I'm not much of a traveller. Once I had a shocking experience in Paris . . ."

There followed the story, an unpleasant room at an unpleasant inn, the indifferent food and wine, the embroidered pouch and the five gold coins stolen in the heart of the night.

"I still think they must have drugged my wine so that I never woke up. It had a very odd colour, I remember, and I found no redress whatever. I feel sure the notary I went to must have been in league with the innkeeper. It was a most unpleasant experience, I assure you. . . ."

Master Albert went on and on and on. Sabina was acquainted with the least detail of the pathetic little story. Richard, as she knew, had also heard it at least once, but he stood and listened, and there seemed no irony or boredom in his expression.

"He is handsome, he is merry and good," thought Sabina, "and he's as courteous as a lord."

Next evening Richard came to supper and brought a small lute with him. He sat a little away from the table littered with pewter and silver, brushed the strings with his lean brown fingers, and sang in French:

> *"My hands in your hands,*
> *My heart in your heart,*
> *My eyes in your eyes*
> *Till death us do part.*
> *My thought in your thought,*
> *My faith in your faith,*
> *My soul in your soul*
> *In life after death."*

"It's a good melody," said Conrad. "Now, please, put the words into our tongue."

Richard did it at once. Anna said she disliked the last two lines because young people had no business to think about death, but Conrad begged the young man to sing it once again.

Sabina said nothing. The fragile little song and Richard's kisses meant one and the same thing to her. She wished she might weep and laugh all at once, and then suddenly she felt drawn towards a silence lovelier than the very language of love. The little song seemed a signature confirming all she felt, all of it far more real and enduring than the dull red wax seals on the marriage-contract. Some day, she thought, idly watching the evening sun gild the apples in their wooden dish, some day she might be fortunate enough to stumble on words which would explain it all to Richard and to herself also. She clenched her hands, looked up, and smiled very shyly.

It was the very next morning that Conrad sent Richard off to the Island on the business of Dame Melburga's dowry.

All alone, Sabina sat by the window in her room and heard the grunting of pigs from the styes and the rasping jingle of the well chain. A tall woman in dull red, followed by a servant, was crossing the forecourt. She was a customer, come to finger, to appraise and, possibly, to buy.

Sabina's small world was shattered and darkened but the great majority of people had no concern either for the shattering or for the darkening, and cloth must still be bought and sold at Stephen's Light. Sabina watched the woman disappear under the porch and turned to stare at the opened chests along the inner wall of her room. There

lay the honest Flemish linen, a length of green silk from
Lyons and another of scarlet silk from Cracow, the buckles
of turquoise and of amethysts, the silver cross studded with
curious green stones from the Levant. All of it was part of
a bride's rich portion—expressed in terms of silk and
linen and jewellery. Here, the wounded imagination leapt
forward, and Sabina saw Richard kissing a mouth dedicated
to holy things, and saw those thin supple arms enclose a slim
proud body once set apart for an entirely different worship.
For a few moments Sabina forgot the disgrace of a broken
engagement and the deep distress of her family. She forgot
everything except the abyss Richard had led her to, and
within that abyss she could not cry because she felt dead.

Yet she ruled herself so that she turned to the window
again. The woman, her servant laden with several bundles,
was leaving the forecourt. The woman had made her purchases and paid for them. The business at Stephen's Light
must be carried on. Sabina saw a buzzard fly over the orchard, remarked the purposeful, swift sweep and, presently,
heard the squeaking of a chicken. She saw the small feath-
ered body flapping in the buzzard's beak and moved away
from the window.

PART II

Dedicated Indolence

IN a small vaulted room off the west cloister, Dame Blanche, islanded in a shaft of sunlight, stood fingering various little boxes spread on top of a big oak chest.

"Kaspar, Melchior, Balthazar," she murmured, one fat yellow hand picking up a tiny metal box. "That's no good at all. It's a charm against fever. It wouldn't help in any other trouble. Oh dear Lady in heaven, that such a calamity should have fallen on this house! And here's a relic of St. Barbara. That would protect anyone from sudden death but, surely, Dame Adela's elopement is far worse than death. . . ."

She sighed and glanced at one of the rings she wore, a fine intaglio engraved with Jupiter, once given her by her father. "Those who wear me," ran the minutely chiselled inscription, "will be beloved by all and receive all they desire."

Well, Dame Blanche wore the ring when she came to the Island but she had to admit that she was not beloved, nor had she ever received all she wanted. She had always longed to work in the garden, and here she was in the sacristy in charge of vestments, altar plate and relics. The relics were all right because of the little attention they needed but vestments and the plate were a source of endless trouble to Dame Blanche who always said that she was born clumsy and could not help it.

The Island was famous for its relics, the most precious among them being a piece of leather from St. Joseph's sandal, a pious gift duly authenticated by a Pope and two learned cardinals. It was castled in pure gold encrusted with fat big pearls from a queen's necklace. Today Dame Blanche left it in its little corner cupboard: she could not see that St. Joseph's intercession would answer their present purpose.

In a square ivory box lay a fragment of St. Gunthild's habit who was ready to offer a remedy whenever cattle were stricken by plague. St. Mechtild averted thunderstorms, St. Walburga was a sure protector against famine and, according to a stoutly believed tradition, St. Radigund helped to make good butter. Indeed, all the saints, represented by the relics spread on the oaken chest. seemed concerned in all things except a fall from grace. But here Dame Blanche's face cleared as she picked up a tiny silver box strapped by a narrow white leather thong. Not a very important relic, merely a tooth of St. Afra of Augsburg, but Dame Blanche quickly remembered the story told by a learned monk from Reichenau about Afra who came from Cyprus, made her home at Augsburg, and kept a brothel there until she was converted to Christianity. She died a martyr's death, amply atoning for all her trespasses. Dame Blanche hoped that Dame Adela would never open a bawdy house of her own. None the less, she had given her heart, once dedicated to

God, into a man's keeping and, surely, it was St. Afra's business, her own stained past considered, to intercede for a fallen sister.

"What a piece of luck," murmured Dame Blanche. "And I'd nearly forgotten we had it in the house."

Yes, the relic would indeed help them. They had Dame Hedwig with her endless and monotonous visions of the anger of God, Dame Elizabeth with her no less tiresome reticence and that oddly ironic smile as though the disaster were something she had expected to happen, and the rest of the ladies all overwhelmed by the appalling scandal, crying and sighing, whimpering and whispering, and, in general, behaving as though the gates of hell were yawning in their faces. Dame Lucia was reported to have made no fewer than five spelling mistakes in a letter sent to an abbess in France, and Dame Anna lost her appetite to the disquieting extent of refusing a fourth fried egg for her supper. Dame Blanche's mouth curved contemptuously as she thought of it all.

And it had fallen to her, Dame Blanche, so often rebuked for her clumsiness with chasubles and candlesticks, to have found the right solution. Now they need trouble no one else at the court of heaven. They must have a procession, and Afra, a saint of their own nation for all she came from Cyprus, might well work a miracle and bring back the sinner—all because Dame Blanche's search had brought the tiny silver box to light.

"I mustn't forget to ask Dame Constance if a litany or a hymn has ever been written in her honour."

The box safe in her pouch, Dame Blanche waddled across

the garth towards the abbess's lodgings. Just as she reached the outer staircase, she heard the chapter-bell and at once decided that St. Afra's intercession was of greater consequence than a chapter meeting.

"My lady," her hurry made Dame Blanche forget the customary curtsey, "all shall be well. I've found the relic of a saint who is certain to help us in this trouble," and she told the story as fast as her shredded breath would allow her.

Lady Isabella heard her out. She spoke harshly:

"Didn't you hear the chapter-bell?"

"But St. Afra—" Dame Blanche faltered, her hands clutching the little box.

"Don't be more of a fool than you can help," said Lady Isabella. "We must find a way out of this trouble, and you come to me with silly stories. You might throw this box into the lake for all the good it's likely to do." She added, her anger thickening: "Try not to spill so much grease over the vestments, Dame Blanche. They are your business."

Half-aware, Dame Blanche tottered down the wide shallow steps. The sunlit garth lay before her, with fat, pink-breasted pigeons perched all round the rim of the stone fountain in the middle. But she never saw them. Her eyes were so clouded that she nearly missed her footing at the bottom of the stairway. Silly stories, were they? Was the Lady a heretic? Nobody really knew what she was like from one day to another. But little wonder that Dame Adela had run away from a house where the head could speak scornfully of a holy relic!

"St. Afra, pray for her," Dame Blanche murmured, and

was uncertain if she were praying for Dame Adela or Lady Isabella. No, she must not pray for the Lady. . . . Here the deep-throated chime of the chapter-bell made her halt. For a few instants she pretended that she stood listening to the bell from the great tower ringing to announce the arrival of important visitors. There would be such a happy bustle by the shore, banners flying, the newly painted barges gleaming in the sun, and then all the ladies in choir, and the fine scarlet carpet spread in the sanctuary, the slow and elaborate *Te Deum,* and later the pleasure of a choice meal eaten in the big frater, snow-white cloths draping every table. But the great bell stayed silent, there was no visitor expected at all, and Dame Blanche remembered that she must make for the chapter-house to discuss a great scandal. She stumbled, and the silver box fell out of the pouch. Dame Anna steadied her, picked up the box, and smiled.

"It's certainly a pity that our afternoon rest should be broken, Madam."

Dame Blanche agreed politely.

"Have you been to see the Lady?"

"Well, yes," Dame Blanche blushed, reluctant to come out with her story. "It's a terrible disaster, Madam. Do you think Dr. Busch is likely to come to the Island?"

"Why should he? We don't really need to be reformed. A single lapse doesn't ruin a whole house, Madam."

"I believe you are right. I don't see why we should be reformed. At any rate, we do stay on the Island. Haven't we all heard about the nuns at Derneburg who dine out almost continually? And those Poor Clares at Nüremberg! Why, they were all sent to Bamberg and Brixen—such a state their house was in! Indeed, you're right, Madam, and I hope St. Afra may yet come to our help. You have, of course, heard about her?"

"Indeed I have. It seems that one must first be a great sinner before one becomes a saint."

"Well," said Dame Blanche doubtfully, "I wouldn't know much about it though I suppose we're all sinners here for all we keep the enclosure. Yet I have read in some old book that monks and nuns should be like Melchizedek—without a care for their parents or any other relations, and I fear we're always cumbered with ours. St. Radegund wore a habit of coarse undyed wool but we wear fine cloth and silk, and the Lady and the prioress have just had gris mantles made for them, and what more expensive fur is there, except, perhaps, ermine? In the old days, there used to be a room set apart where meat might be eaten by the sick only, and we get it every day—except Fridays. All the same, Madam, have you ever thought what would happen to God's mercy if nobody were to sin at all?"

"We shall be late for chapter," said Dame Anna.

[2]

About the end of the fourteenth century, the Island stood desolate, all its roofs fallen in and its walls crumbling down. The once shaven grass in the great garth was knee-high scutch, thistles and nettles rioted in the gardens, and the big bell had fallen from the west tower. It had once been one of the greatest abbeys in the Empire. Now, it offered habitation to crows, rooks, bats and spiders.

There were many causes for the decay. Black Death, famine, a war between the city and a neighbouring duke when the abbey, resolved on keeping its neutrality, suffered both from the duke's men and the townsmen and, finally, so said the pious folk of the city, the mysterious and inexorable will of God. The abbey had known great days of holding friendship with emperors, giving counsel to popes and lavish hospitality to many a royal guest. Its abbots were known for wisdom and sane piety, its sons for chaste, hard living and incredible industry.

The abbey had no glass-roofed houses like those at Dobberan in Mecklenburg, but its vines yielded nothing to the vines of Walkenried and Altenkempen, the watermills it owned on the mainland were as well known as those of Zenia in Brandenburg, and its pear and plum orchards exceeded those of Georgenthal. Its library was famous. To name but a few, Virgil and Lucan, Horace and Ovid, Prudentius and Boethius were represented by manuscripts of matchless clerkmanship, and one of its treasures was a fine early thirteenth-century copy of the Mass sequence for Pentecost, *"Veni, Sancte Spiritus."*

A story still lingered in the city about a freeman's son and a tenant of the abbey, who, all but killed by brigands in the cathedral square, found refuge on the Island. His very name was now forgotten, and little enough was known about him except that he had a pagan bride who drowned herself in the lake and that, in the end, crippled and blinded by the brigands, he turned away from facile love songs he used to compose and wrote the great hymn just before his death. It was also rumoured that on the mainland, not far from the wood between the lake and the road towards the city, strange lights might be seen and weird chanting be heard on occasions. They said it was the bride searching for her young husband, whom she would never find seeing that all suicides were forbidden the golden gates of Paradise.

But the legend had grown misty with the years, and all the grandeur belonged to the past. Indifferent abbots were succeeded by men with no moral sense in them. The great possessions in the Empire and beyond its borders were frittered away mostly in extravagant and absurd lawsuits. There used to be much talk of no fewer than ten rich manors being sold to defray the costs of a lawsuit with the abbey of Quedlinburg—all over an ancient manuscript alleged to have been borrowed from the Island and later appropriated by Quedlinburg. In the end, the abbey faced penury, and no nobleman cared to send his sons to a school where the boys' pittance was reduced to salad and an occasional egg all because the abbey had ceased to be self-maintained and no merchant on the mainland would trust the monks with as much as a small bag of salt. The servants, whether free or no, had all run away. The remaining inmates were wholly unacquainted with most elementary domestic tasks. It was with delight that the city heard the story of a monk who admitted himself unable to make an egg-dish because the egg-shells would not soften after an hour's boiling.

In 1410, the abbot, a kinsman of the Duke of Ferrara, left for Italy never to return. Some years later, they heard of his death but a chapter of two could not very well expect to receive election papers from the Pope and the Emperor. The elder monk, a bundle of manuscript matter in his scrip, was taken in by the monks of Zenia. The younger joined a pilgrimage to the Holy Land and was not heard of again.

But the Island remained, its decay continuing to trouble the city. An ambitious archbishop toyed with the idea of turning it into his own residence, but Monte Cassino, having heard something of the man's habits and debts, preferred to ignore his hints. Some years later, a fire, having destroyed St. Matthias' Abbey in Styria, the Emperor was importuned by the abbess, his cousin, for help. Soon the city heard that the ladies of St. Matthias' were coming to take possession. The burghers shrugged indifferently. The dedicated folk lost no time in giving vent to unbridled indignation. The prioress of the Dominican hospice wanted to know who St. Matthias' ladies might be. Were there not enough religious houses in the city for an alien body to be imported among them, she asked, and she asked often and loudly. The Carmelites agreed, and so did the Archbishop. The Dominicans and the Franciscans for once forgot their differences and talked much about the support of certain unnamed cardinals, and insisted that the case should be referred to the Pope.

But where were the cardinals, and which was the Pope? John XXIII sat in Rome and Benedict XIII at Avignon. The latter, everybody said within the Empire, was an antipope but, in the end, no important letters came to be sent to anyone because the Emperor's wishes could not be overruled.

The city folk, taking no part in the fevered discussions among the religious, preferred to wait and to watch.

The business began badly—with a host of hired workmen from Carniola trooping into the city. The ladies of St.

Matthias', having had one home burnt down, must certainly
be lodged under a roof, and the Island offered neither roof
nor wall. So masons, blacksmiths, carpenters, glaziers and
coopers arrived, demanding both food and transport, and
were given neither. The burghers, made aware of the immediacies of an alien intrusion, wasted no time on discussion. It was merely announced that no man might work in
the city unless he had been domiciled there for a year and
a day. Not a grain of wheat, not a nail would they get in the
city. The foreman pointed out that the Island stood on the
lake; he would get his provender somehow, but the men
must be transported across the water. Not a boat, not a
barge, not a wherry, said the burghers.

In the end, the foreman had to give in. The alien rabble
turned back east, and duly recognized labourers from
among the city folk were hired on behalf of the ladies, and
they crossed over to the Island. Their wages were appointed
by the council, and the city hummed with delight: work on
the cathedral was virtually ending, and here was a heaven-
sent opportunity to stave off unemployment. Yet home
labour proved inadequate for the task of rebuilding the
abbey. The abbess of St. Matthias' sent a silver chain and an
important relic to the city, and the hirelings from Carniola
trooped back, this once nobody hindering them. Soon
enough it became difficult to buy a goose or a bag of pepper
at the market: the newcomers had sharply bladed appetites.

But they had also money to spend. They received good
wages from the ladies and they spent lavishly. They
brought fresh blood and good custom into the city, and for
the first time the burghers began thinking kindly of the

Emperor Sigismund. In the end, the Dominican prioress found that nobody wished to listen to her protests against the coming of the alien ladies. Even the Archbishop declared himself pleased with their arrival. He owed immense sums of money to the bankers of Genoa and Lucca. There were rare relics in the cathedral. The Archbishop wondered if they would be better housed on the Island—for a consideration which would mollify the importunate bankers of Genoa and Lucca.

At last, the last carpenter laid down his tool, and the city heard that the ladies of St. Matthias' were on their way. The Dominicans and the Franciscans made elaborate preparations to receive them but all such invitations were most courteously refused. The forty-five ladies, accompanied by an army of corrodians, serving-women and others, stopped nowhere in the city. Veiled and cloaked, they rode through the streets, disembarked, and took possession. A cardinal came from Rome and another from Mainz, and all the gleaming new buildings were solemnly consecrated. There was a procession, and wheaten bread and broiled pork were distributed to the poor. The Archbishop was invited, and they lodged him in a great room with a marvellous French clock worked by weights and by escapement. It was an absolutely modern and rare toy, and equally rare was the bed coverlet worked in priceless *opus anglicum* in silk and in pearls. So were the finely woven hangings from Lyons depicting Joachim and Anna, hands clasped, lips just touching, with the legend in gold underneath, *Taliter concepta est beata Maria.* But the Archbishop, having supped off several delicately spiced messes, spared little attention on the rich furnishings. He could not forget his debts. In a subtly devious manner he brought the conversation round to the matter of relics.

"We have so many fine ones at the cathedral, but I fear that it may be necessary to part with some of them."

"That, surely, is impossible," said the abbess. "Are you interested in relics?"

"Indeed I am."

At once she rang the bell and told a waiting-woman to fetch the sacristan.

"His Grace is interested in relics."

He found no reply ready to his tongue, and for the next hour they entertained him by displaying their treasures, among them a great crystal, shaped like a dove, with a fragment of the true cross set in diamonds of fabulous value. The Archbishop realized that the crystal dove would pay all his debts twice over. Still, he was a man of breeding, and was duly grateful for a small silver cup studded with turquoises the abbess gave him on their leaving the great vaulted sacristy.

Back in her parlour, she began speaking about the coming feast of Corpus Christi.

"There will be so many visitors, and I fear that our guest-houses aren't quite ready for them."

"Isn't that against the rule?"

Coldly smiling, she leant back on her blue velvet cushions and quoted Lanfranc:

" 'We are all free to add to, or to take away, or to make changes. Many circumstances make for changes in matters which have long been unaltered.' "

"Yes, indeed," said the Archbishop, and sipped his wine rather thoughtfully.

"In this beautiful place," went on the abbess, "we shall serve God as befits our station in life."

The small square windows were open, and from across the great garth came the sounds of the ladies' voices chanting the old Compline hymn:

"Precamur, Sancte Domine,
Defende nos in hac nocte;
Sit nobis in te requies,
Quietam noctem tribue. . . ."

and the simple, quietening lines made the Archbishop forget his debts for a few moments. The abbess patted her little dog and chose a rose-coloured comfit from the dish in front of her. He spoke slowly, looking down on his narrow white hands:

"I have a very deserving chaplain, one Andrew by name, and he has a sister. I wonder if you could receive her in this house."

The abbess looked at the comfit between her plump fingers.

"I shall have to consult my prioress. I am not at all sure about the number of the corrodians we've already got."

"I wasn't thinking of that," the Archbishop said hurriedly. "I meant the girl to come here as a member of your house."

The abbess became keenly interested in her rings.

"But, unfortunately, there is our charter given by the

Emperor Conrad II. We require proofs of noble descent for six generations back."

He stared at her.

"Is it then necessary to be in possession of letters-patent to serve God?"

"To serve God in this particular house? Yes, it is."

"In such a case"—the Archbishop began fumbling for words—"I'm afraid the girl's father was a master baker in the city."

"Indeed?" the abbess smiled politely. "And I have heard that the city is famous for its fine bread. I feel certain that the ladies of St. Dominic will be happy to receive your chaplain's sister. We, unfortunately, are bound by our own charter," and she sighed as though in apology for that particular clause in the charter.

Certainly, the ladies were proud, and it was their pride that kept the least breath of scandal away from the Island. Loose living had long since crept into many an enclosure, but not a hint of any such trespass ever came from the Island. They lived in luxury indeed, but the luxury remained chastely respectable. The old rule insisted on a single meal a day between the middle of September and Easter: the ladies enjoyed three full meals—except on the days of rigid fast. The rule said they must rise and sing Nocturnes in the middle of the night. They duly rose and chanted the Office, and returned to their rooms to find their beds re-made by servants, the fire mended, and a fragrant hot posset ready to hand. The rule said they were to bathe three times a year, at Christmas, Easter and Pentecost, but the ladies used their beautiful new grey-stone bathhouse two and even three times a week.

There came no rumours of crudely vicious scandals but there were many stories about velvet shoes and scented, silken veils, delicate food and perpetual idleness. Sixty-odd servants were soon increased to one hundred and twenty, and forty-five ladies had as many maids to wait on them. The great raftered frater was unused except for important occasions. The ladies broke their fast, dined and supped in their own rooms, and six gentlewomen were in attendance on the abbess at her lodgings, no servant of common birth being allowed there. She rarely, if ever, came to choir, and she gave audiences to her officials only, but etiquette, meticulously detailed and as carefully kept, served as no screen for moral trespasses. The abbey buildings proper were girdled by a high forbidding wall. The chaplain lived in the gatehouse. Stewards and bailiffs and all the numerous working fry had their huts on the eastern half of the Island, acres of wood, meadow and orchard between them and the abbey wall. The ladies spoke to the chaplain, and sometimes acknowledged stewards and bailiffs by a brief nod. The men, who hoed, dug, weeded, planted, tended the cattle, groomed the horses and attended to the blue-painted barges, did not exist for the ladies except as so many pairs of hands and feet.

And contrary to the custom spreading in other religious houses, they hardly ever came to the mainland except for business matters when they stayed at the Dominican hospice.

Still, the city delighted in gossip. The squint-eyed Herda, a cobbler's daughter, hired for a year and dismissed for poor service, soon won the market's respect by the real and imagined stories she had to offer:

"You always knock at the door, and you get beaten if you forget it. You come in and curtsey, and you take care not to stumble over their dogs. All over the place the creatures are with jewelled collars and silk leads! The ladies like their table to be set near the window, and a clean cloth is laid on every day. They eat the finest wheaten bread even on fast days, and always wipe their fingers on a napkin. They have three courses for dinner and two for supper, and they never have beer for breakfast—it's always eggs beaten in milk or wine. Ah dear me, aren't they finicky? I'd get my ears boxed many a time for bringing in a bowl of salad with a little soil clinging to a leaf! They never spit out their cherry-stones and they never ask pardon when they belch. . . . They never think that any hireling's a baptized Christian. It made me sick many a time the way they never look at you when they give an order! All the same, they're lovely! They use a powder made of pearls and rose-water for their teeth, and a paste of pounded corals for their cheeks. Jesu, Mary, they smell so sweet that you think you're near a bag of spices when you stand close to them. And oh the stuff they eat! Nutmeg and saffron in every dish! Candied plums! Citron wafers! Ah me, that was a good life, and a bad Easter to them for sending me off! How can they tell if a body's working or not when they've never done an hour's work in their lives!"

The imperially bred abbess died at the age of ninety. Her successor, daughter of an Italian ducal house, carried on for ten uneasy years, fretted with so many quarrels that the ladies came to lose count of them. Having begun with the Pope, the Italian lady worked her way down to a kitchen scullion, and, near to her dying, remarked that she had no desire to have her spell of purgatory shortened because there would be no chance of a good quarrel in heaven. Having buried her, the ladies decided they must have peace at all costs.

There was Dame Isabella, sister of the Duke of Brunswick, who feared the Turk more than she feared the devil, who crossed herself on hearing a voice raised in anger, and forgave all the injuries almost on the spot; dear, gentle-hearted Dame Isabella who could not bear to hear about the Hussite rebellion because, as she said, it made her sick at heart to listen to such bloodcurdling stories.

"Let's all live together in peace and amity," she would say, and everybody liked her. She was deeply superstitious, and so were they. She liked seeing a wolf at a distance, and crossed herself whenever she met a priest. She believed in brownies and fairies, and so did they. They liked listening to dear Dame Isabella when she read from a small book by one Nicholas Jacquerius about it being lawful to believe that certain things could alter their shape and appearance with the help of demons. In common with all of them, Dame Isabella was terrified of death, and once in a thunderstorm, was heard to recite, *"Salve, Regina"* one hundred times. Again, together with all the others, she was deeply devoted to relics, and the ladies never forgot the occasion when, Dame Isabella being chambress, they were enabled to listen to a pilgrim from France who told them about the relics kept at St. Omer, such as a fragment of Christ's cradle, stone tablets of the Law delivered to Moses and a flower from Mary's garden at Capernaum.

Above all else, Dame Isabella was of their own stock, no uneasily-tempered alien likely to plunge them into the turmoil of dissensions they had endured under the Italian lady. They elected Dame Isabella unanimously, and the casting of their votes was almost superfluous. True, that Dame Isabella was no scholar, but they had no need of a scholar to rule over them. It was a pity that she knew her Latin so badly, but nobody could expect everything, as Dame Blanche said to Dame Lucia. Dame Isabella was of high birth, even-tempered, known to have no irritating foibles, and the rest, the ladies argued among themselves, would surely be added to her by the grace of her office. Dame Elizabeth, then a very young nun, even hoped that the same grace might teach the new abbess not to founder in Latin declensions.

Within less than a year, the ladies thought of that election with horror.

Dame Isabella, power thrust into her hands, became a different person. She leapt from one mad foible into another, and was too busy inventing those foibles to spare much time for anything else. All the ladies were set to make innumerable copies of a long treatise by St. Hildegarde *"On the Subtle Virtues of Precious Stones."* A great beryl was purchased with the money Dame Lucia had set aside for the year's supply of parchment, seeds and spices, and it was set into a crucifix to defend the frater from all peril of fire. The infirmarian was ordered to place a small emerald on fevered brows, and Dame Cosima, upon losing her temper with a bailiff, had to wear a tiny sapphire sewn into a brown silk bag. When a lawsuit in Hanover had gone against the ladies, Lady Isabella sent a messenger to Spain, there to buy a chrysolite ring, the stone engraved with a young man holding a candle in his hand. Such a ring, she told all the ladies triumphantly, was certain to enrich the house a hundredfold. But the purchase did nothing to counteract the consequences of the lost lawsuit.

From the frenzy of the gemmological spell, Lady Isabella turned her attention to medicine. Powdered alabaster, they were told, would now be given as a laxative in place of common herbs.

"But it's so expensive, my lady," murmured Dame Lucia, and was told not to mention anything as vulgar as money.

By the time Sabina came to learn her letters, Lady Isabella was no longer concerned with tooth-powders and laxatives. She was engrossed in collecting old manuscripts.

[3]

The chapter-house faced north, its narrow windows affording views of sky, wooded hills and water. The ladies, on entering, felt grateful to their Maker for the fine day because of a gaping hole in the roof. Habits and veils rustling, they took their accustomed places, a brief prayer was said, and Lady Isabella turned to Dame Lucia.

"You've brought all the papers?"

"They're here, my lady." Dame Lucia bent over a thick sheaf of parchment rolls in her hands.

"Begin then."

They listened, their curiosity rising higher and higher. This was a chapter meeting to discuss the consequences of Dame Adela's elopement, but they heard about the difficulties with the Luneburg salt pans, the default of a farmer-tenant in Styria, the damage caused by the Turks to such and such a manor in Carniola, the loss of this and that and the other, and the ladies' bewilderment grew and grew. What had Dame Adela's defection to do with the diminished income from their watermills at Augsburg? They sat, conscious that the vesper bell might possibly put an end to the business they had not begun.

Dame Lucia came to the end of a recital of losses sustained by several manors in Hanover through worms, lightning and drought. An uneasy silence fell upon the room till Lady Isabella said briskly:

"Of course, all these matters are not for discussion. Now we must come down to our great calamity."

Skirts rustling expectantly, the ladies leant forward.

"What have you to tell us, Dame Lucia?"

"Dame Adela's mother came from our nation, but she was married to an Englishman, and there is the question of the dowry administered by her brothers."

There followed an awkward pause. The ladies were waiting.

"What are the evidences?" Dame Augusta wanted to know.

"The contract," Dame Lucia moistened her lips, "is worded rather peculiarly."

"It is," Lady Isabella nodded.

"Dame Adela's brothers have refused to allow her anything except a share in their mother's inheritance. The late Countess had sources of revenue in the Empire—"

Dame Lucia halted again, and now they all remembered there had indeed been trouble over Dame Adela's dowry after her arrival among them. Her brothers had wanted her to enter a house in England, contrary to her mother's wishes, and Dame Lucia had had to tussle with lawyers, and they in their turn had had to circumvent earlier commitments —either real or imaginary and deal subtly and patiently with the English lords. The terms of the contract were not in money. So much wine, so many bushels of corn, so many fox and squirrel skins, barrels of salt fish, half a bolt of black cloth, all the revenues—except for the cloth sent annually— to be delivered four times a year, on St. John's Eve, the Day of the Cross, St. Thomas's Day, the Wednesday in Passion Week—"for as long as our mother's demesnes yield the said revenues and for as long as our sister continues in the service of God in the abbey of St. Mary and St. Matthias the Apostle"—ended Dame Lucia on a note of obvious gloom.

And now the ladies understood why they had been obliged to listen to the recitals of all the other losses. At once they imagined themselves tattered, wineless and fishless—all on account of Dame Adela's great default.

"She must be made to return," said someone.

That, at least, was obvious to them all. Nobody had any comment to offer until Dame Griselda coughed. She hardly ever spoke in chapter because nobody listened to her, but that day they would have turned to the city's fool for comfort.

"Dame Adela used to be good at prayer," began Dame Griselda, and at once the abbess pursed her lips and Dame Elizabeth frowned. "She also loved the north-west window. The Archangel is shown wearing a surcoat of gold and, if I remember rightly, that young man wore a jerkin of bright yellow, and that," Dame Griselda concluded with the falsely modest air of someone stumbling on a discovery of high moment, "that alone might well have bewitched her.

We need not wait till Michaelmas, my lady. Let us have a special mass sung and ask for the Archangel's intervention."

She finished, and they all knew they had listened too long.

"Nonsense," said Dame Augusta crisply. "She might just as well have been bewitched by Sir Hugo's gold chasuble. She has seen that often enough, I suppose."

Dame Griselda did not dare to point out that Sir Hugo was an old man and not to be compared with the archangel when Dame Blanche broke in:

"St. Afra should be asked to help us, I am certain of that."

"Why St. Afra?" someone raised their eyebrows. "It should be St. Ursula."

"Oh no, surely, you mean St. Mary Magdalene."

Here, Dame Anna bent her head, and everybody could see she was trying not to smile. Lady Isabella's face reflected deep scorn, and Dame Blanche gathered up all her dignity and courage:

"Well, I feel that St. Afra, being of our own nation—"

"But she isn't, Madam. She came from Cyprus."

"And Our Lady came from Palestine," retorted Dame Blanche, her sallow cheeks turning a mottled red when Dame Augusta's calm voice broke across the hagiographical deviation:

"About Dame Adela's dowry, my lady, would it be any use to write to the King of England? The last paragraph of the contract is so peculiarly worded that a capable lawyer might find a loophole in it."

"The King of England," Lady Isabella said impatiently, "is preoccupied with a war in his own country. I understand that the unfortunate young man used to be in the service of the Hansa, but I'm afraid that Lübeck isn't likely to help us. All those cities are so proud of their independence."

A deep sigh rippled up and down the room, and Dame Griselda ventured to speak again seeing that all the others were silent.

"The unfortunate young man, did you say, my lady? Indeed, he's a great sinner. Why, I happened to be in the parlour when two ladies were packing up our small wedding gift to Sabina, and I believe it was Dame Anna—no, I'm wrong, it was Dame Cosima who offered him congratulations, and he said something decidedly odd about Sabina being far too learned. I thought it came as a reflection on this house, seeing that she had been educated by us. Didn't you think it was an odd thing for him to say, Dame Cosima?"

"I don't really remember being in the parlour at all," said the other coldly, "and, anyway, neither he nor Sabina is of any concern to us."

"Sabina certainly is," the abbess broke in surprisingly. "Sabina and Stephen's Light and all the warehouses and other possessions. Of course, she wouldn't wish to marry now. And I really think she used to be good at her letters. I consider it is Conrad the mercer's plain duty to offer his daughter to this house."

Having said it, Lady Isabella leant back in her high-backed chair and glanced about the room. Their instant bewilderment did not take her by surprise. It rather pleased her to think that a battle was about to break under the leaking roof of the chapter-house.

"There are no lay sisters in this house, my lady," Dame

Lucia said in a tautened, nervous voice, and Lady Isabella ignored the remark.

"And we have no room for any more corrodians," said someone else.

"I wrote to Conrad the mercer at the very beginning," the abbess spoke with a peculiar emphasis. "I shall write again—and quite soon. Of course, Sabina shall not come here as a corrodian. I want her to join the community."

Dame Augusta raised her head.

"But there's the charter, my lady. None but nobly born girls may join St. Matthias'."

"We need that dowry very badly—"

"According to the charter—" Dame Augusta's voice trembled with anger, and Lady Isabella repeated:

"We need that dowry very badly."

"And how much did we pay to those glaziers from Antwerp? And how much had to go to the lawyers at Hanover?"

"You are forgetting yourself, Dame Augusta. Do you then wish me to have you suspended?"

"I am sorry," said Dame Augusta, but she did not bow her head and her voice was not coloured with repentance. "My lady, I must say again that the charter may not be altered without the Emperor's sanction."

"I shall get it," snapped Lady Isabella. "I am going to send him a personal letter. Sabina's father is far more wealthy than some of the princes, and the girl's been particularly well brought up. Don't you realize that it's time we began thinking about the future of this house? Do you wish to see all those riches going to the Dominican sisters? They'll get her, and they'll take her dowry without the least misgivings. Hasn't it been well said that the friars and their sisters have banished poverty to heaven?"

Dame Augusta was on her feet again.

"The whole house must be consulted in all matters concerning the charter, my lady. Such is our constitution, and even a letter to the Emperor may not be written without the consent of the chapter."

That was true but none of the ladies ventured to confirm the statement by as much as a glance. They waited for the abbess's reaction. Lady Isabella's plump cheeks flushed an angry crimson. Yet, contrary to their fears, she ruled herself well on that occasion. She did not even shrug or frown. She merely said:

"Let the vote be taken at once. Dame Lucia and Dame Blanche are to count."

About twenty delicate, beringed hands went up in protest. The abbess looked about the room, an ironic smile curving the corners of her mouth. It had indeed been a close battle but she knew she had carried it off.

"Have you finished?" she glanced at Dame Lucia. "Twenty votes against Sabina's admission and twenty-two in favour—with one abstention"—without looking, Lady Isabella knew that Dame Elizabeth had abstained. "So the matter's settled. Nobody may cross to the mainland tomorrow seeing that it is the feast of St. Mark, but Dame Blanche and Dame Elizabeth shall go to the city the day after. You'll spend the night at the Dominican hospice. I shall give you a letter to the prioress but you're not to discuss the matter with her. You shall then go to Stephen's Light and tell Sabina's parents that by a majority of votes this house is prepared to consider the trespass forgotten once their daughter comes here. Of course, I mean to write a personal letter to Conrad the mercer. I did write to him very angrily a few days ago, but he'd better overlook it for his soul's good and his daughter's salvation."

Nobody moved. Nobody spoke. The matter was decided by a very slender majority of one vote since the abbess's was the casting one, and they all knew the house was sharply divided, and some among them felt unashamedly pleased that Dame Augusta, the most bitter opponent of Sabina's admission, was now mistress of novices.

They were waiting for Lady Isabella to give the signal for the withdrawing prayer when Dame Elizabeth spoke for the first time:

"What about Sabina's own consent, my lady?"

"Her consent? Do you imagine that she'd prefer to go to Dominican house? Her parents would surely never hear of that."

"I didn't mean that, my lady. I was her mistress here. I believe I know her a little. I am sure she would never have agreed to marry that man unless she loved him."

"Rubbish! Girls marry the men chosen for them by their parents—yes, even among merchants."

"But I do know Sabina, my lady. Even the man's callousness and cruelty will never change her heart."

"Dame Elizabeth, you've been here long enough to forget all the romances you may have read in your youth."

"My lady, I know that Sabina is odd and sometimes intractable—but I have never known her to run away from things. To come here because of this disaster—"

"It would be an unprecedented honour for her," Dame Augusta spoke between her teeth.

"To come here just because of this disaster," Dame Elizabeth went on calmly, "would be out of character so far as she is concerned. I am not talking about vocation in general terms, my lady. Most of us," Dame Elizabeth's bow included the entire chapter, "were in a way bequeathed here, and we have certainly tried to honour our vows. This is the first grave scandal to happen on the Island. But I am not at all sure about Sabina. I may, perhaps, be mistaken, but if that man were to repent and come back, she wouldn't repulse him, I think. If she were a scholar, she might say that his betrayal of her was an accident, and her love for him— true substance. My lady, Sabina will not come unless her heart be turned to God, and I can't tell if it is so. I feel very strongly that the matter of her coming should be handled quite differently—"

"She shall come once her father chooses it for her," retorted Lady Isabella, and here the vesper-bell broke upon them.

They went to choir and sang the Common of Evangelists, it being the eve of St. Mark, but their minds were so deeply engaged with the matter of the chapter that Dame Agnes, the cantrix, led the wrong antiphon for the second Psalm.

"In velamento," she began, and they duly went on, *"clamabant Sancti tui, Domine, alleluia, alleluia, alleluia . . ."* and there followed an uneasy pause because they did not know whether to chant *"Confitebor, tibi, Domine"* or *"Beatus Vir . . ."* until, quite unexpectedly and out of turn, Dame Augusta's vigorous contralto began the first verse of *"Confitebor, tibi, Domine, in toto corde meo,"* and, the psalm finished, it was again Dame Augusta who

brought them back to order by intoning the proper anti-phon: *"In caelestibus regnis Sanctorum habitatio est. . . ."*

They were all grateful to Dame Augusta but the Office could not engage their entire attention. There were pointed little remarks when a rosary jingled, or a lapdog grew restive, or a lady happened to drop a comfit. Inevitably, they thought of the vote forced on them. They also thought of Dame Adela now braving unspeakable dangers of a hostile world for the love of a casually met stranger, and Dame Blanche wondered if it were permissible to pray for a soul in the state of damnation. She did not know, and she knew it would be no use asking old Sir Hugo because he had long since ceased giving adequate answers in difficult cases of conscience. Perhaps, the Archbishop would tell her. Dame Blanche, her lips shaping the last verse of the 110th Psalm, imagined the scented rushes strewing the floor in the Lady's parlour, the spiced goose, creamed apples and the best French wine served for dinner. Would it be possible for her to ask, whilst offering the Archbishop a portion of the goose, "Is Dame Adela truly damned, Your Grace?"

Dame Augusta nudged Dame Lucia and whispered angrily:

"Vote or no vote, a letter to the Emperor must be written, and I shall also write to my cousin, the Duke. Can you imagine what the girl's stall will be like—with an Agnus Dei on a field of blue for all her quarterings? A merchant's daughter at St. Matthias'! I always said it was wrong to admit her as a pupil! And Dame Elizabeth with all her dreamy nonsense about a special call!"

Dame Lucia muttered conciliatingly:

"Still, a vote has been taken, Madam, and I fear that we

shall need someone's good dowry before long. There have been so many expenses. Why, we may all be reduced to a diet of salad and beans!"

"Nonsense, Madam! What is one lost lawsuit to us, and my little niece is coming here next year. Her portion is big enough, I assure you. I must say poor Dame Elizabeth has tied herself up in knots."

Dame Lucia glanced across the choir. In her stall, Dame Elizabeth sat very still, her cheeks uncommonly pale and her eyes closed.

"You are in her mess, Madam, together with Dame Blanche. Perhaps, you'll discuss it with her at supper."

"I've no intention of mentioning Sabina to her," replied Dame Augusta, and remembered to lower her head at the *Gloria Patri.*

But the majority could not follow the Office. They were deep in thought and perplexity. How could the young man have persuaded Dame Adela? Few among them had spoken to him, but Dame Lucia and Dame Cosima had remarked on the surprising perfection of his manners. He wore a dazzling yellow jerkin and his hair curled all about his forehead. But what did happen? They knew that a habit and a veil, both sodden with dew, had been found on the shore, and two of their gardeners, riding to the city to purchase seeds, had met the young man, with Dame Adela in a blue cloak riding pillion. They said that she wore a crimson hood. Having recognized her, they had not however, dared to stop her. About half a league further, the young man took a sharp turn to a stony lane leading uphill, and the gardeners thought they had better hurry on with their shopping and bring the story back to the Island. That was the last anyone had seen of Richard of Troyes and Dame Adela. Riding pillion, in a blue cloak and a crimson hood! He must have purchased them for her.

With a sense of relief, the ladies stood up for the *Regina Coeli*.

[4]

Dame Augusta was obstinate. She would mention neither Sabina nor Dame Adela at supper, and made an elaborate complaint about there not being enough butter cooked with the young peas. Always obliging, Dame Blanche remarked that the soup was rather insipid.

"I wish I could find that English receipt for a good broth," said Dame Augusta, deftly slicing her cheese. "I had it from my sister, the Duchess, who once spent several months with friends in England. It is made of chestnuts, I believe, with pork liver and yolks of eggs, all mixed with dry white wine. My sister said it was such a success—she had it served almost every day after her return. I do wish I could find that paper!"

"Yes, the Lady is certain to like it," said Dame Blanche politely.

She yearned to discuss both Dame Adela and Sabina, Stephen's Light and other possessions of Conrad's, but she was afraid of Dame Augusta, and Dame Elizabeth remained oddly aloof. She ate her food in silence, and the conversation took to lagging once the culinary themes were exhausted.

At Compline, her stall remained empty, and "It is really

wrong of her to keep away," thought Dame Blanche as she joined in *"Cum invocarem,"* the wimple pushed well under her chin. "It's really wrong," she thought again, and realized they were about to chant the very last *Gloria Patri,* "but all the ladies are agreed that Dame Elizabeth has always been odd. I wonder if she did ask the Prioress's leave," and, raising her voice to join in the brief hymn, Dame Blanche looked at the distant stall where the little prioress, Dame Mathilda, chosen by Lady Isabella for being a perfect and harmless nonentity, was now sleeping peacefully, her face looking very pink and innocent in candlelight.

Dame Elizabeth had not asked the Prioress for leave to keep away from choir. The supper-table cleared by the servants, she remained in her room because she felt that she must stay alone with her thoughts or else go mad. By daytime, she never had the luxury of briefest leisure—being hustled from job to job at Lady Isabella's whim.

The Island had no pupils now, and the few novices were in Dame Augusta's charge. Dame Elizabeth still had the library, her duties there being crowded into the few days before Lent when, in accordance with their customary, books would be distributed in chapter. But, apart from the annual doling out of recognized works of piety, Dame Elizabeth could not now spend as long as five minutes with a book. In her younger days, she would often try her skill at fitting a few Latin rhymes together. Now she knew that Dame Lucia would hesitate to let her have as much parchment or paper as was needed for a day's egg tally.

The ladies thought that Lady Isabella had quite a particular need of Dame Elizabeth's varied services; there was a vaguely defined niche in the life of the house, and Dame Elizabeth, they supposed, filled that niche as well as she could. They did not envy her. From Prime to Compline, Dame Elizabeth's hours were spent in countless, all varied tasks. She could make no complaint about a routine: none came her way. She received visitors, she wrote letters, she taught elaborate stitchery to the younger ladies, she was sent into the herb garden and to the infirmary, into the kitchen and the storerooms, she talked with bailiffs, she interviewed artisans, in brief, she did a thousand and one tasks—always on behalf of Lady Isabella, and she had no official status in the house, and she well knew the reason for it all, and now she thought that she had divined the root of the reason behind Dame Adela's decision to burn her boats—both temporally and eternally.

Dame Elizabeth had spoken boldly in chapter. At supper she would say nothing. Now she was alone, and she welcomed the solitude. Her room faced west, and, sitting by the window, she could—by leaning out—see the lake and the mainland—a milky-grey swathe under the moonlight. The low-keyed chanting was soon ended in the church, silence fell upon the abbey, and to Dame Elizabeth that silence brought both refreshment and anguish.

How well she remembered Dame Adela arriving on the Island, a shy and lovely girl of twelve, with very candid eyes and a smile which made you remember once again that spring never failed to follow the anger of winter. Her freshness, her zest, her winning simplicity, everything about Adela marked her apart from the other novices. To Dame Elizabeth, then, fell the task of training the girl, and the work was pure pleasure. Adela flew from task to task; she mastered her few duties easily and her Latin so effortlessly that Dame Elizabeth, then still engaged in scholarly pursuits, would glance at her tattered copy of Horace and imagine Adela taking her place some day in the future.

Then the girl's mother died far away, in England. Adela never cried.

"Was she not kind to you, child?"

"Oh yes, Madam."

"Don't you feel any grief at all?"

Adela's hyacinth-blue eyes flew wide.

"Why should I, Madam? She's gone to God and Our Lady."

"You can't be sure of that," Dame Elizabeth spoke sharply. "We mustn't take such things for granted. There's purgatory for every one of us. Pray for her soul, child."

"Certainly, Madam."

Then, all too quickly, as Dame Elizabeth thought, Adela became one of the ladies, wore her long veil, and had different duties assigned to her. It fell on the vigil of the Epiphany, and it was Adela's turn to begin the great antiphon before the Magnificat.

"Magi videntes—" she began, and stopped abruptly.

From her own stall Dame Agnes prompted loudly:

". . . stellam, dixerunt ad invicem . . ."

Here, an old nun, having fallen asleep, woke up with a start, and her little dog's sudden whimper broke across the unaccustomed silence.

"Magi videntes stellam . . ." Dame Adela began for the second time, bowed her head, and stood in silence. Dame Agnes lost not a second:

". . . dixerunt ad invicem: Hoc signum magni Regis

est, eamus et inquiramus eum, et offeramus ei munera, aurum, thus et myrrham, alleluia."

"And what," Dame Elizabeth asked later, "happened to you? Such a disgraceful thing to have done—with all those visitors in the nave, too! You are fortunate indeed that the Lady never came to Vespers. Well, what was it?"

"I saw—" Adela began, and at once checked herself. "No, Madam. I saw nothing. It was just like a flash across my mind, and everything else went out. I'm very sorry indeed."

"What in the world are you talking about? What kind of flash?"

"I understood that God so loves the world that everybody will be saved," Adela replied, very much in the convincing manner of a person saying that two and two made four.

"Who told you that?"

"I've read it in books many a time, and I could never understand it. And just at that moment I understood. I felt as though I were standing under an opened sky. But I'm very sorry, Madam."

"Show me the book," said Dame Elizabeth heavily.

Dame Adela ran to fetch a thick leather-bound volume. It was a treatise by Raymond Lull, the manuscript being made at Toulouse sometime in the thirteenth century. Dame Adela found the passage and read feelingly:

" 'God so loves the world that almost everybody will be saved. If it were not so, what would happen to Christ's mercy?' "

"You've no business to read such a book. The man was condemned for heresy." And Dame Elizabeth said to herself: "That's one result of Lady Isabella's purchases! She'll buy any manuscript she finds at Master Herbert's. . . ."

Dame Adela said, her eyes bent:

"I shall not read this book again, Madam, but was the Lady Mechtild also condemned?"

"You're mad to ask such a question. The Lady Mechtild is a saint of God, and you know it."

"But she says pretty much the same things, Madam. She calls God a pure and holy simplicity, and He is everything to her. I love that little book of hers about a perfect abbey with Charity for abbess and Peace for prioress. Oh Madam, she does say such beautiful things. Some of them dart into your thoughts like lightning from heaven. When I read for the first time that 'anger brings darkness into the soul,' I thought I must try and never lose my temper with poor little Gerda even when she spills the posset over my habit."

Dame Elizabeth said nothing.

"Is it all wrong then, Madam?" asked Dame Adela, and her teacher could not reply all at once.

They were good books, undoubtedly, and Dame Elizabeth had read and loved them all in her day. For she, too, had had her own hour of flaming enthusiasm, she, too, had once been informed by longings to lose herself in prayer and contemplation, she, too, had once been convinced of God drawing her closer and closer to Him. It all happened so long ago, she had nearly forgotten it, and now this fresh, flower-minded girl from England made her remember almost too much. Dame Elizabeth put away the volume of Raymond Lull and asked abruptly, her eyes bent:

"What does it all mean to you?"

"I think everything, Madam," Adela said simply. "I

couldn't find any words for it—but it makes me happy both at work and prayer. Once the rushlight went out in the dorter when I was still a novice, and my neighbour screamed—she was so frightened of the dark—but why should anyone be frightened of anything?"

Dame Elizabeth left it unanswered. She spoke in the same unnatural harsh voice:

"You should think a little more about your sins, and not fall into trances when you are in choir. The Lady won't have it, and the house won't have it either. Dame Hedwig's visions mean little enough, they are so absurd that we've learned to laugh at them. But these are very dangerous times, child, and there's so much heresy abroad."

"Is it heresy to try and love God a little more than you know you do?" asked Adela, but the bell ringing for Nones made it easy for Dame Elizabeth to dismiss the girl, yet another of her simple questions left without a reply.

That day Dame Elizabeth wished she might have used less harshness and more candour. But how in the world could she have said to Dame Adela:

"I understand you perfectly because I once went through the whole of that experience. Yes, even though I had many doubts. For instance, it troubled me that the head of St. John the Baptist should be at Angers and also in Constantinople. It troubled me that the same St. Pyro, to whom we sometimes sing a litany, should be known for little more than his perpetual drunkenness. It troubled me greatly that we in this house, who are supposed to follow a crucified Lord, have grown accustomed to so many luxuries. Yet, all those doubts notwithstanding, I was deep in peace. Then it happened that I had a friend at the Poor Clares in the city, and she drew the notice of the Holy Office. She was a good woman, and she said many beautiful and moving things, but they condemned her for heresy, and the Lady was aghast that one of us here should have been intimate friends with a heretic. True that the inquisitors never troubled themselves about me. All the same, I was shaken, and somehow it all died within me little by little. I suppose I was too weak—I couldn't struggle. Now there's nothing —neither delight nor torment in anything at all. . . ."

But, of course, Dame Elizabeth could have made no such confidences to a younger lady.

What happened next, she now searched in her memory. Ah yes, there was that Candlemas procession, and it fell to Dame Adela to sing *"Lumen ad revelationem gentium: et gloriam plebis tuae Israel."* She had been well trained by Dame Agnes, and her clear voice never faltered once as she repeated the antiphon after each verse of *"Nunc Dimittis,"* but the expression on her face left them all vaguely troubled. Singing, she stood a little apart from the other ladies, and Dame Elizabeth, for one, had a sense of a greater distance than the few yards between the singer and the rest of them. Others must have felt something unusual because there followed a little discussion at dinner in the frater, a discussion made possible by Dame Adela's inexplicable absence. Before Compline, Lady Isabella sent for Dame Elizabeth.

"I'll never have you train another novice again. What's happened to that girl from England? Once she'd a trance or something, and today, Dame Lucia tells me, she looked enraptured. Have you been talking dangerous nonsense to her?"

"No, my lady."

"Then what's the matter with her?"

Dame Elizabeth hesitated.

"She's much given to prayer, my lady."

"She's got all her choir duties," Lady Isabella pointed out, and Dame Elizabeth kept silent.

"I see," said the abbess after a pause, "but I'll have you remember once again, Dame Elizabeth, that this house is not a counterpart of the Abbey of Schönau as it was some two hundred years ago. Today, unfortunately, there are many people who begin by seeing a vision and end by being bound to a stake."

Nothing else was said but from that day on Dame Adela was kept away from Dame Elizabeth. The library and the scriptorium were no longer permitted to the girl from England. At meals and in choir she now had the close companionship of Dame Griselda and Dame Maud, both being the most feather-brained inmates of the house. Someone was quick to discover that Dame Adela had a good hand with marchpane and that her embroidery showed great promise. So Dame Augusta kept her busy at stitchery and Dame Cosima employed her for hours at preparing intricate subtleties for the abbess's table, and they might talk about *opus anglicum,* apple-jelly, beetles in the garden and blight on the mulberry trees, in fact, about anything at all so long as they kept away from Mechtild's burning phrases about the simplicity of God. It was also arranged that Adela's accustomed daily hour of meditation should never be spent in solitude, and Dame Lucia often required help with ledgers and tallies, telling the girl that she must learn to apply the maxim *"laborare est orare"* to every detail of the day, and, on occasions, the Lady herself would have her summoned to the parlour there to talk about England and Adela's English kin.

There was nothing for Dame Elizabeth to do but watch from a distance. Adela was still inexperienced. She proved tragically impressionable. Dame Griselda's endless inanities and Dame Maud's constant giggles carried a contagion she was not strong enough to escape. Little by little, her two companions made her wonder whether she had not been foolish indeed in her attempts to scale the heights. The doubt was deepened by Dame Augusta's occasional allusions to the pitiful state of Dame Hedwig capable of imagining a portent in a cock's crow. In the end, the half-fledged bird ceased beating its wings in a cage much too small for her. Dame Elizabeth's heart ached on hearing Dame Augusta and Dame Cosima declare that Dame Adela would in time make a very good nun indeed.

"The lilies she embroidered on the blue velvet cope are pure perfection," reported Dame Augusta, and Lady Isabella looked deeply satisfied.

"They clipped her wings," thought Dame Elizabeth. "Just as it happened to me, and all of it must have caught the poor child at the rebound. They wouldn't let her love God in the only way she could, and she's gone and given her heart to a man, and oh what price! Her own dishonour and another girl's misery. . . ."

Here, the Nocturne bell shattered the silence. Presently, the wind carried the reed-thin singing across the great garth:

"Iam cum stella matutina,
Ad precandum surgimus. . . ."

Dame Elizabeth shivered a little but she would not close her window. She sat very still and hoped that the same God she had once tried to serve would yet befriend Adela.

PART III

Ah, Break the Lute Strings ...

But Adela certainly did not expect God to befriend her; she knew she had damned herself, and she had no illusions about the consequences of the unhallowed dalliance. Nor did she care much to reflect about those consequences. She had a sense of high winds in her thought and strong wine in her blood and, the city left far behind her, she felt that nothing mattered in the whole world except the feel of Richard's body against hers. The smell of leather, the tang of bracken, the unaccustomed gay colours of the new clothes she was wearing, by him bought, such little things seemed to be the entire lettering of a new life. It was all poised within an instant. It had no past and it would not greatly matter if a future were denied it.

They were riding at a furious pace through a rough hilly country to Adela quite unknown. Much later, with the sun behind them dyeing the world violet and crimson, she guessed that they were travelling eastwards. She asked no questions. The deep silence between them was more satisfying than speech.

On the Island, Adela had seen Richard precisely six times. Dame Griselda and Dame Maud had used all the superlatives in their vocabulary as they praised his looks, clothes and manners, and Adela had heard them in silence. His appearance and courtesy had certainly pleased her but it was his first glance at her that had stirred her to the very depths, and his very first kiss had confirmed the stirring. So she imagined that Richard of Troyes had come to her from God and St. Michael to shake the dust of years from her heart, and yet she knew she had been wrong so to imagine since God could never have prompted her to sin.

There, Adela curbed her reflections. Sin or no sin, she could not turn away from the fulfilment in whatever garb it was offered to her. She accepted the instant and drowned all of herself in its depths. Indeed, she must not think— otherwise she might begin reflecting about the girl left behind. Richard had shrugged when speaking of that betrothal. Yes, the girl had pleased him well enough but to marry her would have led him to a yoked condition. He would not have wedded her alone but a whole host of kinsfolk and acquaintance together with a great house and a business concern. Such a pattern, he could now see clearly, would never have answered with him.

Yet on their second day out Richard felt troubled. Dearly as he loved Adela's delicate, sweet flesh, that flesh had been bred in conditions he knew little about. Adela, unaccustomed to rough riding, grew easily tired, and one night under the open sky proved almost too much for her. They reached a small town and could get nothing but a very poor room in a dirty hovel of an inn, with sour porridge and a broiled herring for their supper. Adela, the crimson hood off her head, asked for water for her face and hands. Richard slipped out. In a filthy, smoky room, the fat, swarthy woman sniggered at the request but some water was found. It looked clouded and smelt suspiciously of fish, but Adela dipped her fingers into it.

"We shall soon be in Genoa," Richard murmured. "Do eat some supper, sweetheart."

But Adela could not swallow the porridge and shook her head at the herring.

"Couldn't they let us have a dish of eggs?" she asked.

Eggs cost dear, grumbled the fat virago, the big mole on her left cheek turning an angry purple, and what was the matter with her good herbs and onions, she wanted to know. Richard fumbled in his pouch and produced a persuasive coin. In the end, some hurriedly roasted eggs were brought in, and Adela, taking no notice of the fat woman, began eating delicately, breaking her bread into absurdly small pieces, and carefully wiping her mouth and fingers with a square silver-fringed cloth. The fat woman stared at such incredible manners. In the end, a crooked smile on her lips, she waddled out of the room.

The place was dreadful indeed. Still, the night was before them, their second night together, and they smiled at each other as though they felt secure in their tenure of a castle none other might enter. Richard spread his big cloak over the settle and folded a coverlet twice over to serve Adela for a pillow. From beyond the badly fitting door came the raucous sounds of ribaldry where a few men sat drinking sour beer and playing dice. There came the loud miaowing of a cat and someone's heavy tread across the backyard. A door clicked, and the woman's urgent whisper invited someone to come in. But in their room Richard snuffed out the tallow candle, loosened the wooden slat off the window, and the cool May night came into the sordid place.

"Sweeting. . . ."

Breath held, he listened and had no answer. Tired out, Adela was asleep, and Richard lay down on the floor with far from easy thoughts for company. He knew he would not feel safe until they were aboard their ship in Genoa harbour. Once they got to the Levant, he would earn his livelihood by selling corn or wine. He might even learn something about the dye trade; he had once heard a man say that dyers out in the East were exempt from many taxes, so hard was the craft, so few were the men ready to follow it. But he would learn it, Richard said to himself. Sleep far away, he lay, his eyes wide open to the moonlight. There was a glimpse of a small shapely foot in its dusty stub-nosed shoe and a hand blessedly relaxed in sleep, so pale a hand against the dark cloth of the cloak.

And, watching her, Richard told himself for the hundredth time that he had been bemused and also slightly mad all through the days spent at Stephen's Light. Now he was wholly sane, and ready for adventure and danger, ready for a hard-paved future. Sabina, he thought, may indeed have loved him a little but she would always have claimed him entirely. Adela, asking for such creaturely trifles as a posset, hot water, a dish of eggs, made no larger claims. She loved him wholly but never greedily, and Richard wondered what could have taught her that delirious abandon with which she had come to him.

He had thought himself to be quite knowledgeable about ladies in religion. His service at the Hansa had made it necessary for him to visit many a house. Some among them were cool and shrewd business women, very knowing about market prices and stubborn in all matters which, as they imagined, required haggling. Some were women so castled in piety that they would pass him, their eyes bent and their lips pursed. Some were bored women who dangled their lapdogs, caressed their trinkets, and begged for a piece of gossip, a new tune, and were interested in little more than food and fashions. Here, he remembered one such ready with a kiss in exchange for a length of the new Spanish embroidery in red thread and in black. In brief, ladies in religion were a motley company, but the holy ones were moulded in cold stone, and the lewd ones seemed to offer far too easy a conquest for a fastidious man.

Adela he could not place anywhere. In her very abandon she showed no signs of wantonness. Pious he supposed she could not be. Of high rank, she evidenced no contempt for his own social condition. When tired, she would not complain, and he knew that tonight she would not have asked for eggs if he had not first urged her to eat the porridge: she would have gone hungry and said nothing of it. And she had brought no precious belongings with her, not even her amethyst rosary, nothing but a topaz ring which she took off the very first evening, saying that she could no longer wear it because topaz stood for chastity. She then gave the ring into his keeping and smiled at the ruby pin he wore.

"I'm glad you've got one. It's the sovereign stone, so they say. It's got all the virtues, and I've heard that it even gives hope to those in despair. Why, don't you know that St. John never saw a single ruby in the firmament because that stone signified Jesus who is everywhere?"

Well, he loved her, and it was good to be leaving Europe for good. What with all the unrest among apprentices, journeymen and artisans, the spread of beggardom, the appalling banditry, the muddle of wages, the decline of important fairs, wars and plagues together, Europe seemed hardly a place for a fresh beginning. True that things were not so bad in the Empire as a whole, it was said that Augsburg and Nüremberg held the world between them, so prosperous were they, but how could he find a harbour at either place, having eloped with a lady from the Island? "But she's ten thousand times worth it," said Richard to himself, and held his breath the better to listen to hers, and heard instead a cautious footfall on the landing outside.

"The guard are about," the fat woman's voice hissed through the door. "Get you up this instant!"

Richard leapt to his feet and unhasped the door. It was dark but he heard her heavy breathing.

"Saddle your horse and ride past the little church, and then you'll come to a small gateway in the wall. No warden'll ever let you ride through the city gate, but that wicket'll be opened all right, and you'll find a friend waiting there," she paused. "I'd to part with good money, too, but—there you are—seeing what a decent gentleman you are. . . ."

Here, behind them, Adela stirred in her sleep and began in a clear, accustomed voice:

"Miserere mei, Deus, secundum magnam misericordiam tuam: et secundum multitudinem miserationum tuarum, dele iniquitatem meam."

"Listen to her," said the fat woman appreciatively. "I

reckon our old parson wouldn't have as much Latin to spout, but you'd better wake her, sir. Too much of that chanting might upset the whole apple-cart in a manner of speaking. Now where, I wonder, did you find her? At Bingen? They're always on the run from that house, so people tell me, and I'd a Carmelite here once, and such a good-looking clerk with her, too, but oh dear me, there was such a to-do in the end, and the Duke and the Bishop sent armed men to force her back. Heaven only knows what was done to her later. They drowned the clerk in the river," she added almost conversationally.

"Have you a lanthorn?" asked Richard impatiently.

"There may be one in the room at the back. I'll go and fetch it."

She waddled away, and Richard stood very still. There was no time to lose, and yet he stood still. He would not wake Adela in the dark, he said to himself, and soon enough the woman was back, holding the lanthorn shoulder high so that Richard could see her face, fleshy and moist and informed with a greedy intent.

"Deus, iudicium tuum regi da, et iustitiam tuam filio regis," insisted Adela, and Richard, turning, saw that the crimson hood had once again slipped off her head. The dark blue cloak flowed over her body like midnight water.

"Sweeting," Richard called out urgently, and at once Adela sat up, frowned a little, and said in a confused voice:

"Why, I never heard the bell. It must be late. I don't think I am going to get up. Could I have my hot posset, please?"

"That's the way," the fat woman sniggered. "Why, they

all live like duchesses, waited on hand and foot they are, so everybody says. No posset for you, mistress, and no cooing either. Up you get this instant!" She pushed past Richard and would have jerked Adela's shoulder if he had not pulled her aside.

"Don't you ride too high a horse in this house," she then turned on him. "Out of this place, the two of you, but not before you pay me for my trouble, and you can thank the Holy Lady for my honesty."

A little later, standing, her arms akimbo, by the hearth in a low-ceiled smoky room, the fat woman laughed throatily.

"That was a splendid piece of business," she told her wizened grey-haired husband. "I guessed her to be a runaway nun as soon as I'd seen her nibble her food. So I tipped a wink to our good Hugo, and we are five gold pieces to the good. They're on their way to the mountains now—not that I care a tittle as to what happens to them. Much too proud for my stomach—both of them."

"However did you manage to pull it off?" asked her husband, yawning, and scratching his head.

"It was as easy as eating lard," she told him. "I just said that the guard were out and about, and the stupid donkey swallowed the bait straight away. As though the guard in this place would lose an hour's sleep over a wench from a convent! All I can say is I hope for more such silly folk to come our way. Far more profit in this business than in selling ale and pease puddings. I reckon the Holy Lady had best be given a candle tomorrow."

"Don't you go and buy a fat one," said the husband. "Candles cost dear these days."

[2]

It was Minnie's turn to shell the peas but, through the wide-opened kitchen doors, she heard the ladies' high-pitched voices, and at once she thought:

"Something else must have happened on the Island. Nobody ever tells me anything. I must go and listen. . . ."

She slipped through a side door like an eel through a net, and ran, unashamed of her dirty tatters because unaware of them, one bony hand hurriedly pushing a strand of unkempt flaxen hair off her forehead. Bending almost double, Minnie ran towards the pleached blackcurrant bushes which divided the courtyard from the herb garden. Once there, she crouched low, holding her breath, but she was too late: the swishing of the ladies' habits sounded further and further away. The ladies had obviously gone on beyond the herb garden, and Minnie knew that she might not follow them there. She was more or less on sufferance in the herb garden, but she must not be seen anywhere else —so all the cooks and scullions kept telling her.

"Far too ugly you are for the ladies to see you," Rowena, the chief cook, would say often enough.

In church, there was a corner by the west door, screened off by a tall pillar, where Minnie and all the other wenches like her might attend mass. They could hear the singing, and the tinkling of the bell would reach them when the wind happened to be in the south-east, but it was a murky cold corner, and Minnie hated its shadowiness because everybody knew that just anything at all might creep out of a shadow—a devil with a huge fork, fire spurting out of his mouth, or an enormous spider, or even a bear. On Sunday mornings Minnie must so rule herself as not to cry because she could not see the good lady—so far away in the choir was she, clouded off by whorls and spirals of blue incense. But now the good lady was gone, and there was nobody to tell Minnie what had happened, and the other ladies' chatter was stolen away by distance and a freshening wind. Almost Minnie wished that she might burst into tears when she heard a strident shout from the courtyard:

"Minnie! Minnie! Where's that imp gone to now? Minnie!"

Head bent, she scurried back towards the kitchens. Another serving-girl, her mouth primly set, was shelling the peas. Minnie made a face at her, and was at once cuffed soundly by a tall, grey-coifed woman.

"You miserable little vagrant! Always running away from a job! You'll run to hell one of these days, I tell you."

And she pushed Minnie into a room at the very back of the kitchens, with an enormous fire in the middle, where some four or five women stood watching huge, steaming cauldrons. The place was full of the hissing of holly twigs as the women poked at them with long-handled iron spoons, and Minnie's heart thudded heavily: there was no job she hated more than the annual making of glue.

"They feel boiled enough," said one of the women. One by one, the steaming, slender twigs were pulled out of the cauldrons. Minnie must sit on the floor and peel the top layer of bark off every twig as it came her way. To wrap the finished twigs in elder leaves was the women's business, and the wrapping was child's play compared with the peeling. Minnie's hands were clumsy, and slithers of bark stubbornly clung to the twigs under her fingers. She would try and claw at the bark but it refused to come off, and now one, now another twig would be thrown back at her, and once the bitingly hot wood hit her cheek so hard that she screamed.

"Shut up," said one of the women, "and get on with the work properly unless you want to be hit again!"

"I'd better keep my head down," thought Minnie, "and when they hit me again, it'll be my head and not my face, and it won't hurt so much." She knew that they would hit her again: she could not peel well. Her swollen fingers ached in every joint but they did not ache as much as her heart because the good lady was gone from the Island.

There were dependents like Minnie at every convent in the Empire. Minnie's father was an Augustinian canon, and her mother had been a nun at a small Franciscan house near Nuremberg, but Minnie had never known either of her parents. She had the sharp misfortune not to die at her birth, and a further disaster came her way some five or six years later: she fell on her face so hard that her nose was broken. At least, they told her she had so fallen: she had a vague memory of someone pushing her very hard because she happened to be in the way. Minnie knew she had been in the way all her life, and it did not particularly trouble her. There she was now—with her broken nose, a very large mouth and small pale eyes, and one shoulder reaching above the other. Nobody, certainly not herself, knew her age: she might have been twenty, or thirty, or even older. Many years before she had drifted to the Island in the wake of the numerous women hired for the kitchen work. She had a corner to sleep in, a rag to wear, and scraps to eat, and no lady except Dame Adela had ever taken notice of her.

It happened on a Tuesday before Ash Wednesday when Minnie was told to beat the cod with a hammer in the kitchen courtyard. For two whole hours she must hammer at the fish, and then two women would hack it, and presently Rowena and her minions would cook it with salt, butter and mustard for the ladies' Ash Wednesday fare. Sleet was falling thick that morning, and Minnie's bare feet kept slipping on the wet cobbles, and her bony arms went on raising and lowering the hammer over the silver-pink mass of the fish. Suddenly, her tired, frozen arms made a clumsy movement, and the hammer fell on the violet-red flesh of her left foot. Minnie flung away the hammer and danced for the exquisite pain, and just at that moment Dame Adela appeared in a doorway. She never came any nearer. She never offered help. She smiled and said:

"You poor little waif! It must be so hard for you, God help you!"

Having said it, Dame Adela won a starved and latticed heart. Minnie was poor and little, she was a waif, and the job was far too hard for her strength, but nobody had ever thought of saying so before. She stood still, her mouth gaping, the pain in the left foot almost forgotten. Dame Adela vanished. A few days later, Minnie saw her again. Dame Adela never spoke but she smiled once more, and Minnie had a feeling as though a piece of soft warm stuff had been laid against her throat. That was all, and Minnie could not remember how long ago it had happened because she had no clear idea about the passing of seasons, but a sun had shone over her head ever since until she learned that the good lady was gone from the Island.

The last twig of holly peeled however indifferently, Minnie scrambled to her feet. She thought she would remain in the room a little longer, in spite of its fearful heat. It was best to stay out of sight of the cooks.

The women, their own job finished, took no notice of her. They wiped their faces, shook stray elder leaves off their ragged kirtles, and were loudly pleased with their pittance of hot ale seasoned with butter and nutmeg. The room was thick with the bitter tang of holly bark and the fragrant aroma of the ale, and Minnie's nostrils twitched hungrily. She hoped that, engrossed by the gossip, one of the women might leave her pittance unfinished. It was but a thin hope but it deepened her resolve not to be hustled off to some other tiring job. Minnie stepped away from the fire and leant against a wall. She listened, understanding little of what was said but she knew the women would not molest her whilst they were chattering.

"Of course, she died. They'd no jasper in the house, and how can anyone get through a difficult labour without jasper?"

"Now my brother is going to Essen after Michaelmas. You've heard of their market going all through the week of the feast of SS. Cosma and Damianus? Good knives you get there, and a striped cloth, too, a very cunning pattern, but you must never let water touch it—all the colours run into one another."

"Why, my mother learnt it from some nuns at Regensburg. You sprinkle wine and flour over the hard fur and leave it for a day, and then rub the fur very hard, and it comes up soft and shining. So I told Dame Blanche, and would she listen to me?"

"Much too proud they are in this house! I'd far sooner work for the Dominican sisters at St. Catherine's!"

"Well, I don't know about them, but they're certainly proud and stupid, too, in this house. I once fell on the stairs into the fish larder and sprained my wrist, and there I sat, muttering the good old spell: 'Daries, Daries, Astaries, Disunapiter, Daries,' and Dame Lucia found me, and didn't she beat me hard for witchery, so she said, and there was the sprain as good as gone because of the spell!"

"Beat you, did she? Why, they use more spells than we do," said a younger woman with a bold naked face and moist red lips. "Before they sent me off into the kitchens, I used to wait on the ladies in their rooms, and I'd hear one of those spells so often I know it by heart . . ." and she began chanting:

> *"Mouse, hamster,*
> *Marmot, vole,*
> *Leave the land,*
> *I command.*
> *You are banned.*
> *Up above and down below,*
> *Get you hence!"*

"Witchery indeed," she laughed, baring her yellow teeth, "the ladies could not live without their spells. Why, I heard Dame Griselda say she'd never sit alone in that little room off the north-west cloister, so haunted it is. And they'll never get the chaplain to come with his bell and candle and do his stuff, not they! It's spells for them every time, I tell you. . . ."

Here, unfortunately, Minnie was seen by one of the cooks and ordered to stir handfuls of saffron into a big cauldron filled with steaming milk. She had to stand on tiptoe, so high was the cauldron set, and the smoke from the fire made her splutter and choke, but Rowena, the head cook, stood close by, breaking eggs into the milk, and Minnie dared not stop stirring for a second.

"Open your mouth, girl!"

She turned, gasped, and gaped, and a whole raw egg was slipped down her throat. Almost dizzy by the unaccustomed kindness, Minnie ventured:

"Where is the good lady, the one that is gone from here?"

"Ah," said Rowena, and threw the last of the eggs into the milk. "You've said it for all you are a fool. Proud she was and yet she was good, and I reckon the others drove her away because she was good."

"Is she dead then?" Minnie ventured again.

"Who knows? Stir, girl, stir. . . . Well, I believe it's better for the poor body to be dead. Handsome he was, and slippery, too, an eel wasn't in it to my thinking, and what will he do with her? Not so easy to roam about with a runaway nun in your keeping, I can tell you. Why, I've heard about a duke up in the north who won't have any such goings-on on his lands. Stands to reason, once you're inside the cloister, you've got to remain there. Yet I don't rightly know. Where's the difference in having a bastard inside a cloister or out of it?"

"But she was good—"

"You've said it before, girl," said Rowena, and, the brief kindly mood gone, she slapped Minnie hard on the buttocks. "Go and fetch the onions," she ordered in the ordinary gruff voice of an overworked cook.

[3]

Morning came to Stephen's Light, and Sabina knew that she must get up, wash her face, dress, say her Pater and Ave Maria, and go down the stairs to draw the ale for breakfast. In the kitchen, she scolded a maid briefly for leaving a hatch loose so that a rat had got at the bacon. The scent of clean rushes, new bread and warm ale was just the same, and Sabina moved from room to room, aware of little more except that another day had broken.

There was not much talk at Stephen's Light that morning. The breakfast eaten, Anna said that she was out of Spanish ointment.

"I shall prepare it for you, Madam," Sabina offered, and Anna spoke sharply:

"Let a servant fetch the herbs from the garden. Your father would much rather you stayed indoors today."

So the herbs were gathered and brought to Sabina, vervain, pimpernel and betony. Her quick, deft fingers pulled them all to pieces just as she had done so often before. A big stone jar was brought in, and Sabina carefully poured the wine over the herbs.

"There'll be time to have it strained in the evening," said Anna, and Sabina went into the storeroom, weighted the copperas and the mastic, the wax and the tormentil, and put them all tidily on a shelf. By the evening, these would be mixed with the herb water, and presently the salve would be ready to ease all the accidental sores and wounds in the household. As through a glass darkly, Sabina saw the irony of her morning's labours. Yet all remained as it should have been. You could feel all broken, even slightly mad, inwardly. You could spend what little leisure you had alone in your room and cry for the frost in the spring garden, and such things belonged to yourself alone. Yet your own self was a very, very small thing. It was necessary to remember that Stephen's Light had far more than one room and that it required other moods than those of bitterness and frustration.

The day before had been spent in tumult. Today the place echoed with the normal bourdon of voices. Everybody went about their business. A sprig of vervain crushed between her fingers, Sabina remembered that her father had important callers closeted with him, someone from Augsburg and someone from Milan. From a window she saw two clerks crossing the yard on an errand between Stephen's Light and the warehouses. The timid bell of St. Agnes' rang for Prime, for Terce, for Sext. Busy with her needle, Sabina heard the thin chimes and thought of the Island, her lips tautened, but Anna sat there, hemming a coverlet, and Sabina compelled herself to stop thinking about the Island which today and always would remind her of Dame Adela.

It was a hot and heavy day. Young leafage drooped in the garden. They heard the clucking of hens and the grunting of pigs, and they worked in silence, each aware of a theme neither dared mention. Suddenly Anna stopped sewing and leant out of the window to stare at a kitchen girl, in a bright yellow kirtle, passing by. Anna called out stridently:

"Greti, where did you get such a kirtle from? Where do you imagine you live, girl? In the Painted Street? Don't you know that only Jewesses and harlots wear that kind of yellow? Off with you this instant and never let me see that kirtle again."

Sabina's hand went on moving up and down in her lap. She had not raised her head. She could not very well say: "Does that matter so much? Does anything matter?" and she had nothing else to say.

"Hilda must be falling into her dotage," Anna grumbled. "It's her place to look after the wenches. That dreadful yellow at Stephen's Light! What are we coming to?"

They were called to dinner, and Sabina was thankful to see the table laid for three. Conrad ate and drank after his customary hearty fashion, and in the evening Sabina strained the herbs and mixed the ointment. It was a relief to hear the evening bells break over the city. To others, it may have been an ordinary enough day. To her, inevitably, it had been something of a churchyard of a day. So much had happened that she wondered if anything else would ever happen again, if her entire life would not shrivel into a straitened sequence of common tasks, meals and needle-work, mass at St. Agnes' and at the cathedral, an occasional visit to the market, the company of neighbours with their duly veined conversation about food and ailments and the efficacy of the latest found relic. All would be so ordinary and all would be sane. There was not an inch of room left for any sweet madness, still less for delight.

Only up the narrow stairway, in her room under the high gables, could Sabina cry a little, and then pass her hand over a cold mouth which had once been kissed, and wonder why it did not burn any more.

And a whole grey week had gone when one evening, just before supper, Hilda knocked at Sabina's door.

"The master wants you downstairs," she mumbled hurriedly. "Master Albert was with him after dinner today. It seems they did not talk much about that journey to Paris."

Sabina's throat went very tight.

"What's it all about?"

"Not my place to tell you, chicken, but you needn't look so frightened. There's nobody else coming to Stephen's Light, and you know what I mean without my telling you."

In the smaller of the two parlours, their clothes dyed gorgeously with the evening light, were Conrad and Anna. Anna's cheeks were flushed and swollen with tears. Conrad sat frowning.

"You were happy on the Island, Sabina, weren't you?"

Her hands trembled because he had used a word which could say nothing to her, but she answered quietly enough:

"They were kind to me, sir."

"Well, I think that I am prepared to overlook the Lady's angry letter. I've discussed the matter with Master Albert, Sabina. I mean to write to the Lady within a few days. I want them to take you."

Sabina looked at him steadily. Anna gulped and buried her face in both hands.

"You see the sense of it, don't you?" urged Conrad. "I'm afraid there won't be another man coming to Stephen's Light to ask for you, and what else is there for a decent girl to do? And it's a good house, and you spent enough time among them to know all their customs. And your portion will be a generous one," he paused, and added surprisingly, "but I must have you understand that I shan't compel you if you're against it."

[4]

About a fortnight later, Richard and Adela were nearing Genoa. At the very last inn, about half a day's riding from the city, they fell in with a portly silk merchant from Ulm. He tried to persuade Richard to make for Venice rather than Genoa.

"It's such a good port for the Levant, and there is that famous Fondaco dei Tedeschi, and you'll be among your countrymen there, and that's always pleasant on the eve of a great voyage," he bowed to Adela. "I daresay you'll be glad to see a few of your countrywomen, too. There are few of them in Genoa, I fear."

"But we have friends in Genoa," said Richard, and the fat merchant shrugged and talked of other matters. He said he had a son in the service of the Hansa but the lad was soon to leave it, life being far too hard and not at all profitable on board the Hansa ships, and Richard listened with the air of a man who knew nothing at all about the ways of the Hansa.

"They're not as powerful as they used to be," the man

from Ulm said, shaking his head. "There is Riga and Danzig always quarrelling, and now that the Tsar of Muscovy has annexed Novgorod, the Hansa stands to lose all that trade in the north."

"Surely, the Emperor might intervene there?"

"The Emperor," echoed the man from Ulm in a hollow mocking voice. "Why, sir, surely you belong to our own nation, don't you? Don't you know enough about the Emperor? What's he concerned about except his family affairs and his horoscopes? Believe me, sir, I fully understand your desire to leave Europe. Nothing seems to be going right anywhere. There's a sharp shortage of wool in England and such a dearth of pepper that in some places Christian folk must eat their victuals unseasoned. And all the tolls and the taxes are more than enough to drive a man into his grave. Come to think of it, things are difficult all the world over. You're very young, sir, and you've no idea what it means to come to the evening of your days, spent in mind and in body, and to see no fruit of your labours to come to your children. I've had three ships sunk off the Barbary coast and two wrecked off Sardinia by pirates. No, there's only one place for men of peace to go to, and that's the cloister. There you live without any trouble likely to fall on you, and even if you start a lawsuit, you know you'll win unless you're foolish enough to engage in one against another convent, and even then it depends on what fees you can pay your lawyers. Yes, sir, I've put two of my daughters in religion, and they'll win my soul's salvation as well as their own. It was well worth it—parting with all that money for their dowries!"

So the portly merchant went on, smiling at Adela and

eating his stuffed pike, and they were glad to see him ride eastwards in the morning.

Genoa dazzled Adela. Plunged into that world of narrow, colourful, dirty streets, of tall marble palaces, of crowds of tattered beggars and brown naked children, mule-bells ringing and church bells chiming, Adela clung hard to Richard's arm.

"This seems such a different world," she murmured. "I've never seen anything like it—not even in England. Is this city bigger than London?"

"If I were an Englishman, I'd certainly say it was not, but I don't really know," and presently Richard brought her to the wide sunflooded quays. The wind doing what it pleased with her dark blue cloak, Adela suddenly dropped his arm and stopped talking. There lay the great harbour, studded all over with barges, caravels and galleys and a multitude of other craft, tawny-red, brown, dull-pink sails gleaming sharp under the southern sky. Adela looked and kept silent because she felt she could not tell Richard that the scene had moved her to remember *"Benedicite omnia opera Domini Dominum . . ."* and that she wished she might repeat the verses and felt she did not dare to do so even within her heart.

Richard's friend had already bespoken a room for them at an inn in the Vico dei Macellai, with a carved Turk's head over the narrow doorway. The dark stairway looked incredibly dirty, and the entire place smelt of fish and burnt oil, but to Adela such things mattered no longer. She sat down on the narrow trestle and began untying their bundles to get at a comb, a towel, a fresh kerchief for herself and some tidy hose for Richard. He, astride the only

stool in the room, watched her in silence. Adela looked
much thinner, her face was tanned and weather-beaten,
and her delicate hands were roughened, the nails chipped
here and there. But a grace Richard had remarked at their
very first meeting still lingered about her and, watching her
quietly arranging the few meagre comforts of the room,
Richard once again admitted himself to be a fortunate
man.

"I must take you to the cathedral," he said at last.
"There is a piece of the True Cross set in a marvellous gold
casket, and also the Cup used at the Lord's last supper."

At once a shadow flickered across Adela's face.

"I mustn't cheat," she stammered, blood dyeing her
cheeks a wild crimson. "Richard, I beg you not to take this
as a complaint. I know I've done a wicked thing—but I
must be as honest as I can. There was heaven and there
was you, and I chose you, and you've become my heaven,
but I mayn't kiss a holy relic with these lips."

"Sweetheart," Richard began when her look silenced
him.

He laid aside all idea of argument and, presently, she
followed him to a house in the neighbourhood where a man
from Regensburg had money and a message for Richard.
Their passages to Trebizond were already booked on board
the *Santa Caterina* due to leave Genoa within a week. The
business over, the man talked about the assassination of
the Duke of Milan.

"I think it'll soon be time for me and a few others to return home. The new Duke, whom they call Il Moro, means
no good to Genoa. Trade is certain to suffer."

Adela listened attentively. She had never heard about

the murdered Duke, nor did she understand why his successor should make a man from Regensburg leave Genoa for his native city. She knew so little about the outside world that the conversation might have been carried on in Greek for all the sense she gleaned from it, but it pleased her to discover that there were men of substance and importance who were prepared to see an equal in Richard.

"So in a week's time, sweeting," he said, when they sat down to a dinner of fried fish and pigeons, "we shall be on the high seas." He paused to dip a piece of fish into sauce, swallowed it, wiped his fingers, and added, his eyes staring at the dish, "there's a matter I must mention before we leave Genoa."

Adela stopped eating at once.

"We must get married. My friend from Regensburg knows of a friar who would do it and not ask any questions either."

Adela pushed her trencher away. She did not shake her head. She did not even look at him but her lips shaped a "no" in such a shredded voice that Richard felt uneasy.

"Why not?" he asked, schooling himself to speak calmly.

"I'm your mistress, Richard—"

"You're much more than that," he broke in, and she checked him at once.

"No, Richard, I can be no man's wife. A ring was once put on my finger. That vow I've broken of my own will. I may not, dare not make a mockery of another promise. Do you understand?"

"But where would the mockery be? We're man and wife —in God's sight."

"We never could be, we never could be," she cried so

urgently, her eyes clouded with tears, and Richard stopped all further persuasion.

He had to leave Adela the next day to go and see the skipper of the *Santa Caterina* and, making his way towards the deafening bustle of the quays, Richard wondered if some payment would be expected from him for having broken his betrothal to Sabina. It had seemed so easy to sing a facile little song, to smile and to kiss, and to murmur delicate little phrases about a devotion which had never had any lodgment in his heart. It had seemed almost inevitable for him to weave all those romantic threads into what would have been a good business bargain. So many men did it. He was neither first nor last. Conrad had offered a glittering opportunity, and at the time it had indeed appeared as a satisfying conclusion. But he had not then met Adela. . . .

"And, of course, Sabina'll soon find another bridegroom —with such a dowry as hers—unless some custom of theirs is against it. I suppose I should have sent a message to Master Conrad. Well, there'll be time enough for explanations once we get to Trebizond."

He returned to their lodgings to find Adela white and shaken.

"Has someone been in here and annoyed you?"

"No," she said thinly, "but there was a crowd of pilgrims going down the street, and there were several Capuchin friars with them. I watched them from the window."

"Yes," Richard tried to speak lightly, "I saw them near the quayside."

Adela shivered and turned her face away from him.

"I heard them. They were shouting at the top of their

voices, and in our language, too. I understood every word, Richard. . . ."

She paused as though battling for breath, and he waited.

"The friars kept telling those people to remember that there was no turning back once the hand was set to the plough."

"But that was for the pilgrims," he urged her. "They're on their way to the Holy Land. They've promised to get there."

Slowly, she turned towards him, and he felt shaken by the expression on her face. It was as though all life and light had been wiped off it.

"Yes, they've promised to get there," she echoed leadenly.

"Sweetheart. . . ."

She moistened her lips very slowly.

"Richard, will it hurt you very much if I stayed behind?"

"Stayed behind where?"

"Here. I daren't go back to the Island—but if I stayed here—and worked among the very poor, perhaps, and lived alone, yes, yes, quite alone, Richard—"

For all answer he stooped over her and gathered her into his arms. She did not resist him and, holding her, Richard felt as though the last shred of strength had left the thin body. Her face felt cold and her hands were burning.

"No, no," she moaned, her head pillowed on his shoulder. "No, no, I daren't stay behind. I daren't be alone any more. I'm afraid of this place, Richard, I'm afraid of the bells. They ring in rebuke. . . . They ring in wrath. . . ."

"You shall not stay behind. You're coming with me. In less than a week we'll be gone from here, and the *Santa*

Caterina is a good stout ship, and this is the best time of
the year for sailing—there'll be no rough winds to disturb
you, sweetheart," and Richard went on whispering little
tags and wisps of reassurance and endearment until Adela
sank into an uneasy sleep.

Dawn had barely broken when she woke him. In the
cold grey light he could see her enormous eyes and the deep
flush all over her cheeks. Her speech came slow and slurred
as though her tongue had grown too big and heavy for her
mouth.

"I've got the sickness, Richard. Leave me . . . Leave
me . . . I should never have left the Island . . . Richard, you mustn't go to Trebizond . . . England, perhaps. . . ."

Within an hour she was unconscious. Below stairs, the
innkeeper swore that he would not keep her in his house,
he could not afford it to be said that someone died of
plague under his roof, but an apothecary came and pro-
nounced it to be a fever, and Richard and Adela were left
in peace. The apothecary brought oddly coloured powders,
a very special distillation of poppy seeds and a jar of mal-
odorous green unguent. He bled Adela, forced a powder
between her lips, prescribed a few other remedies, and was
about to leave when Richard stayed him.

"You're coming tomorrow?"

The man shrugged.

"The business'll have to run its course. There's nothing
else for me to do. Don't forget the powders and the cordial,
and keep her warm. There's nothing else for me to do," he
repeated, as though Richard had contradicted him, "and
I'm a very busy man."

"How long does a fever like that take?"

"Hard to say. The lady seems rather exhausted. It may be three days or a week, or even longer," the little man shrugged.

On the fourth day Richard was trying to carry on with the powders and the cordial but Adela was sunk into such stupor that he dared not disturb her. He resolved to have the apothecary summoned again when towards midnight Adela opened her eyes, sighed, and struggled for breath.

"Are you feeling any easier, sweetheart?" Carefully Richard poured a little of the cordial into the horn cup but she would not take it.

"There . . . are no rubies . . . in the city . . . of God . . . so I once heard. . . ."

"Will you have me send for a priest?"

Adela's voice rang a little steadier:

"I shan't cheat now . . . I loved you . . . I still love you . . . Please, stay. . . ."

He stayed, crouching by the pallet, his fingers holding her hand. Soon Adela closed her eyes again. Richard waited, trimming the lanthorn very cautiously lest any immoment gesture of his were to disturb her. But she never spoke to him again.

PART IV

Grey Dawn for Sabina

THE market square was to the north-west of the cathedral and, contrary to all orders, booths and stalls spread with such obduracy that some of them were close by the great west door, and not a few bold pedlars would sometimes display their wares on the flagstones of the porch. The cathedral was the Archbishop's, the market belonged to the city, and the situation was poised delicately. There were shrines and relics inside the cathedral, and they drew pilgrims from all the corners of the Empire. Yet, strictly speaking, the pilgrims' offerings went nowhere except into the ecclesiastical coffers whilst some of the men in the Archbishop's service held the market licence and, all in all, the market could be said to enrich both the clerical and the lay factions. So pedlars' wares were permitted the hospitality of the porch, the sanction being expressed in terms of diplomatically silent acquiescence.

Seen from the steps of the guildhall, the market square suggested a huge multi-coloured bee-hive. Oxen and poultry and pigs, heavily wheeled carts, children and women, black, white, brown and violet-gowned clerics, the city council's men in sober brown, keeping a sharp eye on all the scales, tallies and yardsticks, tax-collectors with their huge leather pouches, and here and there a man in the green and purple livery of the Archbishop's guard, careful not to get in the way of the men in brown because the Archbishop's guard had the right to assert themselves in any church and up the hill towards the great battlemented palace outside the gates, but here, in the city, the council's sovereignty came first, and it was for the council's men to demand the tax on bolts of scarlet cloth from Regensburg and to assess the value of a basket of apples brought in by a farmer's wife.

Here, then, the city bought and sold, heard the world's news, gossiped and quarrelled, laid schemes which had nothing to do with the decisions reached at the guildhall, and breathed amply within a liberty not determined by any enactments of officialdom.

Here, a small space away from booths and stalls, near the corner formed by a merchant's house and St. Nicholas's north wall, men—and frequently women, too—would drift, their business over, and talk to one another, to neighbours and to strangers. Here was the city's strongest heartbeat where often a fantastic fable would be twisted this way and that way until it was almost captious not to see a grain of fact in it. Here, on occasions, an angry interchange of stubbornly held opinions would lead to the bells of St. Agnes' ringing awkward to arm and muster. The city guard never interfered unless the heightened temper of the crowd made it necessary.

"Now then, good people," shouted a man, his cobbler's tattered leather apron crammed with nuts and apples. "See these? My wife's sister brought them in yesterday. 'Take them to the market,' she begged me, and what am I doing now? Taking them back. The tax they expected me to pay on them! Tolls and taxes! That's our life from beginning to end! Pay at the market, pay on the road, pay on the river, pay on the towpath! Think of the Rhine—the whole stretch of its banks dotted with toll-houses! And who gets the money, I ask you?"

"Why, the shaven heads, of course," came a surly mutter from the fringe of the little crowd, and everybody echoed it.

"Thank heaven the lake hasn't got a toll-house. You can still cross over to the Island and pay the bargeman's fee and not be mulcted by any fat-bellied tollman!"

"Yes, you can indeed!"

At once, the grievance of tolls and taxes was swept aside, and the day's most urgent matter leapt to the front.

"Ah yes, good folks, the Island! That young man and his fancy-piece must have made straight for Augsburg and then on for Verona. That's a seven days' journey, and a gossip of mine saw them having the horse watered at Neuss," said the cobbler.

"No, no, neighbour, you're wrong there. It's Wörms they made for, and the girl wore a man's clothes—a red jerkin and black hose, and I heard that she carried a dagger, too."

"Rubbish!" broke in a tall dark man with a broken nose. "They made straight for the mountains. They were going to Venice."

"Wherever they went," began a little jeweller, shaking his red-capped head, "they're gone. And the day before the young man crossed to the Island, he bought a fine chrysolite ring from me. I'd a feeling then that he was not buying it for Master Conrad's daughter. It's a lover's stone, too. Well, what will you, neighbours? It all happened round about St. Valentine's day, and even birds will choose their mates at that time."

"Your memory's gone down a well," said the cobbler roughly. "St. Valentine's day indeed! It happened in May. Choosing their mates! What business was there for a nun to choose a mate, I ask you?"

Nobody had any answer to give him and here two serving-women from St. Catherine's Dominican hospice joined the men.

"Talking about the Island, were you? Well, that is a holy place indeed! I can tell you what happened there this very last Easter. I was serving our prioress with a dish of baked carp, and I heard the story from her own lips. The ladies were having their procession to the sepulchre, and it fell to that wanton to be one of the three Maries, and she should have sung that very holy song. I've no Latin and I can't remember the words, but our prioress said they were very deep and holy—all about loving the blessed Jesus in life and in death also. Well, when it was the wanton's turn to begin, she couldn't sing a single word and turned as white as her wimple, and cried so loud that everybody could hear—even the herdsmen who were far away, 'I've no love for Him—either living or dead,' and down she fell, and just at that moment a large toad crept from under a blackthorn bush, and it was only after Sext and it grew as dark as the night. The ladies all ran back to the cloisters, and they never had a procession that day."

"Well! What a story!"

"Our prioress never tells stories." The woman's sallow
cheeks reddened in fury, and a fat baker soothed her:

"Nobody said a word against your prioress. It's the
Island we're talking about! So proud they are, and yet there
was a witch and a wanton among them—for all her high
birth—running away with a merchant!"

"Not even a merchant," said the cobbler. "He'd no place
of his own. He was in the service of the Hansa."

"Still, he dressed finely enough," a woman retorted. "His
sleeves were always slashed lengthwise in that new Italian
fashion. Why, he once came to my man's shop and wanted
a doublet of green velvet made in the same way—but none
among our men had much notion about the slashing."

"Why, that's easy enough, I should say," smiled the
jeweller. "Take a pair of shears and cut away to your
heart's content. There's nothing more to it, is there?"

"Nothing more to it!" the tailor's wife bridled up. "Do
you imagine that fine cloth is just like a sheep's back?"

But sartorial details roused no lasting interest. The Island was half-way across the lake, Richard of Troyes had
gone and taken one of the ladies with him, but Stephen's
Light stood within the city gates, and Sabina was the daughter of an important burgher, so they must remember her.

"Yes," sighed the woman from St. Catherine's hospice,
"that's what comes of riding too high! They must even
choose a foreigner for a bridegroom, our own folk not being
good enough for them! And look at the girl's mother—
strutting about like any lady of rank with a long mantle
and her heart-shaped head-dress! Yes, much too proud
they are!"

"Still that young man was no great catch!"

"And they don't aim high," said the jeweller. "They are decent folk. I've heard that they buy no other fish save herrings in Lent, and their maids never gather herbs but say a Pater properly, and they pay all their accounts without any argument, too."

"Herrings!" the woman curved her mouth in contempt. "That's because they're mean, and as to mumbling a prayer in your herb garden, well, what is there to it?"

"Nothing at all," the cobbler sneered at her. "The friars are at prayer most of the time, and someone said they've banished poverty to heaven."

"Don't you dare say such things to me," the woman clenched both fists. "There's our prioress, and she won't have honey eaten in the frater—so strict they are."

"Now, now," said somebody. "Leave the friars alone. Far too much is heard of them, anyhow. But I must say that Master Conrad's no friend to poor folk. It's all on his account that we weavers have no right to buy wool for ourselves. We're only allowed to work at it for the mercers, and it's they who batten on us, and it was Master Conrad who urged that law to be brought in."

"Right you are, gossip," piped a reedy voice from the back. "He's no friend to the working people. Why, he had me fined last Martinmas. He said that I had put salt in the dough—as though an honest baker ever would! But what will you, neighbours? Nobody ever listens to us. . . ."

"They will some day," said the weaver, his scarred face darkening. "It's always monks and burghers today. It can't last so for ever. But I think the shaven heads are the worst. If you deal with them, you must pay on the nail. Go to

Allenbach, neighbours, where the shaven heads of Reichenau sell their wine. Let you be dying of thirst, they'd never let you have a drop unless you pay hard cash for it. Remember that black hungry year five winters back? St. Eugene's granaries were bulging with corn, and did they let anyone have a bushel of it?"

"You're right, gossip. I dropped a sack of flax on the road past St. Eugene's the other day, and their cellarer—may he rot in hell—happened to ride past, and he claimed it at once."

"Never mind," cried the weaver. "Our day shall come in the end—but tell me, neighbours, has anyone seen Master Conrad's daughter?"

Heads were shaken, and the jeweller said pensively:

"And what's going to happen to her now?"

"Well," said the tailor's wife, "Otho's sister who works in the kitchens at Stephen's Light says it's the cloister for her."

"But who's going to get the house and all the rest of it?" asked someone. "Master Conrad's got no nephews that I've ever heard of, and the city will never stand for a nunnery being set up at Stephen's Light."

"That's all you know," said the woman from the Dominican hospice, and pursed her lips importantly, but nobody believed that a rich burgher's daughter would enter such an unimportant house as St. Catherine's, and the woman's carefully repeated "That's all you know" was wasted on the crowd. Their minds once again turned to the elopement.

"If they do get caught," reflected the cobbler, "it may well be the gibbet for him, and she'll be sent on a peace journey. They still do that, gossips. Why, at Essen, a Franciscan sister went that way, and they'd no fewer than four masons to do the job. A slow death, neighbours. Plenty of time to make your peace with God, I reckon."

"That's against the law now," scowled the weaver.

"Who says so?"

"I do."

"And I suppose my nephew's brother-in-law is a liar, is he?" demanded the cobbler.

"I know nothing about your nephew's brother-in-law."

"I suppose you don't. By all I hear, all his friends are respectable folk. And he happens to be a mason at Essen."

"And he walled the nun in with his own hands, I suppose?" laughed the weaver.

"He knows the men who did the job."

"What a story!"

"A story, did you say?"

"And I'll say it again if it pleases me—"

"But it doesn't please me," shouted the cobbler, letting go his apron, scattering nuts and apples all about him. Within an instant, his arms were bared to the shoulder, and fists went to work with a will until a brown-coated man from the city guard ran up, gave a clout each to the cobbler and the weaver, ordered one of them to pick up the scattered fruit, commandeered an empty basket from a woman, and calmly walked away with the booty.

[2]

Such gossip never crept into the parlours at Stephen's Light. Conrad would not allow it in his presence, and all the maids were afraid of Anna's heavily beringed hand. Still, the men about the yard and the warehouses and the women in the kitchens brought stories from shop and market and any street corner, and it was easy to whisper when scraping the grease off a skillet. Moreover, the kitchen was safe enough because Anna hardly ever appeared there. Whatever the disaster fallen upon the house, the season's duties could not be denied. There was soft fruit to sort for preserving, herbs to dry, fresh mint and penny-royal to sprinkle in chests and presses.

At the back gate, the paupers' dole was duly distributed in honour of a marriage never to be celebrated. For the space of one morning, Hilda and three maids carried large trays of mutton and ham pies, broiled fish, wheaten bread and baked apples smeared with honey and studded with poppy seeds. There was an abundance of food and drink, a marked absence of talk, and Hilda, arms akimbo, took care to keep the people from poking their heads through the gate. Thus, very few questions were asked, and those received no answer and, the last baked apple pushed into the scabby hand of a blind beggar, Hilda slammed the little gate and waddled back to the house, conscious of a difficult and unnecessary task well done.

"Anyway, there's never any waste at Stephen's Light."

Anna would have endorsed the words. Not so Sabina. She felt all wasted inwardly, and it did not seem to matter greatly whether or no there should be waste outside.

After that first outburst when, drowned in a sense of loss deeper than any words could reach, she had slashed to ribbons her wedding-kirtle, Sabina had no more tears to shed —not even when alone in her room. She wondered if she had become a changeling. She felt as though anything done by her or for her were something apart, happening in a world in which she now moved by the sole virtue of a continuous pretence. She tried not to think about Richard— but to her annoyance, because such reflections could not but anger her, her thoughts would oftener and oftener turn to Dame Adela. Richard's had been a vulgarly crude betrayal. The matter of Dame Adela suggested no easily understood vulgarity. She had betrayed not only herself and two other people but God, the Holy Lady and all the saints, and such a trespass seemed inconceivable when Sabina remembered a quality about Dame Adela once made evident in the church on the Island. Then, with her cold pure face raised towards the altar, Dame Adela had indeed looked all caught up into adoration and love, and that was something that Dame Elizabeth had once hinted about. Sabina felt uneasily convinced that such adoration and love could not have been faked. They were wholly beyond her, and yet she thought that she could recognize their true quality. It was all very puzzling. If Adela loved God and had promised herself to Him for all eternity, how could she have come to exchange such a portion for the love of man? Sabina could understand nothing, and she could only think of it in terms of a very thin, timid candle burning in a sun-flooded room. She doubted if she would ever learn anything once she was among the ladies. Dame Elizabeth, Sabina remembered, had a peculiar reticence. She certainly would never talk to her, Sabina, about a matter as painful as Richard's defection.

Once she was among them . . . Sabina blushed, and

here was her mother, her plump fingers busy with a mountain of black cherries, saying:

"It's the best thing for you, girl. The ladies know you well enough, and I'm glad to say that your father's forgiven the abbess for that angry letter she sent him a while ago. You'll take your silver posset cup and the sapphire buckle and other things." Anna pressed both hands on the cherries packed tight into a stone jar and sighed a little. "Indeed, you must take enough gear with you. It's such a rich house, and we can't have a daughter of ours go there—ashamed of her dowry. Your father"—here Anna checked herself rather awkwardly and turned her mind to a different matter. "Ah yes, your father said you were not to be beaten for tearing that silver damask kirtle to pieces, but you were wicked to do it, Sabina. There was ample stuff in it to make a cope for the old man at St. Agnes', and we'd already promised him one for Christmas."

"But I wouldn't have liked to see the kirtle turned into a cope, Madam."

"That wouldn't have concerned you," Anna retorted, and pushed an empty jar towards Sabina. "Pack the cherries in, will you? Why, what's the matter?"

"I was just going out with Hilda, Madam. There are lemons to buy and a few other things."

Anna frowned.

"Your father'd much rather you did not go shopping for a few days," she spoke heavily, and somehow Sabina asked no questions. The cherries packed, she slipped to the back of the house to wait for Hilda's return. Hilda presently appeared, the satchel bulging with lemons, a big rent across the shoulders of her bodice, mud drying on her skirts, and a scratch across her chin.

"Heavens! Did you tumble down somewhere?"

"I'm not yet blind enough for that," Hilda snapped, and flung the satchel away so that the lemons made a bright yellow scatter on the flagstones of the porch.

"Then what happened?"

"Never you mind, chicken, and you've no business to come and stand in the back porch at all. Get you to the parlour and go on with your needlework. Isn't there enough for a young lady to do in a house but she must waste her time waiting for an old servant by the back porch?"

Sabina did not move.

"You are going to tell me what happened?"

"Well, since you want to know, I gave the fishmonger's wife a good slice of my mind, and she threw some mud at me and tried to claw at my shoulder, too." Hilda chuckled proudly. "But I was too sharp for her. She lost two of her front teeth, and she'll never wear her green kirtle again—I tore it from waist to hem."

"How could you have such a brawl in the street?"

"It was in a shop, and it was well worth it. I won't have anyone saying things."

"What things?"

"Never you mind, my darling. It's all in at one ear and out at another with me—but did you expect me to stand there and have a she-devil tell everybody that my young mistress had made a rascal go clean out of his mind? To say that you'd given him something in his wine so that he couldn't look at any young woman without desiring her. Did you expect me to listen to such poison and do nothing

about it? I hope she's still spitting blood, that I do. I'll gossip her again if I get another chance. And then to have the
sauce to tell me that the young villain must have got scared
of all the learning you've got!"

"Never mind any of that, Hilda. I won't have you brawling with anyone, you understand? What does it matter
what anyone says? Just think what my mother will say—"

"Need she know? I'll have a good scrub before I go near
her."

"Brawling in a shop, and with me going to the Island,
too—"

Hilda stooped for the scattered lemons.

"A tame ending, indeed," she muttered, "and I can't see
much sense in it either. One apple rotting on a tree doesn't
mean that the sap's gone. One man failing you, and off you
go with a mouth far too pretty to mumble prayers all day
long. What'll you do with your body once you're on the
Island? What I've always held is that a body must be ruled
—but within reason. There'd be far less lechery in the
world if priests could live in honest wedlock with their
women, and you know it, and there isn't a weaver in the
city but thinks the same way. And just why is that learned
and saintly gentleman, Dr. Busch, riding up and down in
the Empire, I ask you? Putting religious houses in order,
so pasty-mouthed folk will tell you. Ah, take the younger
ones out of the cloister, give each a husband and a child,
and the world'll be a lot cleaner—to my thinking—"

"Stop—"

"Ah my darling, I'm old now and ugly enough, but I was
once seventeen, and I knew a man and I bore a child, and I
reckon life would have been a sorrier business without them

for all the sorrow I've had. Well, you haven't gone to the Island yet."

"Stop." Sabina stamped her foot.

"And who else is there to talk to you about it? The mistress can't say one word without the master prompting her, and the master is not a woman, my chick. Most men imagine that any girl has it in her to follow in the steps of the Holy Lady. Wicked rubbish that is! I tell you that life'll be hard for all you'll lie under satin coverlets and eat delicately."

"You're mad and also wicked. The ladies are good. I know them."

"Did I say they were wicked? No, far too proud they are, my chick, to fall into any common wickedness—seeing they're all daughters of kings and dukes."

"Leave off talking to me. If I were to tell my mother, you'd get a beating and be sent away."

"But then you could never tell her," Hilda said sensibly, and somehow they made their peace over the scatter of lemons.

A few days later Sabina called Hilda into her room.

"Here's some money. Please buy a wax candle and light it at St. Sturm's chapel in the cathedral. Here's some more for a pound of turmeric. And"—Sabina paused and fingered a gold coin and a pink silk girdle. "Call at old Gunta's this evening. Let her light her fire and look into it. You'll ask her just two questions. The first is—'where?' and the second—'how?' Now have you got it all clear?"

"Well, yes," said Hilda, and stared at the gold coin and the silk girdle with such obvious regret that Sabina broke in:

"Never you mind! You may think it's too much for old Gunta—but you'll give both things to her."

It was dark when Hilda slipped into the room and laid a small bag by the candle on the table.

"Here's the turmeric, my pet, and your candle's burning all right. I gave the money and the girdle to Gunta. She never looked at either, and her place smelt so foul that it sickened me. But she lit the little fire at once, and she went on muttering so long I quite thought she'd never finish. She must be going out of her wits, chicken."

"But the answers! I want the answers!"

"I've got them word for word, my darling, which is very clever of me seeing that I didn't understand your questions. 'Where?' I asked her first, and Gunta replied." Hilda knitted her forehead and went on slowly, minting every syllable. " 'In the place of the heart.' " Here, the smoke got into her throat, and she coughed a little, and then went on, "A pleasant place, her own, hard to hold."

"You haven't made it all up?"

"St. Ursula strike me dead if I have. Now, the second question was 'how,' and Gunta's answer was queer, I must say. 'By speaking strange words to an elderly man.' That, I must say, doesn't smell of the Island—except for the Archbishop, perhaps, but they say he hardly ever goes there now."

But Sabina said nothing. Hilda waited—only to be thanked and dismissed. Sabina hardly heard the closing of the door. She lay, her arms behind her head. The intent behind the first question had been simple enough: where would she live and fulfil herself? In the place of her heart, "a pleasant place, her own, hard to hold." Had Gunta, by peering into the flames, seen her, Sabina, at Stephen's Light? But how was that possible? Yet Stephen's Light was truly and supremely the place of her heart. But the second answer was even more involved than the first. "How?" she had asked, and Gunta had answered: "By speaking strange words to an elderly man." Did that mean that she, Sabina, would never go to the Island but would marry—of course, at her father's pleasure—marry some elderly burgher in the city and treat him strangely? And how could the first answer dovetail with the second? Sabina fell into an uneasy sleep, the riddle still unexplained in her mind.

She asked Hilda if Gunta had been sober that night. Hilda shrugged.

"Well, I could see nothing there except some clouded beer in a crock."

"And nobody saw you go in?"

"Oh dear no. Don't you fret yourself, my pet. Old Gunta's practice is not what you might call flourishing these days. For one thing, she's grown rather hard of hearing, and nobody wants their little secrets shouted about, do they? And for another, most people—so I hear—are mortally frightened of her. They say that she smears her body all over with an unguent the devil himself gave to her, and everybody knows that it'd be no use getting her for witchcraft—she'd neither drown nor burn because of the ointment. Anyway, I hope her answers were of some use to you, my pet?"

But Sabina said nothing.

That night she dreamt that she lay in Richard's arms, with Adela watching closely, a piteous little smile curving her mouth. Then Richard vanished, and Adela moved

closer and laid a very cold hand on Sabina's breast and said:
"You've seen him go. You could never hold him. He's like
spring water and as cold. See what he has done to me," and
here Adela began dissolving—slowly and horribly, her
face, shoulders and arms turning into runnels of clouded
water, and some of it brushed against Sabina's cheek, and
then she woke with a start and felt the salt of her tears
sharp and hot on her mouth. An owl screeched in the orchard, and Sabina fumbled for her beads.

That was her punishment, she thought, for sending Hilda
to old Gunta's to get unhallowed counsel, and Sabina trembled remembering the horror felt at the gradual dissolving
of Adela's body. It was a punishment and also a warning.
Her mother was right. To go to the Island would be the best
thing for her, but here Sabina remembered Stephen's Light.

She sat up and pushed open the wooden slats of the bed.
She stared at a corner of the room etched clear in the
moonlight, a chest with a silver bangle on it and the round,
steel mirror, a pale brown kirtle spread on another press,
and the oak floorboards grooved and cradled. Sabina lay
still and looked on. There had been her wild inarticulate
passion for Richard. There had never been any wildness in
her feeling for Stephen's Light; she had loved it steadfastly
and deeply all her life, and she knew that she would take
its persuasion with her wherever she went, that she would
always cherish in her memory the serene intimacy of its
corners, its candid windows, and the satisfying severity of
its stone and timber.

Here it came to Sabina—and poignantly—so that she
must struggle against tears—that—whatever dowry her
father were to give her, Stephen's Light could form no part

of it. Master Albert had said so. Stephen's Light was no mere house but a living vein in the body of the city, a great and firmly rooted business with all its warehouses and lands, and Master Albert had made it clear that the city council would never permit any religious body to take possession of it. He had told them about a baker's brother having lately willed the premises and the goodwill of the business to the monks of St. Eugene, and the city had contested the will, and in the end, the premises only—but not the goodwill—were ceded to the monks. So Stephen's Light would have to go to one Peter, a distant cousin of Conrad's, a prosperous leather merchant at Würzburg. Her father had once met him, a stout elderly man much respected at Würzburg and beyond, with a timid shrivelled wife and ten sturdy children, one of whom, Sabina supposed, would reign at Stephen's Light when all of them were gone.

Therefore, she told herself, old Gunta's answers were rubbish. Sabina would never hold the place of her heart, and there was no other choice for her. She thought of what stories she had heard about learned ladies in France and at the Italian courts, who were supposed to be capable of writing a Latin sonnet during dinner and of discussing philosophy in Greek in between the dances at a banquet. Sabina was neither lady nor scholar but she knew her letters and the abacus, and such modest accomplishments might be found useful on the Island.

A few days were gone, and Master Albert, important in a formal fur-trimmed gown, sat in the parlour at Stephen's Light, all the writing materials spread on the table before him. He had been invited by Conrad to come and draft the petition to the abbess together with a private, less starchily worded letter, and the household knew that their master was not to be disturbed. Old Canon Bruno, Hugo the mercer and Barbara his wife were coming to dinner, and Sabina was sent into the kitchen to beat up the eggs for a cinnamon batter. Suddenly, a back door was wrenched open. Startled, Sabina dropped an egg. The pale yellow trickle spread over the flagstones and stained the toe of her crimson slipper.

"Jesu, Mary," shouted the cook from the doorway. "Run for the mistress somebody! A gardener from the Island's in the city. The Lady is dead. Nobody knows why—but I'd say they must have poisoned her. Easy enough to slip things into the wine. . . ."

[3]

At her last chapter, having forced a reluctant vote on the nuns, Lady Isabella had behaved sensibly for the first time during her abbacy. "Let us admit a burgher's daughter into this house," she had said, and left them all perplexed by the unexpected curve in her approach to a difficult and—as most ladies thought—an unnecessary problem. Lady Isabella had given no reasons for her decision, and their bewilderment plumbed uneasy depths. Their charter, as they still thought, was sacrosanct; it formed— so far as their life was concerned—the very backbone of the same tradition to which Lady Isabella paid homage to the ludicrous extent of not allowing a single printed book to be brought to the Island because the printing of books, in her opinion, cut right across the hallowed texture of inviolable tradition. Now she was insisting on a violent departure from the old pattern, and she would offer neither explanation nor excuse for the precedent.

It flung the house into a fever, and Dame Blanche and Dame Elizabeth, chosen to carry the message to Stephen's Light, were not allowed an instant's peace. For the first time in anyone's memory, the house was sharply divided, and the opposing faction was led by Dame Augusta—with her Brunswick and Wittelsbach kin, in whose opinion Dame Adela's defection seemed but a soap-bubble compared with the attack upon the charter. She went about, dropping her exalted kin's titles like so many sharp-jagged pebbles, wondering what the King would say and hinting that the Duchess might never again come on a pilgrimage to the Island. The world, said Dame Augusta, was indeed falling to pieces, and houses like their own were the last anchorages for high rank and true blue blood. They should remember all the peasant revolts in recent years, and the growing pride and insolence of indifferently bred burghers was but another challenge to their way of life. Already, Dame Augusta pointed out, there were corners in the Empire where high birth counted for nothing at all. Her cousin, the Duke of Brunswick, but lately widowed, would he take a merchant's daughter for his second wife, demanded Dame Augusta, and the ladies' good breeding forbade them to remind her that one of her own nieces, from the same exalted house of Brunswick, had but lately married a banker from Augsburg, the ink being barely dry on the man's patent of nobility.

"There are no ambiguities in the charter. It says most plainly—each candidate must produce evidences of six generations of noble blood. That girl could not count one. I've nothing against her personally, but of course it was a mistake to have her come here as a pupil."

Dame Augusta talked much and persuasively. She was so obviously on fire with her loyalty to the house that even those who had voted for Sabina's admission could not but agree with her arguments, though they were careful not to be too obvious in their acquiescence since Lady Isabella's displeasure was no light matter even for the best connected lady on the Island. Alone among them all, Dame Elizabeth chose to differ from Dame Augusta.

"I've no idea if Sabina will ever come or no, but I confess I am glad of the Lady's decision. She's perfectly right."

"But you spoke against it in chapter, Madam."

"Yes, I'm against any compulsion, Madam, and I feel that Sabina would hardly care to come once her own wishes were consulted. But I meant that the Lady was right in a different sense: we've no business to keep our doors closed against tradesmen's daughters."

"Madam," for an instant Dame Augusta's voice nearly failed her, "that I should hear such a thing from you—who come from the house of Meissen! And wasn't your own mother a Hapsburg?"

Dame Elizabeth shrugged.

"There's been far too much talk about high descent, Madam. Aren't we rather apt to forget that the Lord's blood was shed for all the sinners in the world?"

A few among the ladies present bowed their heads in approval, but Dame Augusta merely crossed the garth to engage yet another willing audience in a passionate argument for the defence of the charter.

Meanwhile, Lady Isabella kept to the privacy of her lodgings. She even banished Dame Lucia, saying curtly that she had no leisure for any further business that day.

Lady Isabella knew she was right, and yet it hurt and angered her that she should be right. Five hundred odd years lay between her generation and the granting of the charter by the Emperor Conrad. The face of Europe had changed beyond all recognition. The hurried and flurried pedlars of those days had vanished, giving place to stolid, shrewd burghers who, ensconced within the proud walls of their towns, knew how to impose their way of life, their customs, laws and influence upon Europe, and dukes now meant little to those who, on occasions, knew how to brave Imperial displeasure. So much of life's surface was informed by the exigencies of business, and still more lay behind each fresh business venture. It was a new society where effort, hard work, individual ability and initiative answered for banners, escutcheons and pedigrees written on dusty sheets of floriated parchment.

Lady Isabella was sharply aware of such things. She knew that things were changing everywhere in the Empire, certainly in Italy and—very likely—in England, and the change in conditions had been shaping for a few generations back, and the Dominicans and the Franciscans had taken due note of it. The prioress of St. Catherine's hospice in the city had a master baker for her father.

New blood was certainly needed. High descent no longer mattered, and it hurt and angered Lady Isabella that it should be so.

It was a hot, heavy day, and its burden oppressed her.

She felt slightly sick, and she wondered if the blood in her head were coming to a boiling point. She snatched at a bunch of herbs and drank a little cooled beer. The nausea soon left her, but she chose to spend the rest of the day by herself.

At supper, however, it was the duty of Dame Lucia and Dame Blanche to make their appearance. Lady Isabella toyed with a sliver of roast meat and sipped her wine in silence, occasionally glancing at her two little dogs asleep on a white fur rug. The servants came and went in silence, and through the opened window the mingled scents of a summer evening stole into the room. The two ladies would have liked to talk, but Dame Lucia's tentative remark about the rising cost of gold-leaf was received without comment, and Dame Blanche's enthusiasm over a new French subtlety of pistachios, wafers and cream, shaped and painted to resemble a peacock, led to a mordant remark:

"Can't any of you think of anything except food?"

That aggrieved them both since their minds were full of chapter matters but of necessity they held their tongues. Lady Isabella retired early, Katryn, a novice, being on duty outside her bedroom. A little earlier, the girl had dropped a heavy silver candlestick in the abbess's parlour and been soundly cuffed for her clumsiness so that she lay down, her face damp with tears. Suddenly, Katryn woke up, startled by stertorous groaning behind the closed door.

"The Lady must be at prayer. Perhaps, she's sorry for her bad temper," thought the girl, when the groaning was followed by a heavy thud. That did not sound devotional, and Katryn dared greatly, rose from her pallet, and raised the door hasp. In the cold moonlight she saw Lady Isabella prostrate on the floor, her face upwards, the coif fallen off her head, and her arms flung wide. Katryn smothered a scream and tiptoed nearer. The Lady's mouth seemed oddly crooked, her eyes were wide open, but she did not see the girl, nor did she appear to hear Katryn's stammer:

"What can I do for you, my lady?"

There was no answer and, frightened, Katryn turned and ran to clang the iron bell at the top of the outer staircase. The bell rang loudly enough to be heard all over the Island but, on running back, Katryn saw no change in the Lady except that the breathing sounded a little more laboured. She ran back to the top of the staircase, and gasped with relief on seeing Dame Augusta and Dame Lucia hurry across the garth.

"The Lady! The Lady!" screamed Katryn. "She's lying there on the floor, but I swear I never pushed her out of bed. By St. Ursula, I never pushed her—"

"Hold your tongue, child," said Dame Augusta, "and for mercy's sake stop clanging the bell. The whole house will have heard it by now."

Soon enough, all the ladies, their ill-adjusted wimples and veils flapping about, appeared at the foot of the staircase, and Dame Elfrida, the fat little infirmarian, was the first to reach the abbess's room. One quick glance from Dame Elfrida was enough to make Dame Augusta send Katryn and another novice to Sir Hugo's lodgings, and a younger lady to the infirmary for the death-cloth and to the sacristy for the blessed ashes. Other orders were promptly given by Dame Lucia and Dame Blanche, and nobody thought of taking notice of the pink-cheeked little prioress. Sleep still in her eyes, she knelt in a distant corner, nobody remarking her.

Soon the great vaulted room glimmered with the lights of several tapers. Four servants, sleep slurring their speech and clouding their eyes, spread the death-cloth on the floor, and it somehow fell to Dame Augusta to sprinkle it with ashes in the form of a cross. Lady Isabella's heavy body was laid upon the cloth and, in the scent of musk, burning wax and orange water, the ladies knelt and made their clear responses to the litany mumbled by Sir Hugo.

". . . *Omnes sanctae Virgines et Viduae*," he muttered, and they replied:

"*Orate pro ea.*"

"*Omnes Sancti et Sanctae Dei. . . .*"

"*Intercedite pro ea . . .*"

Lady Isabella lay motionless, her right hand flung out. Candlelight played on the three great rings she wore—the diamond for strength, the ruby for happiness, the sapphire for purity. The coif had not been put back on her head, and the ladies tried to avert their eyes from the thick tumble of silken iron-grey curls. Dame Blanche, kneeling, held the taper placed between the plump white fingers which had obviously done with the clasping of things, and large blobs of wax kept dripping on the abbess's scapular. All the windows and doors stood wide open, but the night was so still that each candle flame looked like a carven blue-orange flower.

Meanwhile, Sir Hugo quavered on, praying that Lady Isabella's soul might be delivered from all the perils of hell and from all tribulation even as Noah was delivered from the flood, Isaac from his father's hand, and Moses from the Egyptians. These petitions ended, he began:

"*Delicta iuventutis et ignorantias eius, quaesumus, ne memineris Domine. . . .*"

Dame Elizabeth knelt in the doorway. Here was the utmost simplicity, she thought, about the only true thing left in their lives. Abbesses and nuns had been speeded on their last journey in exactly the same manner for more than a thousand years. Enclosure no longer kept, poverty and silence forgotten, luxuries admitted into the cloister—but all of it ended in the same way—with a coarse black cloth spread on the floor, ashes strewn upon it, wax dripping, and the appointed words read before the falling of the ultimate curtain. A death-bed in the house, thought Dame Elizabeth, was about the only link left between them and their saintly founder. She tried to open her mind to the stern and lovely amplitude of the moment, and found that she was indeed able to forgive that woman, whom the exercise of grievously unlimited power had so speedily delivered into the arms of petty tyranny. Forgive her Dame Elizabeth could. Pray for her she could not.

Here the prayers were interrupted by the familiar imperious voice:

"I won't have such muttering over me. Here, somebody fetch me orange water. . . ."

Kneeling, the ladies seemed sculptured in their amazement. A breath of wind stole through the room, the taper in Dame Blanche's hand went out with a timid hiss, and Sir Hugo dropped his book. Lady Isabella's mouth twitched once or twice. She tried to move her head, and her eyes were full of angry astonishment. Then her head jerked a little, and the sound slightly resembling the rattle of dry peas against stone made Dame Elfrida cast a hurried glance at Dame Augusta, and there was Dame Lucia picking up Sir Hugo's book and finding the right place for him.

"*Subvenite, Sancti Dei, occurrite, Angeli Domini, suscipientes animam eius, offerentes eam in conspectu Altissimi. . . .*" In a trembling voice Sir Hugo ambled on through the rest of the prayers, and then Dame Blanche was the first to rise from her knees. She made a deep curtsey to the corpse, turned, curtseyed to the little prioress in her corner, and began backing out of the room.

Dame Elizabeth stood still. Then she stirred and caught Dame Blanche outside the stairway. She spoke in a whisper since none of them might now raise their voices until after the funeral.

"Our mission to Stephen's Light, Madam. . . ."

Dame Blanche carefully straightened the wimple under her chin.

"Ah Madam," her whisper was peculiarly honeyed, "now it surely rests with the prioress and the two senior ladies, of whom Dame Augusta is one," and she bowed and went down the steep stairway.

Dame Elizabeth followed her slowly. The prioress was well known to be unable to give a definite order about the pickling of winter cabbage, Dame Blanche stood next in seniority to Dame Augusta, and the mission to Stephen's Light bade fair to be postponed to the Greek Kalends.

Meanwhile, a novice had reached the church, and the

peal of the bell broke over the Island, telling everybody that the thirty-first ruler of the house of Our Lady and St. Matthias had gone to her reward.

Dame Elizabeth's room had been tidied by the servants, and her cowl lay ready on the press. She knew she must now go to choir and take her part in the first office for the dead. But for a few moments she stood very still and thought of Sabina sadly and tenderly.

[4]

The life of the house followed the customary pattern except for the absolute silence in the cloisters and the garth. Ladies, sitting down to meals in their rooms, took care to close the windows and not to speak too freely when the servants were about. The prioress, Dame Blanche, Dame Augusta and the infirmarian were in charge of the funeral, and the abbot of St. Eugene and an abbot from Mainz were among the invited dignitaries but, except for Lady Isabella's numerous princely kin, no laity were asked, though a generous enough dole would presently be distributed to the poor of the city.

"Surely, some of the more important burghers should be invited to the funeral," remarked Dame Elizabeth, and Dame Blanche smiled.

"My own opinion is of no importance, Madam," she spoke with an exaggerated politeness, "but there seems to be a feeling among the ladies that, living on the Island, we are not really bound to the city. After all, it is a good hour's ride from the shore, isn't it? Naturally, the Archbishop will be among the guests," she added.

Dame Elizabeth found she had nothing to say.

The matters of food and wine, wax candles and bedding required for the guests must needs occupy everybody's mind since no really important decisions might be taken until after the election of Lady Isabella's successor. With visiting abbots and other clerics of standing present in the nave, the ladies refrained from bringing their lapdogs into choir, and all the appointed offices were sung with care and precision:

"*Quia apud Dominum misericordia*: *et copiosa apud eum redemptio. . . .*"

Yet, all the customary ceremonial notwithstanding, a sense of urgency informed the Island. There were endless little sessions of three or four or five ladies together, and nobody suggested that Dame Elizabeth should join any such session but she could easily guess at the burden of all those conversations. An election was the most important event in their lives; its result would colour and determine the courses to be pursued down a number of years. Dame Elizabeth had no doubts about the identity of Lady Isabella's successor. Now one lady, now another, would drop an accentuated curtsey on meeting Dame Augusta. Delicate hints were dropped in the garth and the cloisters and even in choir. This window must be kept closed because Dame Augusta disliked draughts. Care must be taken with the yellow plum crop because they were Dame Augusta's favourite fruit. Kitchen wenches must be rigorously excluded from the herb garden because Dame Augusta did not like to see them there. With the election still distant, the mind of the house was made up.

By Michaelmas, the election papers had reached the Island. Sir Hugo, too deeply rooted in age and foible to be troubled by the result, sang the mass of the Holy Spirit. One by one, the ladies recorded their votes, the novices being meanwhile locked up in their dorter. Despair brushing against her mind, Dame Elizabeth cast her vote for the insignificant little prioress. Later in the morning they all went to the chapter-house to learn the result. A wild October wind sent rivulets of rain through the gap in the roof but they waited in decorous silence, trying not to take too much notice of the raindrops falling upon their heads and shoulders.

Dame Augusta was elected, two votes only being given to the prioress. At once, habits rustled, veils were re-adjusted, as the ladies got up, smiling and clapping their hands, certain, as they were, that this time no unfortunate mistake had been made.

The fuss and the bustle preceding Lady Isabella's funeral were as nothing compared to the fevered busyness of the installation. Dame Augusta, having rather briefly acknowledged her unfitness for the high office, wasted no time on repeating the conventional protests. With both capable hands she plunged into the treasury. Silk hangings from Lyons, priceless embroideries from Barking, a new setting for the jewels in the processional cross, new crimson and gold upholstery for the abbess's throne, all these began coming to the Island. Some of the finest craftsmen from Nüremberg were engaged—at a high expense—to re-furbish the ladies' coat-of-arms over the choir stalls. From a quarry in Thuringia came a load of finely veined grey stone, and the choir was entirely re-paved. A definite order was given to a master builder in the city for the re-roofing of the chapter-house. Sir Hugo had two cassocks made of the finest Flemish cloth, and even the kitchen wenches were given new brown kirtles. Christmas was round the corner, but of the end to the preparations there was no sign, and the day's motto became "hurry, hurry," lest Lent were to overtake them. Lady Augusta and the two senior ladies spent their days surrounded by parchment, inkhorns and quills, and at the lodge the portress kept receiving bales of presents. There was a reliquary from the Emperor, containing a finger bone of St. Matthias, a sapphire ring from the Duke of Brunswick, and a pink pearl chaplet from a Wittelsbach lady. Everybody admired the gifts, and went about conscious that the eyes of the whole Empire were—however briefly—turned towards the Island.

Dame Elizabeth knew she could not expect any preferment from Lady Isabella's successor. She felt no regrets because the least important office would have burdened her. Degraded from her seniority she knew she could not be except for a trespass she was not likely to commit. Constantly and fussily employed by Lady Isabella, Dame Elizabeth certainly wondered a little about her duties under Lady Augusta. Within a bare fortnight she knew she had no duties. She must, inevitably, acquit herself in choir but the chanting of the Office began and ended her activities in the house. Nothing was formally taken out of her hands because nothing had ever been formally placed under her care. Dame Elizabeth was not informed that she would no longer be required at the guest-house, in the scriptorium, in the stillroom, at the abbess's lodgings. She was merely left alone, and now Dame Griselda was the second lady to share her mess, and Dame Griselda's incessant chatter about all the doings in the house was no feather-weight penance to Dame Elizabeth.

Meanwhile, the city, too, had sent its gifts, and a bolt of blue French damask together with a small bag of seed pearls came from Conrad the mercer, so Dame Elizabeth heard from Dame Griselda.

"Oh dear Madam," she twittered, pecking at her spiced ham, "the guest-house will be positively crowded. None of us knows where the Duchess of Brunswick is to lodge with all her ladies. You can well understand why Lady Augusta decided to invite no burghers at all. There just isn't an inch of space left anywhere—unless, that is, we were to lodge the burghers in the stables. Of course, the poor folk will come for their dole. It's to be a particularly rich one, too, roast pork and honey-bread, apples and other things. Lady Augusta is determined to practise charity in widest terms, so she told us all today."

At last, the great and tiring day came and went. Now they reached the eve of Candlemas, and Lady Augusta summoned her first chapter. There were various documents in connection with Dame Adela's elopement, letters from lawyers about her unpaid dowry and suchlike papers. Presently, Dame Lucia coughed and said nervously:

"Here is the petition of Conrad the mercer together with a private letter addressed to your predecessor, my lady." She peered at the sheets in her hand and explained, "It was written the morning after Lady Isabella's death before any official information had reached the city."

Nobody moved. Lady Augusta raised her face. Across the great vaulted room, her clear grey eyes fell on Dame Elizabeth.

"Yes, I remember perfectly." She paused. "Such an admission, as we all know, would be against the charter. Do the ladies wish the matter to be put to the vote? I must, however, remind them that it would mean a grave new departure." Here Lady Augusta paused again and fingered the pink pearl chaplet hanging from her girdle. "With the charter once altered, always provided that the Holy Father and the Emperor gave their consent, there would be created a precedent. Will this house be wise in creating it? Far be it from me to deprecate the manner of life chosen by our sisters of St. Dominic and St. Francis, but our way has always differed from theirs. The Blessed Lord and His Holy Mother"—here Lady Augusta bowed her head—"call the high and the lowly alike to their service but it is clearly their will that there should be the high and the lowly."

Amiably, eloquently, Lady Augusta discoursed for several minutes. At the end, not a nun but was convinced that it would be schism and heresy combined to interfere with the charter in the least particular. All the faces reflected deep satisfaction. Lady Augusta was undoubtedly proud but at least she proved herself consistent in her pride. They had had more than enough of inconsistencies under Lady Isabella. They agreed chorally that they had no wish to put the matter to the vote. Lady Augusta rewarded them with a stately bow and a smile.

"Dame Lucia, you shall now inform Conrad the mercer that it is against the rules of this house to receive his daughter as an inmate."

Slowly, Dame Elizabeth rose to her feet. She knew that the battle was lost. She had not been degraded but so pointedly ignored that she realized her voice would carry no conviction among them. She also knew she must speak—if but for the last time.

"May I remind you, my lady, that this matter was decided at an earlier chapter?"

An indignant rustling broke over the room. Lady Augusta picked up a quill and began examining its tip with great interest.

"And it was carried by a lawfully taken vote," said Dame Elizabeth in a high ringing voice. "How can the chapter go back on their decision?"

She paused. The indignant murmurs thickened. Still Lady Augusta said nothing.

"No written answer was then sent to Conrad the mercer —but does our honour permit us to find a loophole in that omission? My lady, I was not sure and I am still not sure whether Sabina would ever come among us. But that is not the point. I feel that we can't afford to ignore, still less to insult the city. Indeed, I feel certain that we'd do so at our own peril. A few years ago the armies of the Sultan ravaged Carniola. Who is going to defend us, women, if such trouble were to break out nearer home? But that is not all, my lady. May we, dare we, close our doors against decently brought up Christian girls merely on the ground of their low origins?"

Now Lady Augusta's mind had shaped her reply. She looked at Dame Elizabeth with pity.

"I don't think that this house is prepared to bear with inconsistencies, Dame Elizabeth. If I remember rightly, you once argued that the girl's admission would depend on her own consent. Now you have argued the whole case from a totally different and most irrelevant point of view."

"My lady, Sabina must be given an opportunity to refuse. Surely, this touches upon the honour of this house seeing that the vote was lawfully carried?"

Now Lady Augusta's smile vanished. Her voice was icy.

"Do I then have to remind you, Dame Elizabeth, that this is no way to speak in chapter? By the guidance of the Holy Spirit, I was elected to rule this house, and it follows that its honour is in my hands. The matter is settled." She clapped her hands and the ladies rose for the prayer.

As two by two they left the chapter-house, they took very obvious care to avoid Dame Elizabeth.

PART V

A Woman at Stephen's Light

SOME Italian players were passing through the city, and Conrad, in common with a few other burghers, invited them to Stephen's Light. In the biggest of the four warehouses, they gave a performance of "The Life of St. George" and a drama about St. Catherine of Alexandria. They looked a sorry, tattered lot of men, and it was decided in the city that they should not be allowed to stay above a week, no inn, not even the Silver Fish, willing to give them shelter. Hilda said that some of them were known to lodge in the Painted Street. She argued that they all looked like men who did not much care how they came by the money jingling in their pouches, and she had all the windows shuttered and the doors barred the afternoon they came to Stephen's Light.

Once St. Michael had crowned St. George with a tin diadem patchily covered with gold-leaf, a hunchback came forward and played the lute. His grey hose were badly torn and his grey jerkin liberally smeared with grease, but his music was good, Anna said, and ordered that saffron was to be added to his portion because of the pleasure he had given them. So she said to Hilda in the hunchback's hear-

ing, and at once he bared his head and swept a grotesquely exaggerated bow.

"I speak your language a little, Madam. I do thank you for your generosity."

"We liked your playing," Anna said politely. "Where do you come from?"

"Genoa," and he bowed again as if to thank Anna for the further privilege to him accorded by her question. "People often tell me that I can play. But to amuse and to please anyone is easy enough. To offer people comfort is a much harder task. In Genoa, last summer, I fell in with a gentleman of your nation, Madam, and he was sadly bereaved, his lady having just died of a fever, and I played some of my airs to him. I heard him say to someone that my music was like good oil poured over a wound."

"I'm sure it must have been," said Anna, her voice barely screening her indifference to a stranger's bereavement in a remote and unknown country.

"I heard later that the gentleman was supposed to know the city. He was a man of affairs and much respected. There ran a rumour that the young lady had been a nun, but I felt pretty sure that was a malicious fable."

"Your dinner is about to be brought to you," Anna broke in a little sharply and led the way out of the warehouse, Sabina following her.

She had heard every word. She had kept silent. The man had come from Genoa and had once played to Richard— to comfort him, and Adela was dead and, presumably, damned. All the madness and the cruelty and the grief leading to an early death in some filthy alien lodging house. . . . But she must learn more, Sabina said to herself. She would give a gold coin to the man if he told her more. She must know more, she must know everything. She would choose a moment and slip to the back and there wait by the little gate. The players, she knew, were taken to the great bakehouse, neither the cook nor Hilda allowing them to come into the kitchens. A little money had already been given them, and a barrel of wine which had gone bad and been left outside to catch the frost. In the doorway of the parlour, Sabina heard her mother and Hilda talk about the larded beef cheek and baked cod.

"Let the lute player have a little saffron with his meat and give him some jam to eat with the wafers," Anna was saying.

So much given them to eat, and they looked hungry enough, and a whole barrel of wine was theirs, too, and what was she, Sabina, about, with her secret little plan of slipping a ducat into a vagabond's dirty hand—at the back gate, too? Was she going mad again because Richard had been mentioned by a stranger?

"But I must know more," Sabina assured herself.

The men seemed to take a very long time over their food and wine. It was certainly risky waiting there, in the bitter cold, in the dark-blue shadows, by the back gate. Cloaked and hooded, she waited. At last, the bakehouse door opened, and she heard heavy, lurching steps and broken, thick voices. Would they all be drunk? She pressed her shoulders against the wall. The ducat burned between her folded palms as she saw the hunchback come nearer and nearer.

"Stop," she breathed urgently. "That man in Genoa? You were telling my mother about him," hurriedly, clumsily she unfolded her hands and let the coin drop into the hunchback's readily waiting palm. "What was his name?"

"They called him Master Richard," smirked the man. "They said he was on his way to Damascus—but I wouldn't know that."

"Did you truly play and talk to him?"

The man hesitated.

"Madam, I'm a strolling player, and our kind aren't much known for honesty. I am not honest. I played to a motley company, and he may have heard me through the wall. I don't know. I never saw him nor spoke to him—but I certainly heard his story."

"And"—Sabina swallowed hard, "she—she died?"

"Of a fever, they told me. He had to change his lodgings. The innkeeper was frightened of plague, so I heard."

"Had he gone to Damascus when you left?"

"I wouldn't know for certain, Madam."

Barely thanking the man, Sabina turned and ran into the house. So it was true. Adela was dead and so was Richard so far as she, Sabina, was concerned, but it eased her oddly to have spoken with the hunchback.

So the players went on their way, and the city promptly forgot them. There were far more exciting matters to discuss.

The Archbishop, the abbot of St. Eugene, the Dominican and the Carmelite prioresses were alone invited to Lady Augusta's installation.

"I don't like it," said Conrad to Anna. "I sent Hugo with my gifts to the Island. And the petition and the letter went so long ago, and I have heard nothing at all. It would take time to get ready Sabina's dowry and all, and there are so many legal papers to draw up, and yet I have not heard a word from the Island. Who does she imagine I am? A common artisan?"

"Well, I suppose they could not do much till after Lady Isabella's funeral, and now they're all busy with the installation."

"Yes, and no city folk are to be invited. I don't like it at all."

"Perhaps, they mean to have their feast for clerics only."

"Do they indeed? If you were not a woman, you might go to the Golden Cross, or the Black Eagle. I don't know how many dukes and duchesses there are—with all their attendants, too. And some of them are on the Island already, and Hugo said he could barely make his way to the lodge—so many people milling about! Why, the portress boasted that they were getting ready for five hundred guests!"

"There are the beggars," Anna mumbled. "Hilda has seen one of the bailiffs. There'll be pork and wheaten bread for the dole."

"Well, wife, we're neither high-born nor do we belong to the gutter, but my stuff and my money used to be good enough for them in the past, and I don't like it at all."

Anna sighed and turned to her spinning-wheel. She had already heard more than enough from her kin and acquaintance. The landlords of the Black Eagle and the Golden Cross were indeed pleased with the Island. So were the paupers. So were the Archbishop's men proud of their new green and violet doublets. But the Archbishop's men had nothing to do with the city, and innkeepers and beggars were by no means its only inhabitants.

"It's perfectly plain to everybody," said the fat, pale-eyed Mathilda, wife of Master Albert, the lawyer. "That proud woman is determined to ignore us all. As though Master Albert had not been entertained by high-born gentry during his visit to Paris. I pray that your daughter will not be maltreated by them all on account of her origin."

"Oh no! Her father would never allow that to happen."

Meanwhile, the great day came and went. The royal visitors had gone It was Candlemas, and still no reply from the Island came to Stephen's Light.

On a bitter wind-swept morning a muddied rider came down the street leading to Stephen's Light. Near the gate a girl in a scarlet hood hurried by, a trug of carrots in her arms. The man reined in and shouted:

"Do you belong here?"

She nodded.

"Give this to your master, will you?"

A folded piece of parchment, held together by a thin black cord with a dangling blob of red wax, landed on top of the carrots.

"Good shot!" laughed the man. "Run along, girl, and give it to him at once."

But Conrad was closeted with an important visitor from Ghent, and nobody dared disturb him. It was almost dinner-time when Hilda brought the letter to him. He broke the seal so roughly that tiny chips of red wax were scattered all over the table. He began to read, and in an instant his fist banged so furiously that a ginger cat, startled out of his sleep, ran out of the room and a pewter standish rolled down to the floor. Anna hurried in.

"So I am not good enough for them," Conrad was thundering, his face crimson. "Wife, send someone to fetch Master Albert at once. I'll fight them tooth and nail. And that's what they mean by God's service! My daughter not good enough to enter their house! By the Cross and St. Sturm. . . ."

No dinner was eaten at Stephen's Light that day. Master Albert came, read the brief, frostily worded letter, and shook his head. The occasion was distressing enough for him to refrain from any allusion to his journey to Paris, but he could be of no use at all, and he said so.

"But, surely, you are a lawyer, man," Conrad shouted at him.

"I tell you there's nothing to be done."

"Nothing to be done? My money not good enough for them? It answered all right when Sabina went to get her schooling on the Island. Dare they suggest there's a slur on her character because of that rascal from Troyes? They'd better see to their own affairs."

"No, no," Master Albert said hurriedly. "It is all to do with their charter. See, they quote from it. A charter, my friend, is a legal document. It is binding."

"Well, then, I'll go to the Archbishop."

Master Albert shrugged.

"They are not dependent on him, I fear."

"I'll write to the Pope then. Is this a Christian land or not? And Lady Isabella did promise. There was nothing in writing, but I heard quite enough. She summoned a chapter, and the matter was put to the vote and carried through."

"She is dead, my friend. And there has been no contract."

"And they dare call themselves Christians."

Master Albert folded the parchment, put it away, and stroked his beard.

"I shall sue them—contract or no contract," roared Conrad, and once again the lawyer shook his head.

"My friend, I once had a client who got involved in a lawsuit with the monks at Zenia in Brandenburg, and I knew my client was in the right, but the monks won on all points. First, once you begin fighting them, they'll tell you that no superior is bound to keep the promises made by a predecessor, and such a point is valid at law—particularly when there's been nothing in writing. And finally there's their charter. I beg of you not to waste your money in such a lawsuit."

"I'll make their name stink in the city."

"But they wouldn't care in the least," and Master Albert added carefully: "I feel sure the Carmelites will be happy to receive Sabina."

"I'd much rather she remained a Christian," Conrad retorted.

[2]

For all Sabina knew to the contrary, that lute-player may well have told a fable, and Adela might be still alive. With Richard's fortune or misfortune, so she had schooled herself to think, it was no longer fitting for her to be concerned. But Lady Augusta's letter was no fable. Sabina read it twice through. Her mother's grief and her father's wrath

were both hard to understand. She put the letter down and
shrugged.

"Well, sir," she looked at her father, "I suppose I'd have
been a sparrow among peacocks if I'd gone there."

Anna burst through her sobbing:

"What rubbish! Look at the Carmelite prioress! She's a
high-born lady, but most of the sisters are not, and it's a
poor house, too. They can't always afford purslane for
breakfast, and they never have candles in their cells. And
nothing except good has ever been heard of them. They're
so occupied in prayer that they're hardly ever seen in the
parlour. A sparrow among peacocks! Why should those
ladies on the Island be like peacocks, I'd like to know."

"She shall not go to the Carmelites," shouted Conrad.
"No child by me begotten shall go to any religious house.
Poor or wealthy, good or bad, they're all alike in one thing,
yes, they are, they are hypocrites, and I wouldn't mind if
the Pope in Rome were to hear me."

Sabina looked at her mother.

"Shall I go now and finish the nut jam, Madam?"

"What does the nut jam matter?" wept Anna. "If
you'd only have enough sense to cry, girl! Can't you see
what it means? One disgrace on top of another," and here
Conrad stopped his pacing up and down and seized Anna
by the shoulder.

"What did you say? Another disgrace? What disgrace
is there that a daughter of ours should have been refused
by such a house? Disgrace indeed! I won't have you use
such a word! I see now that I'd no business to send that
petition at all. And let this be an end to the matter!"

Sabina heard. She gave her father a peculiar look but she said nothing.

"And as to the girl going to finish a job in the kitchen," went on Conrad, "well, I for one was pleased to hear her mention it. Of course the jam must be finished. Why shouldn't she finish it? What's the good of crying and sitting with your hands idle?"

"Well, it has upset me," Anna began in so small a voice that at once his huge arms went about her shoulders.

"I know, I know, and, perhaps, I'd no business to shout at you—but let's be sensible together. Let the girl go and see to what she's got to do in the kitchen," he added, with a clumsy effort at playfulness, "isn't that the way you brought her up, and a good way it is, too."

Sabina waited for him to finish, and then she asked:

"Have I your permission to think about it, sir?"

"You're not to think about the Carmelites or any such place," he flung at her, and Sabina shook her head.

In the kitchen, ignoring the curious glances and furtive whispers among the maids, Sabina, standing very erect, measured out the honey for the nut jam, spoke a kind word to a girl for the faultlessly pounded walnuts, carefully poured the honey into a huge iron kettle, and beckoned to another girl.

"See that the fire's kept even and go on stirring for the space of ten Paternosters, and then I'll come back."

She turned towards the crazily perched ladder, smiled at Hilda, and there was the landing and the privacy of her own room—for a few moments.

In the parlour, her mother's sobs beating on her ears, Sabina had stood dry-eyed. In her own room, she wept fiercely and briefly. She had submitted to her father's earlier decision, and had had the Island much in her thought and her prayers those last months. She had remembered Dame Elizabeth. She had never reflected whether she had a calling or no but she had begun feeling drawn to that life which, on its surface, at least, carried the chrism of a special dedication. Now Sabina wept because a dream was shattered for ever. There were no dedicated people in the world. There were just ordinary, well-bred women who chanted the Psalter and a few hymns, ate their meals, delighted in gossip, and clung to their high descent to the exclusion of all else. Her mother had leapt to a vehement defence of the Carmelites. There Sabina could not gauge her. She, at least, had known no other religious house than the Island. She could no longer think of it as a religious house at all.

But her tears were few, however fierce. Her father had been right in saying that was the end of the matter. She had asked his permission to reflect on something else. She had explained nothing. She must think it all out very carefully before she was ready to speak to him, and she must get ready all by herself. Here, not even Hilda might come to her aid.

A full week had gone when, coming into the parlour, Sabina faced Conrad. Her mother, as she knew, had gone to visit a friend. Sabina's face was white and her hands shook slightly.

"Will you let me stay on here at Stephen's Light and help you, sir?" she began without the least preamble, and the look Conrad gave her said plainly that he thought she had mislaid her wits. None the less, she hurried on:

"Sir, don't you remember that visitor from Ghent who

told us about one Alice Chester, a draper's widow in Bristol in England? He said there were other women in that city who were engaged in trade. And Alice Chester is said to import iron from Spain and to send wool and cloth to Flanders and to Portugal. She's got a son to help her, and the man from Ghent said that she was much esteemed in Bristol. He went there once, and he saw the fine house she had had built—with a shop below and a big hall above it. I've thought much about it, sir. It needn't be impossible for women to be in our trade, need it?"

Conrad did not answer the question. He merely said:

"Of course, I know all about that woman in England. My people at Antwerp have had many dealings with her. But she's a widow."

"The man I was betrothed to is dead to me," said Sabina quietly. "Sir, I know my letters and a good smattering of Latin and something about figures, too. The rest—and I do know there's much of it, I must learn. Sir, won't you allow me to be of some use to you? Otherwise I'll be sorry I wasn't born a boy."

"To be of use to me? You're of use here."

"I don't mean needlework and preserves only. I don't think that it's good for any life to be empty. Marriage and religion aren't for me. I fear I'll never forgive the Island," Sabina's voice shook at the brief spurt of vehemence. "I shall never set my foot inside a religious house again!"

"You know nothing about the trade, and there's also the gild. What do you imagine they'll say?"

"You're one of the senior members," Sabina reminded him, and still Conrad frowned.

"You know nothing of the trade," he kept repeating.

"Sir, I didn't know the alphabet when I began learning it."

He did not answer her, and Sabina knew she had no further arguments to marshal. She had spoken daringly enough. She could do no more. She only hoped that—whatever his decision, her father would speak before Anna's return, and Sabina checked an absurd impulse to fling her arms round his neck and to win his consent with her kisses.

Conrad turned away from her and began contemplating the wintry scene in the garden. His hands were thrust behind his back, and Sabina, aware of the pointed gravity of the moment, held her breath. Suddenly he swung round and stared at her.

"You said you could learn? Learn then and remember that I make no promises. I give you a year, and I shall watch you, and I refuse to be made a laughing-stock in the eyes of the gild—and you'll have to answer for every mistake you make. Is that clear?"

"Yes, sir," said Sabina, aware that he needed no words from her, thanked him very briefly.

Conrad having spoken, Anna's tears, protests and adjurations carried little weight at Stephen's Light.

Yet from the beginning Sabina knew that she would have to swim out of her depths. She had a bunch of mostly unrelated facts tucked away in her memory, and she had little more than that. She had indeed heard much about great fairs at Erfurt and Leipzig, at Magdeburg and Regensburg, but she knew nothing about their background, and to the fair in her own city she would go—always accompanied by Hilda—for no weightier purpose than that of making some light and amusing purchases. She knew that the best cloth of gold came from Syria and the best silk stuffs from Lyons, that some towns in Normandy made a good grey cloth, and that there were mercers of note at Lille and Beauvais. She had heard enough about the linen of Ypres and the fine curtain material woven at Arras. She knew that her father had dealings with England, the Low Countries, Spain and the East through a middleman at Antwerp. She had met visitors from Alexandria and Tyre, from Famagusta in Cyprus, from London, Toledo and Florence. She had a pretty clear idea about the several provenances of spices, wines, dyes and scents which filled the shops in her own city. She had listened to many a conversation about bad inns, piracy on the open seas, wickedly high tolls levied by bishops and abbeys, some of the amounts rising to sixty and even seventy per cent of the total value.

Sabina knew, too, that times were hard and business ventures complicated through the internal feuds in the Empire, that the nobility kept aloof from all trading concerns, that clerics were greedy, and that the working man thought himself downtrodden and underpaid. Sabina had never seen the sea but she had often been to her father's warehouses on the river banks, talked to keelmen and watermen and watched the flat-bottomed, single-masted boats sail down to the west. There was one big painted map at Stephen's Light, and Sabina knew how to trace a ship's course from Genoa, along the west coast of Italy, down to Sicily, curving round the Greek peninsula, along the north coast of Candia on to Rhodes and Cyprus and further still, to Syria.

All that knowledge was echoed in the very heart of Stephen's Light; it was at one with the measured rhythm of its days, its severe beauty, the feeling of pride, poise and security her home had always stirred in her.

But Sabina also knew that she was almost wholly ignorant. Now she saw that the lovely persuasion of Stephen's Light belonged to the years which were behind her. The place still stood in beauty but from now on her own response to that beauty would have to be made in far more exacting terms than any she had ever known. Sabina found that reality was stone-paved, that it meant hard work, difficulties, disappointments, mistakes, and even frequent spells of frustration. Letters were left unanswered, agents defaulted, ships were seized by pirates, warehouses set on fire by discontented workmen. To learn her father's trade was not merely to run the smooth wavelets of silk between her fingers.

And Conrad had given her one bare year to master the rudiments, and she must learn them under the most hampering conditions since, being a girl, there were so many avenues barred against her. She might not attend gild meetings and public auctions, or spend hours at the wharves, or hear men talk at inns, or even pay visits to shops without being accompanied by a maid. Sabina must learn from within Stephen's Light, and learn much: the endlessly involved threads of buying and selling, the maddeningly unpredictable fluctuations of supply and demand, the intricacies of book-keeping, the moods of money markets and, most importantly, the moods of such business men as kept in touch with Stephen's Light.

She was now allowed a chair and a corner of her father's large table in the counting-house, and presently two or three ledgers were confided to her care. Book-keeping as such meant little trouble to her, and often enough she would cease considering the narrow columns of figures whenever an important caller was in the room. Then Sabina listened, every cranny in her mind opened wide to receive more and more information, to put it away in her memory but not before she had weighed every particle of it in her judgment.

One morning, a man from Ghent called to discuss the matter of frieze and kersey. The best of those, as Sabina had already learned, came from England. The man mentioned the shortage of English wool and warned Conrad that the prices would rise. Sabina waited for the visitor to go. Then, in none too steady a voice, she offered her first independent opinion to Conrad.

"Suppose we were to wait till the prices hardened, sir?"

"But I must send in my annual order to Antwerp. I couldn't afford to run short of frieze or kersey."

Sabina was ready for that—not with hollow persuasion but with a chaplet of convincing figures. She reeled off the names of all the warehouses, so many bolts of frieze, so many bales of kersey were in stock.

"I see that we bought a little above the usual quantity last year," she went on, "and if you were to ration the sales a little this year, we could hold out." She added calmly: "But I think the prices might be raised just the same. Indeed, I have heard that Master Luke's to raise his within a few days."

"Of course! Master Luke's already got his stuff in," Conrad explained, but Sabina shook her head.

"I rather doubt that, sir. A man of his came to borrow a bolt of frieze from us two days ago."

"Did Martin let him have it?"

"Yes. On my instructions. I hope I did not do wrong, sir, but you happened to be out. I saw the man myself, and learned that Master Luke would keep the frieze back until he had the rise in price confirmed from Antwerp," and Sabina laid down her quill, propped her chin in both hands, and added: "As a matter of fact, sir, our stocks stand so high that it wouldn't harm us to let Master Luke have a little more of both kersey and frieze—naturally at this year's wholesale rate with a small commission added. I am sure Master Luke would be grateful."

She did not expect Conrad to reply at once. He did not. He stared at her long and hard, and Sabina recognized that peculiar stare given—though seldom enough—to those in his employ whom he knew he could trust.

"I believe you'll do well enough," he said at last and left the counting-house without looking at her.

[3]

Having buried Adela, Richard lingered on in Genoa. The berth booked on board the ship for Trebizond had long since gone by default. The surly innkeeper, frightened of a death, had insisted on his leaving, and Richard found a corner at some poor hovel of a place nearer the harbour, a mere slip of a room partitioned off the only living-space the house afforded where indigent pilgrims, wandering stu-

dents and such thinly moneyed fry came for a few hours, a
day, or a night, and then moved on towards future uncer-
tainties. Richard never met any of them. What few friends
he had in Genoa kept telling him that there were generous
openings for a man of his quality at Akko and Damascus.
They said that he knew the trade so well—and what was
more valuable still, that he knew the world. Why, there
were opportunities as far as China, they said, for a clever
man who knew the value of money and the value of a good
argument, who had been employed by the great Hansa,
and had rubbed shoulders with many merchants of note.

Richard heard it all, and he did nothing. Weeks slipped
by, and his friends ceased urging him. He stayed on at that
hovel. Little by little he gave up shaving and washing, and
you could hardly see the little lute and his other belongings
for the thick layers of dust upon them. Aware that he had
money, the fat innkeeper brought food and drink into the
room at such times as pleased him. Sometimes Richard
fed. Sometimes he did not.

He could never have admitted so to any man of his acquaintance but he felt as though he had been branded for a
double murder—even though at times his mind grew so
confused that he could not think very clearly. Yet never
could he escape from that sense of guilt—however clouded
his consciousness might be. For Richard was now convinced that Adela had succumbed to the undoubted hard-
ships of their long journey together, and in that sense he,
and none other, had certainly killed her. And now, alone
and bewildered, he had begun thinking about Sabina.

He had not thought much, if at all, about her till Adela's
death. It was now, with heavy grey inertia wrapping him

like a shroud, that he wondered whether what to him had been a mere feather-light brief dalliance could have meant much more to Sabina. It seemed as though Adela, having gone from him, had left a curious legacy to his memory. Alone in that sordid Genoese hovel, Richard reflected much and often on Stephen's Light.

He knew well enough that he would have married Sabina for the contract, the rich possessions, a burgher's dignity, Conrad having told him that the city would waive the customary condition of domicile for a year and a day before admitting Richard to all the civic privileges. So he would have married Sabina in exchange for all those, and by now he would have been a citizen of one among the finest cities in the Empire, his uneasy alien condition a thing of the past. He would have indeed been yoked, but he would also have had Sabina, Stephen's Light, much honour and a certain amount of leisure his earlier days had never known.

Instead, Richard had gone to the Island, and the same incurable restlessness which had once flung him far away from his native Troyes and made him exchange the humble security of his father's steading for the challenge of an uncharted journey in search of freedom and of chances, that same wildness had again welled up in him. And much more than that. To Sabina, Richard would have given loyalty and, possibly, a measure of genuine affection, but worship, he knew well, he could never have brought to her. That would have shocked her. In her world, men reverenced their mothers, respected their wives, not too obviously, and paid worship to the Virgin alone. Richard knew that well. None the less, he had always hungered for a corner within a shrine, for a cup into which he might pour all of himself, body and soul and mind. He might have given his body to Sabina—but she would have refused a lien upon his soul. There was a simplicity and also a certain clear hardness in her which recoiled from any heightened feeling, any overcoloured emotion. Sabina, so Richard now told himself, would have made a paragon of a wife.

So the very first time he had seen Dame Adela across the garth on the Island, aloof, lovely, a little lost, a little sad, Richard knew that here, indeed, he might fall down and worship and lose all of himself in the shame, the madness and the splendour. All the time the senior ladies were arguing about a stranger's unpaid revenues, Richard kept that shining image in his thoughts. Then it happened that she, having been told to bring a certain document to him, came into the parlour, and she came alone. Her gait, her voice, above all, her look, confirmed it to him. He felt that she had been asking a question and that to her he had come as an answer, and there was nothing else to it because it was everything in a swift, terrible, shamefast manner. Adela carried the air of someone with a secret to communicate, and that secret was herself, and it was then that Richard realized there had been no secret at all in Sabina.

He belonged to his age, and he had few illusions about ladies in religion but Adela, having come into his arms, still kept some of the cold purity he had seen and loved when first meeting her on the Island.

Now she was dead, and her dying had closed the door on his peace. She would not have him fetch a priest to her, and he would not pay for a single requiem mass on her behalf. And it proved to be her death that flung light across the darkness of his sin—sin not against her but against

Sabina, to whom he might never return, and now he refused to consider the future.

Autumn had gone to give place to a harsh, windswept winter, and Richard continued in the same condition. The innkeeper did not worry greatly on his account. Richard gave him no trouble and paid for the food even when he left it uneaten, and the lodgers' personal concerns and tumults had nothing to do with the infinitely more important matter of bills settled as soon as they were presented.

One stormy evening, the room beyond the flimsy partition was crowded with casual guests. There came the constant jangling of tankards, the innkeeper's heavy footfall, an obscene jest, a whirl of oaths. Then a voice began singing the old song which insisted that churchmanship was preferable to any other walk in life, and presently the singer reached the verse about the merchant folk:

> *"Mercatores videas, quali cum labore*
> *Vivunt, ut familiae praesint cum honore;*
> *Undas maris transvolent magno cum timore,*
> *Ubi res et corpora perdunt cum dolore. . . ."*

Indeed, thought Richard, idly watching the spluttering of a tallow candle in his corner, that was the whole pattern of a merchant's life, hard work, perilous journeys, continuous struggling after wealth and, if you did not perish on the road or at sea, you died in your bed, but come to die you must, and here he heard the final verse:

> *"Vide, fili, clericos purpura splendentes;*
> *Ipsi sunt divitias vere possidentes. . . ."*

and the clergy, prelates and others, arrayed in all their purple, reached the same straitened inexorability at the end of the road. You might be buried in purple, thought Richard, but where was the difference between that and being laid down in soiled, tattered sacking? He stared at his flickering candle. He knew that it would do him good to get up, trim himself up, and join the men at their singing and drinking. They were talking German, Sabina's language, which might have been his own, and he had gathered enough of their talk to know that they were all on the point of leaving Europe, all of them hoping for richer and easier opportunities elsewhere. All the quaysides in Genoa teemed with such folk, determined to earn their passage eastward, men who were weary of Europe's fatigue, who were tired of tolls, taxes, ill-paid work and the sharp-clawed hand of penury never too far from their throats. Richard had met many such. He wished to meet no more. Today, their very eagerness to strike new roots jarred on him who, according to himself, had done with the shaping of new ventures.

None the less, he could not escape their talk.

"Rich indeed the clergy are," confirmed a hoarse voice after the singer had obligingly turned the song into the vernacular. "Who ever heard of an abbot paying a fine to a layman? And they've got the impudence to say that taxes and tolls are good for the soul!"

Someone shouted for more ale. Someone else reedily talked about a recent riot among the linen weavers at Ulm.

"Of course," the hoarse voice insisted, "all wages should be properly graded. Stands to reason that a dyer has more skill than a wool-comber, but it's always the fullers and the cloth-binders who make trouble. That's what happened in Ghent, and they went the wrong way about it, too. It's not shouting and looting that'll get us there some day—it's just doggedness."

"Ah well," broke in the lute-player, "we've done with all of it now. I suppose you happen to be a dyer?"

"I am," confirmed the hoarse voice, "and I'm a widower with no children, and I'm going East. They tell me that dyers are needed there, not, mind you, that there is no justice in our cities once you get away from the noble and the cleric. I was fond enough of my own city, but I somehow couldn't stay on once I was left alone. Still, there's some justice there for the working man, say what you will about all the other places."

"And which is your wonderful city?" mocked the lute-player, and immediately and angrily the hoarse voice shouted a name which made Richard start from his pallet.

"And it's a fine city for all I've left it," boasted the hoarse voice. "Hardly a man that's been out of work there for many a year, and the Archbishop himself daren't meddle in anything, and I can tell you there'll be talk about my city in the four corners of the world. . . ."

"Why? Did your burghers mate an elephant with a bear, or what?"

"I have never seen an elephant there," retorted the hoarse voice. "There'll be talk all because of a young woman who's turned a master mercer—"

A loud guffaw interrupted him, and the lute-player laughed louder than all the rest.

"Ah, my friend, and I happen to know a tale about a

wench at Nüremberg who took to wearing arms. It didn't
last long. They soon clapped her into prison."

"I know nothing about the woman from Nüremberg,"
roared the hoarse voice. "But with us it is true. She's a rich
mercer's only child, and they betrothed her to a foreigner,
and he went and eloped with a nun from the Island, and her
father wished her to join the ladies, but they said, 'Ah no,
your money smells good indeed but your blood stinks,' just
in their usual arrogant manner, and now the young woman
sits in her father's counting-house, and she's learned the
trade fit to shame a man, strike me St. Sturm if I lie, and
they all think a lot of her, so cool in her judgment and fair,
too, for all she's a woman."

Here a chair was scraped along the sanded floor, and
the man from Ulm said reedily:

"Come to think of it, gossips, it's true. I've heard of it at
Würzburg where the young woman's cousin lives."

"There you are," said the dyer, "and now it's time I
went off to see a skipper. God rest you all."

They who remained went on talking but Richard ceased
to listen. He stayed very still. It was odd that he would prob-
bably never see the man, or hear his voice again. It was
odd and yet it answered Richard's mood. More than that:
it proved the first finger of light glancing across his inward
darkness. It so moved him that the very next morning he
got up, put himself in decent trim, made as good a meal
as the mean little place could afford, bought a horse, and
set northwards.

Adela's death had left him at the edge of despair. The
dyer's story had convinced him that amends were not only

desirable but inevitable. Richard did not imagine that Sabina, were he to meet her again, would spare a single look for him, nor did he altogether wish her to do so. But return he must. He had not a shred of a plan in his mind. There seemed nothing except a compulsion he realized he must not ignore. He could explain nothing. He did not wish to have anything explained. He vaguely thought that he might be imprisoned on return. Certainly, there would be a heavy fine to pay to Conrad for the broken marriage-contract and, possibly, another to the Island for the abduction. His resources might not be adequate to cover both fines, in which case a long term of imprisonment would fall to his lot. He thought of those eventualities briefly and impatiently. Nothing mattered except that he must return.

Yet he travelled slowly. He said to himself that he need not hurry, that what he was going to do might be done next month, next year, or even later. He travelled slowly because he sensed that he must have enough time, not for the vain purpose of inventing excuses and explanations for his trespass but for the sake of finding himself entirely. Sickness overtook him at a little hamlet the other side of the Alps so that it was spring again by the time he came back into the city, the third spring since the days when, an acknowledged bridegroom, he used to walk about those streets.

Richard's beard had grown, his features were altered by illness, and none recognized him as he rode into the great forecourt of the guildhall. He had certainly trimmed himself up during the last lap of his journey but there was nothing in his manner or his clothes to tempt any of the guard to rush forward and hold the horse's bridle for him.

They loitered about the place, eyeing Richard curiously, but they did not appear concerned about his business, and he surprised them by tossing a gold coin at them.

At once, a man sprang forward. Richard nodded briefly and asked:

"Are the Council in session this morning?"

They were not, he heard, but Master Luke happened to be at the guildhall. Would the gentleman be pleased to see Master Luke?

Richard tugged at his beard. Master Luke, also a mercer, was Conrad's distant kin and one of the three witnesses to the marriage-contract which had not been honoured. But did any of it really matter? Yes, said Richard, he would be pleased to see Master Luke, and the brown-liveried man brought him to a small dark room with barred windows where the fat little mercer stood up and looked, no recognition in his eyes.

"I'm Richard of Troyes, sir," Richard said quickly, "and I have come back to the city to make what retribution is necessary for the wrong I did to Master Conrad two years ago."

As soon as he had spoken, he felt as though he had come to a point where it no longer mattered whether they would imprison or torture him, or let him go. His words had rung dull and wooden in his ears, and now he stood, breathing jerkily, and through the barred windows, the early spring sunlight played on the dark green hangings and the wide oak trestle under a picture, and Master Luke's crimson gown suggested a raiment put on for a festival.

But there was no sense of a festival in the fat little man's manner. He slumped back into his chair, his eyes blazing.

"You—you—are a scoundrel," he brought out at last.

"And I'm here to admit it, sir," Richard paused. "There are monies of mine deposited at Lübeck, and I'm prepared to pay any fine the city may determine."

"A fine?" panted the little man. "Do you then imagine my cousin would touch a penny of your money?"

Richard said nothing.

"Have you come back thinking anyone would welcome you here?" shouted Master Luke. "Are you hoping to slink in at Stephen's Light by the back door?"

"Certainly not. I'd never dream of thrusting myself on them."

"You won't be allowed to thrust yourself on anyone." Master Luke banged his fat fist on the table with such fury that the small painted box full of cuttlefish powder rolled off to the floor. "Yes, we'll make it certain that you don't force yourself on anyone in this city."

"I quite expected it, sir."

"Did you? Don't stand there adding lies to your other trespasses! You thought you'd get off with a fine! We'll show you what we think of fines in this city!"

Richard did not reply, and suddenly it appeared as though Master Luke had no further words to use to him. A handbell was rung, the guard appeared, a few sentences were flung by Master Luke, and Richard found himself being led to an underground room furnished with a pallet and a stone jar of water on the floor. A little daylight trickled into the room from a lattice set high up in a wall.

"I left my horse in the forecourt," Richard turned to the guard.

"Prisoners have no possessions," answered the man, and

soon the rusty screeching of a bolt confirmed Richard's condition. Oddly enough, he felt at peace. He flung himself down on the pallet and slept more soundly than he had done since leaving Genoa.

And there he was left for many a day. Food would be brought in twice a day, but the guard were taciturn, nor did he try to make them talk. He asked for nothing. His bodily needs were few and they were answered. He supposed that sooner or later the Council would try his case. He knew enough law to realize that nothing more than a fine could be extracted from him. He also knew that his detention was not strictly in accordance with the law, and even that did not trouble him. His business had been to return, and he had returned.

[4]

Nobody told Richard about it but a feverish mood held the city at the time. To begin with, Lady Augusta, having done with her installation and with various outstanding pieces of business, had found leisure to turn her attention to Dame Adela's abduction. Nothing seemed to have been done about it. Dame Lucia vaguely alluded to certain letters either written or about to be written by Lady Isabella, but it was obvious that apart from a furious missive sent to Stephen's Light, the house had not moved at all in the matter. So Lady Augusta was preparing herself for action, and her preparations leapt to a frenzied pitch on receiving the news that "the dastardly young man" was back in the city and that Dame Adela had died in Genoa.

Dame Lucia was excused no fewer than five liturgical offices so busy was she in helping the abbess to draft the preliminary document to the Archbishop. All the details of Richard's crime must be set out. Dame Adela was a *sponsa Dei*, and for the outrage committed the man must be treated in a manner meted out to all felons. He must be flogged and branded, and imprisoned for a number of years, if not for life, and heavy damages must be paid to the abbey. Dame Adela, being dead, could not be restored to the Island, but it was imperative that her body should be brought over from Genoa—at the young man's expense—and re-interred on the Island. As to the damages, they would have to be assessed according to Dame Adela's dowry fallen in abeyance since her elopement. Dame Lucia was not allowed to quote from the dowry contract since, as Lady Augusta pointed out, it was not necessary to vex the Archbishop with such paltry details.

Dame Lucia hesitated.

"The contract is the strongest legal proof we have, my lady. I fear it will be absolutely necessary to produce it."

"Surely, you can make a copy of the clauses dealing with all the revenues without bringing in that very unfortunate last paragraph?"

" 'for as long as our sister continues in the service of God in the said House of Our Lady and St. Matthias, the Apostle,' " Dame Lucia read aloud and frowned. "I can certainly copy out the relevant clauses about the revenues, my lady, but I am positive the original will have to be produced if you wish to make a case of the matter."

"I have no intention of doing so," said Lady Augusta.

Her messenger delivered the letter at the Archbishop's

palace and was told that the answer would be sent to the Island within a few days.

But the Archbishop felt most unhappy. Lady Augusta's exalted rank considered, he could not very well write and tell her that her knowledge of the law equalled that possessed by the city idiot. Richard was a layman, and a layman's trespass in a case such as his was punishable with a fine and no more. Still less could the Archbishop bring himself to tell Lady Augusta that she could not have chosen a worse moment for framing her complaint. Richard was back, and the Council were keeping him in polite detention at the guildhall, but the city's mood was anything but kindly so far as the Island was concerned. Richard had grossly insulted one of the most important burghers but that—in the eyes of the common folk—was of a feather's weight compared with the Island's refusal to admit Sabina. Moreover, the city still remembered that not a single townsman had been invited to Lady Augusta's installation.

The Archbishop sat and pondered on what news his dependents brought to the palace. Richard of Troyes, on his return, had seen Master Luke, and Master Luke's wrath had fallen on the young man's head. But Master Luke was only one among twenty councillors, and it appeared that not even Master Conrad, most concerned in the grievous business, had evinced the least desire for a savage revenge. The Council were now determining the amount of the fine to be paid into the city funds, Master Conrad having refused any personal redress. And Richard of Troyes was being kept in very polite detention, the Archbishop's secretaries reported, with baked pike and spiced goose for his provender and plenty of good wine.

"Why are they keeping him there at all?" wondered the Archbishop, and raised both hands in horror on being told that a rumour had taken firm root in the city about the Island prepared to go to any length to avenge Dame Adela's abduction.

"The people must have gone mad," he told his chaplain.

"Well, your Grace, it is evident that the Council are prepared to humour the people by keeping that young man in safe custody."

"But, in heaven's name, man, do they imagine the ladies likely to cross over from the Island to inflict bodily injury on that young man?"

The chaplain shrugged.

"They'd imagine anything," he said briefly.

Within a few days, Lady Augusta, hearing nothing from the Archbishop, dispatched a second messenger to the palace. The old man wrote to the Council who replied with great courtesy. Yes, Richard of Troyes had returned to the city, and they were considering what sum was due from him on account of a broken marriage-contract. They also informed the Archbishop that, in their opinion, the young man had behaved with great propriety and honesty and that he was resolved to do all in his power to atone for "the trespass by him committed in what concerned the household of Master Conrad the mercer." The Council's letter made no mention of Dame Adela because that matter lay wholly outside their province. Having read the letter, the Archbishop knew what he had known from the beginning: that there was nothing for him to do.

Not so Lady Augusta. Receiving no reply from the palace, she sent an imperiously worded message to the Council. She no longer demanded either punishment or damages: simply and starkly she said that Richard of Troyes must be delivered to the ecclesiastical courts. In default of which, she threatened the Council with the Emperor and the Pope.

The twenty councillors met to consider the letter. They had it read aloud by the clerk. The burgomaster suggested that the contents amply warranted the letter being left without an answer. The matter was put to a vote and carried unanimously. But none of the twenty councillors chose to remember that the clerk was the husband of a masterful and most garrulous woman. Within a bare few hours, the whole city heard of Lady Augusta's threat. The matter of Richard of Troyes' return, the never-failing wonder of a young woman handling business at Stephen's Light, a most moving sermon by a wandering Dominican missionary, and the tale of a mermaid being washed ashore somewhere in France, everything was at once swept out of people's minds.

"Threatening us with the Emperor, is she?"

"And the Pope, too! Don't you forget the Pope, neighbour!"

"We'll threaten in our turn, gossips!"

A crowd rushed to St. Catherine's hospice, it being rumoured that one or two ladies from the Island were staying there. The terrified portress assured the people that there were no visitors in the house but the angry crowd would not believe her, and the whole place was searched and ransacked from cellar to garret. Their anger still unslaked, they ran out and made for the market square.

"Threatening us, are they? A pack of filthy foreign sluts, that's what they are!"

"And they say there's a cousin of the King of France among them!"

"And they gave tainted meat for the dole, too. I've heard it at the Silver Fish, neighbours, that old Hugo and his wife both died of stomach disorder that same day. Pork was bad, they said."

"Neighbours," roared a weaver, "they say that the Council are keeping that young man at the guildhall all on account of those black-gowned bitches threatening to have him poisoned. It's up to us to see that it doesn't happen—"

"Yes . . . Yes. . . ."

"Off to the guildhall," the weaver shouted, and they all stampeded after him. The guard checked them in the forecourt, and the mob saw that bare fists, billhooks and suchlike would be no match for shining halberds and daggers. They drew back but they would not stop shouting until a shaken councillor appeared on the steps and assured them that young Richard of Troyes was perfectly safe.

That evening, the mob wandered off to the lake shore and amused themselves by burning four of the abbey's ten barges.

[5]

Some four or five leagues to the west of the city, Conrad had a deep-moated mill built on two storeys with a high gabled roof and four turrets. It was in charge of a trusted dependent of his, and it stood in a thick grove of oaks and walnut trees. Oaken sawdust from the mill would be sent to Stephen's Light where Hilda used it for killing ants and

moths. To the mill Sabina would often go as a child. Hilda
and the men went there to get nuts, sawdust and flour, and
to have an hour's mellow gossip with the miller's wife. Sabina want for pleasure, it being understood that such ex-
cursions were a reward for a fairly long stretch of good behaviour.

The mill said little enough to her but she loved running
about in the grove specially in walnut-time, and Gunta, the
miller, would sometimes amuse her by climbing into the
fork of an old tree, a flute between his lips. He could not
play well, but still a tune of a kind would always compel
Sabina to dance a measure on the short stubbly grass until
the women called her in to dinner. Replete with hare pie
and larded milk, Sabina spent the afternoon in watching
beetles and ants run about. There were no other children to
join her in a game, but she never felt bored. It was good to
ride back to the city, in the cool of the evening, her little
arms entwined round Hugo's neck, the smell of wild straw-
berries drifting to her from a wood on the right.

Now there she went again, neither for idleness nor yet for
amusement, but to meet a bailiff from one of her father's
distant farms, to walk with him over the grove, and to mark
the trees chosen for felling. It was the first expedition of
such a nature for Sabina; she felt proud at being sent by
Conrad on a business which marked still more deeply his
gruff appreciation of her efforts.

"I trust that young bailiff well enough," he told her,
"but I want you to use your own eyes, too. All that timber
is to be shipped down to Hanover—but you may choose
one little tree for yourself," and he added without looking
at her, "a walnut chest is a pleasant piece to have in any

room, and there are many good craftsmen in the city to make it for you."

Having once said, "I believe you'll do well enough," Conrad had gone no further in his approval. He never had sugared words on his tongue, and Sabina felt she had no need of them. The fact that he left her more and more at her leisure to study his most important ledgers, that he never questioned her presence in the counting-house whilst he was interviewing callers of note, that he expected her to pay frequent visits to the warehouses, that often enough he would toss brusque questions at her and nod his head at her replies, all of it proved that Conrad had long ceased to consider Sabina's request as a piece of great foolishness.

Anna, too deeply rooted in custom to accept such a new departure with pleasure, did not, however, venture to go against Conrad's wishes, and Hilda's attitude went a long way to determine that of the rest of the household: "I knew you'd get somewhere, my chicken. And aren't I glad? An empty life is like a cup for the devil to fill. Put your mind into the job, and, please God, some day your heart'll be turned somewhere. No don't frown at me, my pet. I know what I'm talking about." Suddenly she remembered: "Why, that's old Mother Gunta all over! 'Where,' and 'how' you asked of her. And hasn't it all come true? 'In the place of your heart . . .' here at Stephen's Light, and you got it by speaking to the master. Yes, my darling, old Mother Gunta's got the true gift all right—not that I'd care to go there too often. . . ."

So now Sabina rode to the mill, and the man's small, brown-cheeked wife met her, the toothless mouth wide in a smile. There was not much comfort at the mill but a clean straw pallet had already been put in a corner and a great jug filled with ice-cold water from the well brought up the crazy ladder. There were boar's brawn and honey bread for supper, and Sabina heard that Egbert, the bailiff, was expected early next morning.

Sabina told a girl to unpack the hampers she had brought, gave the miller and his wife two stone bottles of wine sent by Conrad, a piece of good English stuff from Anna, a jar of cranberry jam, two iron spoons and a skillet. The supper eaten, Sabina slept in the scent of corn husks and to the music of running water.

The woman brought her milk for breakfast, and Sabina, sleep still clouding her thoughts, stretched out her hand for the small stone jug, and then asked sharply:

"What's happened?"

The woman crouched low on the floor, her hands clasped. Egbert, the bailiff, was down below, she said at last, her eyes bent.

"Is he drunk then? What's happened?"

"He hasn't come straight from the farm," mumbled the woman. "He stayed in the city for a bit—"

The stone jug slipped through Sabina's fingers.

"My—my father—"

"No, no," hurried the woman, "both master and mistress are well—all thanks to St. Pirim, but Egbert's heard that someone's come back to the city. . . ."

Sabina leapt from the pallet, pulled a shift over her naked body and a cloak over the shift, and ran down the steep ladder into the yard where Egbert, his jerkin dusty, stood with his back to her.

"Who's come back to the city?" she called out.

Egbert turned, his face deeply red.

"Madam—" he began, and she broke in:

"Tell me at once, do you hear?"

His eyes avoiding hers, he told her.

"And the master thought that you might like to stay on at the mill for a bit, and he said it was to be as you chose."

"Wait for me here, please. I shall be down again in a few moments."

Sabina turned towards the stairway again. The woman had gone but another crock of milk and a wooden dish of apples were put by Sabina's pallet. She drank a little milk and ate two of the apples. She put a thick grey kirtle over her shift, and carefully plaited a green ribbon into her hair. Then she went below, and the miller's wife watched her, arms crossed on her shrivelled breast.

"Thank you for my breakfast," Sabina said. "I'm going home after dinner. Please, have a sack of oak sawdust ready and some of those loaves my mother likes so much, and I might just as well take some flour with me. See that the dinner is early."

"My man's brought in a couple of trout."

"Ah good! They're nice to eat when broiled in wood ash, aren't they?"

"Yes," said the woman, and her bewildered glance followed Sabina across the yard. With her own ears the miller's wife had heard Egbert tell the story of that young man being back in the city, and yet there was the young mistress, discussing her dinner and sawdust and flour, and going off into the grove as if nothing at all had happened.

"I suppose," muttered the miller's wife to herself, "that once your heart's truly broken, you don't bother much about picking up the pieces."

Sabina was in the grove. She chose her own tree, had the rest marked for felling, and came back to the mill. Never a word had she said to the bailiff about the story he had brought from the city. She ate the broiled trout with relish, watched the horses packed with sacks and hampers, thanked the miller and his wife for their services, and rode off back to the city and Stephen's Light. She must ride past the guildhall where, as Egbert had said, Richard lay, and she rode, looking straight ahead of her.

Anna met her, tears falling down her cheeks, and Conrad stood, observing her closely. Sabina said she hoped that her mother was not in any bodily discomfort.

"Discomfort? What are you talking about? I am in agony, that's what I am. For a man like him to dare and come back here after all he had done! Truly, he must be worse than a Turk!"

"The miller's wife sent you some of those crescent-shaped loaves you like, Madam." Sabina bent to untie the smallest of the hampers. "They were so pleased with your gifts— particularly the wine and the kersey."

"What do I care about a miller's pleasure? Sabina, I'm telling you—"

"But I've heard all about it, Madam. I think Hugo has taken the sawdust to Hilda. Oh, and I was to tell you, sir, that the young saplings have rooted well." She placed a dozen or so of small loaves on the table and bowed to Anna: "May I go and trim myself up, Madam? The wind was rather rough and my hair needs combing."

"But," Anna stared in bewilderment, "don't you understand what I've been telling you?"

"Perfectly, Madam, and you've told me everything. There's nothing more to say, is there?"

Anna stepped back, her mouth open wide. Conrad said nothing, and neither his wife nor his daughter could tell that he stood there, so tall and stately in his dark green gown, praising Sabina in his heart since he could never bring himself to speak of such things.

"She's proud," he thought, "and with the right kind of pride, too. Ah yes, she'll do well enough."

And he was not to know that, her own door closed upon her, Sabina must clutch at the bedpost to steady her trembling knees. She had heard the story early in the day, and never an instant had she had away from other people's eyes, and nobody—not even her parents—must know of the gnawing burning ache which now made her bite her lips and informed her eyes with wildness. Richard had indeed died for her, and now he was back, but nobody must be allowed to imagine that he would ever rise again for her, and in the end Sabina so ruled herself that at supper she could say calmly enough:

"Why, yes, Madam, as I said, I heard the story from Egbert." She paused to pick up a chicken leg from her trencher. "I suppose everybody must needs talk about it."

Less she could not have said. More she would not say, and when Anna began repeating some deeply involved story which included the Council, the Archbishop, Lady Augusta and Dame Adela's death, Conrad frowned.

"I'll have no gossip in this house," he said levelly, and Anna, compelled to silence, fell to discussing her food.

[6]

Lady Augusta, having been virtually snubbed by the Archbishop and ignored by the Council, having heard about the burned barges and the riot in the city, came very near the verge of madness. It did not matter that the ferment in the city was said to have calmed down, the guard having restored order. The young man was said to be lodged in incredible comfort at the guildhall, and it did not appear that any measures at all would be taken against him.

"It's the end of the world," declared Lady Augusta. "But we've still got an Emperor and a Pope. I shall write to them both. Poor Dame Adela must have a Christian burial —at least."

Nobody in the house, least of all Dame Elizabeth, felt particularly happy until a pleasant diversion made Lady Augusta turn her face away from wrath. The widowed sister of the Duke of Holstein, a cousin to the abbess, came on a visit to the Island. She was a fat, pallid woman devoted to her lapdogs, astrology, and the pleasures of the table. She always wore a great opal buckle because a Spanish scholar of note, who had once cast her horoscope, had assured her that opals afforded best protection from all peril by land or water. The countess's visit to the Island had been postponed several times because of horoscopes being unfavourable to travelling, but now at last she was among them, and all the ladies hurriedly agreed that she could not have come at a more propitious time: a cousin's company would surely assuage Lady Augusta's frayed nerves, and a cousin's counsel make her turn to a more profitable course of action than that expressed in terms of vituperative letters to the mainland.

The countess arrived with her seven lapdogs, her gentlewomen and gentlemen in waiting, her tiring-women, an astrologer, and a pet monkey. All the parlours now rang with loud voices. The garth and the cloisters looked gay with brightly coloured clothes, and the ladies felt they amply deserved such a pleasurable deviation from the commonly trod paths. The excitement soon spread from the guest-house to the kitchens and all the other back regions of the abbey. Even Minnie, spent though she felt under the burden of inevitably increased tasks, sensed that she was getting her share of it all when Rowena, the head cook, tossed a couple of sweet wheaten cakes into her lap.

The ladies spent much time in admiring the visitor's gifts—a big square crystal reliquary with a bone of St. Linus, St. Peter's successor in the chair of Rome, a pair of Spanish silver candlesticks, fine kerchiefs of say and cambric, a big box of amber and coral buttons, and a quantity of fashionable embroidery in red and black silk. There were pretty Moorish collars for the abbess's lapdogs and a fine linen cloth for the high table in the frater. In her turn, the countess admired the copes and chasubles in the sacristy, the trees in the orchard, and the star-shaped flower beds in Lady Augusta's private garden. She volubly approved the new paving in the choir. At last, Lady Augusta brought her to the herb garden, and she stood, heavy and shapeless in a fur-trimmed violet gown, and gestured with her plump white hands.

"Here, cousin, I do feel at home. You should see my herb gardens at Bingen. Now, of course, you know, that if you

sow parsley on the eve of Lady Day, it will be above ground
in less than a fortnight?"

Lady Augusta murmured that she had never heard of it.
She did not add that she would have found it hard to recognize parsley if she saw it.

"And never, never," continued the countess in an urgent
voice, "let them use horse manure on the beds. Sheep
dung is really the best."

"But we have no sheep on the Island."

"You should have. Look at the ladies at Maria Dingen.
Their sheep paid for quite three lawsuits of theirs." Here the
countess allowed herself to be led back across the garth.
"By the way, cousin, do tell me where you get your wool
from? Believe it or not, but I have heard about some mercers in Hanover who are known to mix hair with their wool.
Isn't it iniquitous? And they haven't yet passed any law
against it! And oh the prices are rising and rising!" She
raised both hands in horror. "My brother, the Duke, tells
me it's all on account of the raised wages, and I can't
understand it because corn is cheap enough and a working
man has no palate for anything but coarse bread which he
can still buy for a copper."

They were mounting the steep stairway to the abbess's
lodgings, and Lady Augusta, having had several days of leaf-
thin courtesies, was longing to plunge into the heart of the
day's burden, to make the countess listen to the tragic
story of Dame Adela's abduction and death, of the Archbishop's indifference and the burghers' insolence, but good
breeding forbade such an outpouring unless or until the
visitor herself offered an opening, and the countess was
now busily discussing food and fashions. She had just been

on a visit to Ferrara, its duchess being a distant relation of hers.

"All the gowns and men's doublets also," she was saying importantly, "must have shields on the shoulders, and the hem of the skirt must be flounced." She raised her heavy violet skirts a little the better to display her own flounces. "And not to forget, cousin, ordinary veils have quite gone out of fashion. The Duchess gave me one braided all over with gold and nacarat silk, and I saw her wearing one that was ravishing—made of some transparent pink Eastern stuff and worked all over with a spider's web pattern in gold thread."

"That sounds very beautiful," said Lady Augusta.

It had been a hot day, and she felt weary. She knew she did not wish to discuss fashions, manure, herbs, or the delicate subtleties served at the Ferrarese court. Also she wanted her dinner rather badly. But she compelled herself to say again:

"That sounds very beautiful."

Not the trite remark but Lady Augusta's tone of voice served her a good turn. She had spoken in very low-keyed accents, and the countess's mind forsook the gold-threaded veils in Ferrara.

"You look out of sorts, cousin. I'm afraid this Island must be a damp place in the winter. Take care that you don't get the flux. And I can't say that I felt drawn to your city. One of my tiring-women fell and hurt her knee, and I had to leave her behind at the inn, and I must say I didn't think the people were at all obliging or even respectful. One of my attendants asked for some salve and was given a jar with some green stuff in it, and it stank so horribly

I felt it would do no good at all. Yes, I must say it again—you look out of sorts, cousin."

Lady Augusta's cheeks went a mottled red. Here was the opening she had prayed for, and she snatched at it avidly. She told the story to the end, adding:

"And do you wonder, cousin, that I should be looking out of sorts? There is nobody here except those impertinent fat burghers. Why, one of them was even daring enough to suggest that his daughter should be received in this house!"

"What? A merchant's daughter at St. Matthias'?"

"Precisely! Do you remember poor Lady Isabella? She was imprudent enough to allow the girl to get her schooling among us, and that inevitably must have given her father all sorts of foolish ideas. However, that doesn't matter so much. Dear cousin, what am I to do with an archbishop who won't answer letters, or with city councillors who absolutely ignore me?"

The countess looked grave.

"I'm glad you've told me all about it. Of course, I'd heard some talk but I didn't like to be the first to mention it. You may remember Adela's aunt at Quedlinburg. She always said that Adela was a nitwit."

"She behaved as though she were, and now she's dead, and the Archbishop—"

"My dear, I shouldn't waste any more time on him. In my opinion, your case is quite clear, and Adela's people would never dare to default."

"Did her aunt say so?"

"Oh no, she's far too clever."

A pause fell. Then Lady Augusta murmured:

"I was thinking of writing to Frederick. Whatever people

think of him and his foolish preoccupations, he's still Emperor and a relation—however distant. And, of course, there's always Rome. Yet I am not quite certain what I had best do," she added impulsively: "Dear cousin, I was rather hoping for your advice."

"I am going to do it on your behalf. I shall send for Don Diego at once on my return to Bingen."

"Who is Don Diego?"

"A most pious and learned Spanish gentleman." The countess crossed herself. "May God preserve him in all eternity!" She touched her opal with appreciative fingers, and Lady Augusta remembered her cousin's passion for astrology. She waited politely.

"Yes, yes," went on the visitor. "Don Diego and none other shall tell us whether the stars are in favour of your taking the case to the Emperor and Rome. You can leave the entire matter in my hands, cousin."

Lady Augusta bowed. It would have been against all good breeding to admit that she had no faith in any astrologer and that she had hoped for solid counsel and, possibly, family backing in her dilemma. It was with a sense of relief that she heard her gentlewoman's steps outside the door.

"Let's go and dine," she invited her guest.

On the same day, between supper and Compline, Dame Elizabeth felt that she must have some quiet and solitude. She again had the enjoyment of the little vaulted room in the north-west cloister, but the whole place teemed with visitors, and she could not escape their loud voices either in the garth or in the garden. She slipped through the little gate at the southern end of the garth, walked past the de-

serted kitchen gardens, and found herself in the orchard
when, from the direction of the pleached pear-tree walk,
she heard someone's low-keyed sobbing. Dame Elizabeth
quickened her steps. In the ebbing daylight she saw a figure
crouching at the foot of a tree. She bent and peered, and
recognized a girl from the kitchens whose name, as Dame
Elizabeth thought, was Minnie.

"What are you doing here? You should be indoors. And
why are you making such a noise?"

Awkwardly, slowly, Minnie pushed a strand of matted
hair off her forehead. One look at those eyes made Dame
Elizabeth soften her voice:

"Your name is Minnie, isn't it?" She did not wait for the
girl to acknowledge it, and hurried on: "Has someone
beaten you too hard? Or are you hungry?"

Minnie got up to her feet and slouched forward a little.
Her lips moved at last:

"The sun's setting, Madam, the sun's setting. Once she
looked at me and spoke kindly, and she smiled, too, and
now they've killed her. I'd have let myself be killed to save
her, but now she's dead all because she was so good, and yet
she is not at peace. She can't be because I've seen her."

"Stop! Who are you talking about?"

"Why, the lady who went from the Island some while
ago. I can't remember how long, the lady who left with a
young man, so they say in the kitchens, and I've seen her
walking about in the orchard and wringing her hands because she's not wanted anywhere, and I can't make her see
that I want her."

"Stop," said Dame Elizabeth again, "and go indoors. It's

time you were asleep. Do you know any prayers? No? Then cross yourself three times, do you hear, and if you see anything like that again, come and see me. You know me, don't you? My room is in the north-west cloister."

"Madam, I'm not allowed to go there."

"If anyone stops you, unless it be the Lady, tell them I've sent for you. Say nothing else. You must not speak of having seen anything, you do understand?"

"Yes, Madam, but I have seen—"

"And I have heard you," said Dame Elizabeth and turned away.

Her face beaded with sweat, her hands trembling, she crossed the deserted garth. She supposed that all the guests had gone to the frater there to drink their evening cup of wine and eat some wafers. Slowly, she made herself reach the cloisters. The heavy oaken door of the little room closed behind her, Dame Elizabeth fell on her knees by the window. She did not clearly know what she was to do until she found herself praying dumbly for the grace of prayer to be given her again.

Later, at Compline, she wondered if Minnie could indeed have seen Dame Adela's ghost wearing the blue cloak and the crimson hood worn by her on the night of her elopement. Minnie, so Dame Elizabeth had once heard, was known to be simple of mind but foolish folk were often granted revelations and showings which stayed hidden from those whose faculties were unflawed. It was in keeping with Dame Adela's character that she should have taken pity on a ragged little waif among them, and it was also obvious that Dame Adela, her tragic end considered, would now be seeking for peace and not finding it. And what more natural than that she should appear here, on the Island, where she should have ended her days?

Dame Elizabeth knew that she had no business to keep the story to herself. It was her duty to go to Lady Augusta because incense must be burnt in the pear-tree walk and holy water sprinkled there, and the uneasy ghost urged to depart in peace. But Dame Elizabeth also knew that she would not go to Lady Augusta. She caught herself wondering whether blessed water and a few appointed words mumbled by Sir Hugo had the power to bestow peace on anyone, least of all, on a poor unanchored ghost. . . . The daring thought left Dame Elizabeth untroubled.

PART VI

"What Bird Will Nest in Winter?"

THE countess's promise to provide the ladies with a horoscope from a stranger in Spain was presently communicated by Lady Augusta to Dame Lucia and Dame Blanche.

"I had hoped," she could not help saying, "that I'd be given different advice. However, the gentleman in Spain and his possible findings need not interfere with what steps there are left for us to take."

"About Dame Adela's dowry?" asked Dame Lucia.

"Why, yes."

"There's a very capable lawyer at a place near Nüremberg, my lady," offered Dame Lucia, and Dame Blanche lost no time in murmuring that in her humble opinion a saint's intercession might yet restore all the lost revenues. Lady Augusta frowned and dismissed them both. She, at least, had no intention of pinning her hopes on a lawyer's ability, and Dame Blanche's hagiographical fervour was not much to her taste at any time.

After the visitors' departure, the ladies settled down to their accustomed ways. They had heard enough gossip to last them through the winter, and the countess's women had brought some new Italian and French receipts, in particular one for a sauce to eat with roast chicken made with ginger, orange-peel and red wine. There was also a new and moving Christmas hymn the countess had discovered in Italy, and Dame Constance at once began teaching it to the novices:

> *"Verbum de patre natum,*
> *Lumen de lumine,*
> *Nuper est incarnatum*
> *De matre virgine,*
> *Verbum abbreviatum*
> *Homo de homine. . . ."*

From her room in the north-west cloister, Dame Elizabeth heard the fresh unproven voices stumble through the lines and Dame Constance interrupt them with a mordant reproof:

"Don't, please, be so shrill at '*Lumen de lumine.*' It isn't an alleluia to soar up to the ceiling. Now, all of you, once again!"

And Dame Constance was right, thought Dame Elizabeth. "Light of light" had such a calming sound, and it suggested those very last moments before day-break. The words were widening, too. Here she remembered a few stray lines from the Pentecostal sequence supposed to have been written—at least an old legend so affirmed—in the very room where she now sat:

> *"Veni, sancte spiritus,*
> *Et emitte caelitus*
> *Lucis tuae radium. . . ."*

Dame Elizabeth raised her head from the needlework in her lap and glanced about the small vaulted room. If there were any truth in the old legend, it was precisely within these walls that—some two and a half centuries before her day—a crippled young man, whose very name was now forgotten, blinded in a street fight on the mainland, had written the stirring poem on the light of the Holy Ghost and died, his work ended. The room was now supposed to be haunted though nobody had ever seen or heard a ghost there except ladies like Dame Griselda and Dame Maud who were prepared to find traces of the supernatural in the very dust under their feet. Dame Elizabeth's finely boned hands were very still. She kept quiet as though expecting the old walls to share some of their secret with her. No such sharing came to her, but, unaccountably, she felt quietened as though the prayers she could not make had been both heard and answered.

Here, she remembered Minnie and her story. She had expected Minnie to come to her, but the girl had not been, and the thought of Minnie and Dame Adela brought Sabina to Dame Elizabeth's remembrance.

"They all say she is fully occupied these days, but I still hold that she should have been given a chance to make her choice. It was unkind. It was not just. . . ."

Dame Griselda and Dame Maud still shared their meals in Dame Elizabeth's room. Now, with the supper bell having rung, they appeared, and their brittle shrill chatter filled the little room.

There had been a fire at St. Catherine's hospice, they told Dame Elizabeth, and a jeweller had been robbed in the night, but all the weavers and apprentices seemed quiet enough.

"It's because we are in winter," said Dame Griselda. "I suppose it would be difficult to run about and set houses on fire in the bitter wind and the sleet. Isn't it odd that such troubles should always happen in the fair season?"

Nobody had anything to say to the sage remark.

"You know, Madam," Dame Maud turned to Dame Elizabeth, and offered a dish of lemon-flavoured wafers to her, "that the Lady has written both to the Pope and to the Emperor. At least, we all think she has because Dame Lucia has been secreted with her the whole afternoon. So I have heard. Of course, Dame Lucia has kept her counsel about it all."

"She has not," retorted Dame Griselda, choosing a filbert. "She has told several ladies that she knew perfectly we would see justice done at last."

"About Dame Adela's dowry?"

"Why, of course."

"And what of that dreadful young man?"

"Unfortunately it appears that nothing can be done except inflict a heavy fine. He's still in the city, and they seem to make quite a hero of him because of his return. Personally," said Dame Griselda, "I could never endure fools in my life. There is a common saying about the extremes meeting. I fear I've never found it to be so in my case." She waited pointedly, expecting a ready endorsement from the two ladies, and bit her lip at their silence.

They had finished their food, the servants came to clear and, the door being opened, two or three ladies passed, heard scraps of conversation, and joined in.

"We all wonder if that young man came back because of the girl. Has she seen him?"

"Well," Dame Griselda pursed her lips importantly, "I know she has. Rowena saw it happen in the square. Sabina rode past him and cut him dead."

"That sounds good. The girl's got some pride, at least."

"Well, she may have," said Dame Maud, "but it's quite dreadful her having gone into the business. Imagine a young girl sitting in a counting-house! It's most unbecoming. . . ."

Dame Elizabeth shook her head.

"Why should it be? She's always had a good head for figures."

They all looked at her in pity, and Dame Elizabeth wished that she might be able to call at Stephen's Light and to talk to Sabina and she felt sad, aware that it would never happen.

So Christmas came and went, marked by no other excitement than that at the second mass Sir Hugo forgot the commemoration of St. Anastasia and that the green geese served for ladies' dinners were horribly overspiced. At Candlemas, Lady Augusta's candle went out during the procession just when the ladies were chanting *"et gloriam plebis tuae, Israel."* Everybody exchanged furtive glances, and Dame Blanche shivered because for a candle to go out at such a moment was the very worst of omens. She somehow succeeded in keeping her fears to herself but they came to be amply justified within a few days.

Dame Blanche was in the sacristy, horrified to find several moth holes in the dark green curtain which was to hang between altar and choir during Lent. She knew she would never get it darned in time. She rummaged in a press and came on a pair of grey-rose damask curtains. Their colour looked certainly festive, and she decided to send young Dame Prudence to the Lady for the instructions. Dame Blanche was folding the moth-damaged curtains for darning when Dame Prudence ran into the sacristy, her face ashen.

"Good heavens," a mass of dark green cloth slipped out of Dame Blanche's hands. "What's happened now? Has a bull got loose?"

"It's the Lady," babbled the girl. "Dame Cosima says we're all to dine off dry bread and herbs today. Something dreadful has happened, Madam, and the Lady is so furious that I didn't dare mention the curtains."

"Well, I suppose I shall have to use the grey-rose damask then."

"No, no, Madam. The Lady wants you at once."

By a blazing fire of apple-logs, Lady Augusta sat, her face livid. The scattered pink pearls of her chaplet lay on the rug at her feet. The square oaken table was strewn with several sheets of parchment. Dame Lucia and Dame Blanche halted in the doorway and curtseyed deeply. Lady Augusta flashed such a look at them that they all but staggered backwards.

"My lady," murmured Dame Lucia.

"My lady," gasped Dame Blanche.

"Close the door behind you," Lady Augusta ordered, "unless you wish every fool in this house to hear what I've got to say."

The door closed, they waited. Lady Augusta stamped her foot.

"Can't you see these papers? Read them! Read them at once! What did you think I had you come here for?"

Dame Blanche stood still. But a brief year before, Lady Augusta had been the chosen darling of the whole house. Dame Blanche remembered that Lady Isabella had, too, been the chosen darling in her turn—before her installation. Where, then, was the much vaunted grace of office when two pleasant, amiable, well-bred ladies could—in so short a time—develop such a grasp on tyranny? Dame Blanche shivered and bent her eyes. She heard the parchments rustle between Dame Lucia's hands and prayed that she might not be commanded to offer an opinion because she knew she had none to offer.

The countess, on reaching her home at Bingen, had decided that even Don Diego's advice would hardly be adequate in the case of Dame Adela's dowry. So the lady told the whole story, including Sabina's rejection by the chapter, to her brother, the Duke of Holstein. The Duke brought the story to a cardinal, and the cardinal remembered it when he got to Rome. The letters, now received by Lady Augusta, never alluded to any fine due from Richard of Troyes. They made no mention of Dame Adela's dowry. They dealt with the question of Sabina's admission. The cardinal, to Dame Lucia's deepening horror, chose precisely the same arguments as those used by the late Lady Isabella at her last chapter: the social pattern was changing, and it was not fitting for any religious house to be wholly governed by the archaic considerations of blood and rank. The cardinal added that the matter was so regarded in the highest quarters in Rome and that he had already communicated with the Emperor about the necessary changes in the charter of the House of Our Lady and St. Matthias, the Apostle.

Dame Lucia finished reading and stammered:

"Do you wish the chapter to be summoned at once, my lady?"

Lady Augusta stared as though she could not believe her ears.

"Another chapter? Yes, and what happened at my very first chapter, Dame Lucia? They would not even vote about it. They rejected the whole idea out of hand. I am certain that my predecessor had been right—but how could I force a decision at my very first chapter, tell me that, will you?" shouted Lady Augusta, and neither of the ladies dared to remind her that the chapter's decision had been taken at her own most adroit persuasion.

"Now the matter is settled for us," Lady Augusta leant back in the chair. "Both of you shall have to go to a burgher's house and eat humble pie all because a thoughtless cousin of mine has mishandled the case. And I shall write to Rome and inform them they have been obeyed, and I don't really care if they expect us to open our doors to the women of the Painted Street."

"Dame Constance will novice the girl, my lady," murmured Dame Blanche.

"That'll be none of your business," Lady Augusta turned on her. "Now leave me and remember, both of you, there is to be no chapter."

None, of course, was held, but within less than half an hour the entire house learned about the letters from Rome. There were urgent whispers even in choir, and someone heard Dame Constance affirm that the draughtiest corner in the chapel would be too good for Sabina.

Alone, Dame Elizabeth doubted if the girl would ever come but, wisely, she kept her counsel. She longed to escape the anger and confusion of it all, and towards the evening she made for the orchard there to come face to face with Minnie.

"Why haven't you been to see me?" she asked not unkindly.

The girl stood silent, twisting and untwisting her unshapely red fingers, and Dame Elizabeth could not see her face for the matted hair hanging over it.

"I suppose you had nothing else to tell me?"

"I've told you once, Madam. You said I was not to speak of it. I've not said a word, but I have seen the good lady since. . . . Why, I saw her yesterday, and she was crying fit to wring your heart, and her hands were full of oxslips and marigolds. But she was crying, and I could not get near her."

"Have you remembered to cross yourself three times morning and evening?"

"Not always."

"Try and do that." Dame Elizabeth waited, but Minnie had nothing else to say.

Across the garth, the ladies' voices were loudly arguing about the escutcheon to be placed over Sabina's stall.

"But she'll never come here," thought Dame Elizabeth, "and I suppose it's better so."

But she wished she had been chosen by Lady Augusta to go to Stephen's Light.

[2]

Conrad would never allow gossip in his house. None the less, much of it found its way under his roof. Hilda might well rebuke servants for their chatter but she could hardly leave Anna's questions unanswered, and Anna, sharply resentful of her husband's ban on the whole topic, lost no chances of snatching at any spicy morsel brought by Hilda whenever Conrad happened to be out of hearing. And Sabina inevitably must know why Richard had come back. To admit the wrong he had done and to pay the fine, Hilda said, adding that the mood of the city had been quick in changing towards him. They all commended him for his courage more so since the ladies on the Island were known to clamour for savage reprisals.

"But, surely, the ladies will be satisfied with a fine?"

"The way they're going on, my pet, they're not likely to see a copper coin paid over to them. Threatening with the Pope! Threatening with the Emperor? That's not the way to get into the city's good graces. Little wonder some of the rougher folk went and burnt those barges."

But Sabina was not interested in arson.

"What's happening at the guildhall?"

"They lodge him well enough, and even Master Luke has been heard speaking politely to him. I shouldn't be at all surprised if they were to give Master Richard some employment later on when all the fines are settled. There's something in a man who comes along and says openly he's done wrong." Here Hilda glanced at Sabina in a peculiar way. "Still, dear heart, who would drink twice from a tainted well, as the saying goes!"

Sabina merely turned away and began combing her hair.

The rioters had not been near Stephen's Light; Sabina had the peace and the safety of her father's counting-house for her work and her own room for the occasional spells of privacy, but Hilda's reference to a tainted well disturbed her far more than any shouting down the street would have done.

"And why should any of it disturb me?" Sabina asked herself one morning and, on raising her head, was pleased to see Martin, one of the senior clerks, come into the counting-house.

"There are the ten loads of Italian silk brought over a fortnight ago. The master sent me to say they've all been checked but he has not had the copy of the acknowledgment sent to him."

"Ah yes," and Sabina blushed, aware that she should have written out the acknowledgment without any such reminder. "Of course. . . . Of course. . . . I'll write to Lyons this very day."

Martin pulled at his girdle and murmured:

"You meant Florence, Madam, didn't you?"

Too honest to screen a blunder, too proud to admit it, Sabina frowned.

"Please tell my father it shall be done today."

But the wisp of an incident left behind it the consciousness of a flaw in the armour of her inward discipline. "I mustn't waste any more time on such thoughts," Sabina said to herself as she began drafting the formal note to the silk merchants in Florence. "It is stupid and wasteful," she thought, and the badly mended quill jabbed so hard that the ink spluttered all over the date and she must needs make a fresh beginning.

Indeed, it was both stupid and wasteful. Sabina knew that Conrad would never hear of a renewed betrothal, nor was she certain that such a renewal would ever resolve her inner uncertainty. Every time she tried to search her heart, she inevitably remembered Hilda quoting the old proverb about a tainted well. Had all of it been a poisoned well indeed, or had its waters been merely clouded? How could she tell? Yet, after long hours spent over the ledgers, it seemed permissible and even sweet to remember the madness of a particular spring, to think about a Spanish lute played in the twilight, a fragile French song, and the wild compulsion of a man's mouth against hers. There were moments when Sabina wondered whether even her pride could prevent her from feeling like an autumn leaf tossed here and there by sharp-fanged November winds, and there were different moods when she found herself able to pray that she might never see Richard again.

Her father would never mention the matter at all, but he must have heard much, and it was evident that the city had been moved by the manner of Richard's return. They lodged him well, and they might yet employ him. But, thought Sabina, whatever happened, he must never be allowed to carry his repentance to the threshold of Stephen's Light.

[3]

It would have been better if Lady Augusta had taken counsel with those whose prudence excelled her own, or if she had schooled herself to wait until she might steer her course in calmer waters. But, humiliated and angered by the letters from Rome, she thought that action, however swift and unreasoned, answered best. On hearing that everything was quiet on the mainland, she decided that Dame Lucia and Dame Blanche were to go to Stephen's Light at once. She sent them off accompanied by a bailiff and two serving-women, and she gave them no instructions beyond saying:

"You shall stay the night at the Dominican hospice. Here is a small present and a letter for the prioress. Be careful, both of you, how you answer her questions. I don't want any gossip spread in the city. Surely, the truth is grim enough."

Dame Blanche was too frightened to speak but Dame Lucia ventured:

"Is there no letter for Conrad the mercer, my lady?"

"Why should I write to him? It is quite enough for him to be told that a cardinal in Rome thinks it fit that his daughter should be admitted into our house. There'll be ample time for letter-writing later on."

"Do we then say nothing else, my lady?"

"Yes," snapped Lady Augusta, "you might say a *Veni, Creator* on your way to Stephen's Light."

The two ladies crossed the lake and rode into the city, an uneasy silence between them. They had no doubts that Conrad would be staggered by such flattery from a cardinal in Rome. None the less, they felt that the abbess might have reinforced their arguments with a letter sealed with the great seal of the abbey. They duly murmured their *Veni, Creator,* and Dame Blanche added prayer to St. Ursula, but the unhappy sense of their going empty-handed haunted them all along the way.

The unease was hardly dispelled by the sight of Hilda standing in the porch of Stephen's Light. Hilda they knew well—but this once the old woman did not choose to recognize the visitors. Dame Lucia asked for Conrad in an admirably firm voice. For all answer, Hilda stepped aside and held the door open for the ladies to enter.

It was so warm in the parlour that they unbuckled their cloaks at once. Pulling at their wimples and smoothing down their veils, they murmured to each other that the stony severity of the room was pleasing to find in the house of so rich a man as Conrad. Then Dame Blanche peered out of the window and remarked on the fine weather, and Dame Lucia admired the small white statue of St. Sturm in a corner.

"Oh yes, Madam," Dame Blanche bowed slightly, "but it would have been more suitable to have a candle burning in front of it."

Dame Lucia shrugged. They fingered their beads, examined a plain oak coffer and listened. But there were no sounds of any steps outside the door. Dame Blanche remarked on the unusual shape of the windows in the parlour, and Dame Lucia frowned.

"Madam, I fear that very unmannerly old woman could not have announced our coming. Really, it's such a pity that the Lady did not give us a letter."

But here the door opened none too hurriedly, and they looked up to see Sabina.

Dame Lucia spoke loudly:

"Good morning, but it's your father we've come to see. . . ."

And Dame Blanche flustered:

"Dear child, it's so long since we saw you—"

"My father is coming," Sabina said, curtseyed to both ladies, and beckoned to a maid behind her. The two ladies at once remembered that they had breakfasted very early, and they watched the wine, pink-coloured wafers and a dish with preserved cherries set on the table.

"My father will be here in a moment," said Sabina again, and invited them to take the high-backed chairs and some food and wine. She filled the horn-cups and passed the wafers in their shallow dish, and the two ladies took heart from the obvious civility in her manner. They sipped the wine and nibbled at the wafers, and made trite little remarks about the weather and the promise of the vineyards, and Sabina made her replies in the same cool voice. She was just about to refill the horn-cups when Conrad, with Anna behind him, entered the room. The two ladies rose, and Dame Lucia said that they had a message to deliver from the Lady.

"And we'd like to do so in private, sir," she added, and made another little curtsey so that Conrad must bow once again.

"If it concerns my daughter, Madam, she'd better stay in the room, I think."

The two ladies coughed uneasily and glanced towards Anna but Anna stood, her eyes bent. Then they glanced at each other and gave an unnecessary tug or two to their wimples.

"Does it concern Sabina?" asked Conrad.

Dame Blanche bit her lips, and Dame Lucia shrugged.

"Well, since you wish Sabina to remain here," she paused, but Conrad said nothing, and she went on: "we have a message from Lady Augusta to you, sir, a message of the greatest importance. You may remember that there happened an unfortunate muddle at the very beginning of her abbacy?"

"I remember no muddle at all, Madam. I received a clearly worded letter from Lady Augusta which told me that my daughter could not be admitted into your house on account of her social status."

"Yes, yes," Dame Lucia agreed. "I remember it perfectly, sir. That's just what I meant. Such a letter, sir, should never have been sent to you at all."

"But it was sent, Madam, and I was given to understand that such were the wishes of the entire house."

"It was all most unfortunate, sir. Surely, you will remember there was Lady Augusta's installation and all, and now just recently she has heard from Rome." Dame Lucia paused to lend weight to her use of the word. "Yes, from Rome, sir, and the house will be happy to receive Sabina."

There! She had done. Proudly aware of her matchless diplomacy, Dame Lucia leant back, wishing that she might wipe the sweat off her temples.

All was quiet in the parlour except for Anna's laboured breathing and the click of Dame Blanche's rings against her beads. Dame Lucia drew another breath and ventured to look at Conrad. That dark fleshy face told her nothing at all. Unease stirred in her. It was almost as though everybody were waiting for her to go on, and there was nothing else she might say. She clutched at a mere straw of a post-script:

"Of course, you will duly receive a letter from Lady Augusta, sir."

"If there should be any occasion for her to write to me," Conrad replied suddenly. "My daughter has heard you, Madam. Well, Sabina?"

She raised her head and said quickly:

"It is for you to answer the ladies, sir."

"Well then," Conrad straightened his huge shoulders, "that's what I think of the matter. No man will ride a horse which has thrown him badly and no woman cares to look twice in a cracked mirror."

The two ladies were not successful in smothering their gasp. The sharp-edged pause was broken by Sabina:

"I share my father's mind. . . ."

Dame Blanche stared at a ginger cat coiled in his sleep on a broad window-sill. Dame Lucia wiped her fingers very slowly.

"You've had your answer, ladies," Conrad told them.

Dame Lucia tried to steady her voice but it rang croakingly:

"Is that a reply we can possibly carry back to the Lady, sir?"

"It wouldn't be as harsh as the one I had from her. You tell me that letter of hers was a mistake. Well, I prefer to abide by the mistake."

"Sir, for a house such as ours it is a great concession even to admit to a mistake."

"That may well be so—but you must forgive a burgher if he does not understand much of these matters."

"But what is Sabina to do?" Dame Blanche broke in. "Surely, surely, sir, there is her soul to think of."

Conrad frowned so that Sabina knew his patience was tautening for a snap.

"I did think of her soul," he said sharply, "when she was in great trouble. By God's grace, it's all behind her, and may I say again that you've had your reply, ladies."

Not the words only but the emphasis made Dame Lucia and Dame Blanche remember that their horses had waited long enough outside Stephen's Light. They must ride back to the Dominican hospice and answer the prioress's difficult questions as best they might. Of Lady Augusta's reaction to the failure of their mission they preferred not to think at all for the moment. They got up, clutching their beads, and Sabina, too, rose and bowed to each lady in turn. They stopped, a thin finger of hope brushing against their hearts but Sabina's very first words crushed that hope once and for all. Those words were like deftly handled, sharp-bladed scissors which cut through the whole weft and woof of their argument. The ladies stood and listened, at once horrified and fascinated.

"You spoke of my soul," she began in a clear voice, "but let that remain between my God and myself. I'll allow no intruder there. Once I might have been happy among you, but I've since learned that I wouldn't have found God served under your roof, at least—not in the way I understand such service. You've put cunning and pride where humility and charity used to be once, and you use the poor as though they were rejected by God himself. Does the wearing of a scented habit justify your claim to follow the Lord and the saints? Does the daily chanting of the Psalter teach you the true way to Paradise?" Sabina flung at the ladies, her brown eyes on fire. "My father has now allowed me to help him in his business, and I try and give my whole mind to it when I sit in his counting-house, and that, after all, is a worldly matter, that's only trade which you despise so much. But how many among you think about God's business when you sit in choir?"

When Sabina had done, there crept a tension into the room as though—having heard one thunderclap, they were fully justified in expecting another. At last Dame Lucia said:

"Sir, had the Lady known about it, we would never have been sent on such a mission." Here she paused to gather herself up for the final shaft, and her voice thickened with horror and anger. "I assure you there could be no question of welcoming a heretic among us."

Their veils rustling loudly, the two ladies left the room.

[4]

The perilous word had left the place chilled. Dame Lucia had used it out of her despair since a charge of heresy might not be so easily woven out of a girl's impassionate phrases. And Conrad knew it to be so even if Anna did not. Conrad approved Sabina but he had no time to spare for her because, the door closed on the ladies, Anna at once broke into piteous sobbing. She had been silent throughout. She did not say much now. Both hands pressing to her temples, she swayed to and fro in the chair.

"They'll take her away! They'll take her away! They

took away that girl at Nüremberg and they burned her. Oh Sabina, how could you say such things? They'll take you away. . . ." Eyes glassy, mouth fallen-in, Anna stared as wildly as though the faggots for the stake were already brought into the room.

"Go to the counting-house," Conrad said to Sabina, and then took his wife's damp hand in his. "Stop it," he urged her. "Don't let the servants hear you. Nobody can take Sabina away. She goes to mass and keeps all the fasts, and the old man at St. Agnes' knows her too well. Do you understand what I am telling you?" Conrad bent over Anna. "As to myself, I'd be the first to curse those women through every gate in the city."

"So would I," Anna gulped, "but they can't hurt her, can they? I thought they looked so spiteful—"

"They'll have the Council and the whole city against them if they try any mischief," he said so weightily that she knew she could indeed believe him.

Meanwhile, in the counting-house, Sabina waited for Conrad. She rather hoped he would stay with her mother for some time because she needed time to return to the day's ordinary matters. She felt so angry, disgusted and shaken.

She had schooled herself to exile all thought about the Island from her mind. Once, a long time ago, as it seemed to her today, she had come to cherish the dream of a life among them, her inner self clothed with a desire to serve God in their company. Not once or twice but on many occasions it had seemed to Sabina that she would thus find peace and learn to see Richard's cruel departure as a sign that she had never been destined for a life in the world.

That dream had been broken in the most wounding manner imaginable. They had not even tried to see if Sabina would answer their purposes. They had rejected her because her father could not have produced a proof of a single generation of nobility, and their refusal had brought Sabina into an unfamiliar climate. It had not shaken her faith in God nor disturbed her adherence to the important practices she had followed since childhood. But it had certainly made her suspicious of many religious surfaces, and the suspicions had greatly troubled her.

Now, inexplicably, they had found her acceptable. Sabina thought little about the letters from Rome. It seemed to her that, with one dowry gone by default, the Island had decided to see if their shattered fortunes might not be mended by securing her portion. In that she was unjust but the little she knew was not enough to convince her of the injustice in her thoughts.

"Never shall I go to them . . . Never . . . Never . . . And if I am a heretic, they are blasphemers. . . ."

Here Sabina heard her father's heavy footfall on the stairway outside the counting-house door. She longed for bean water to refresh her burning face, but there was none in the place. She wiped her cheeks with a kerchief and got up, her knees trembling.

But Conrad was coming in for a different purpose. He had comforted his wife as best he knew. He would neither comfort nor rebuke Sabina. They were together in his place of business. The matter discussed in a parlour of his private house did not belong to the counting-house.

"I saw Martin early this morning," he began, without wasting an instant on preambles. "He said there was a mat-

ter of importance you wished to discuss with me. I can spare
the time now. What is it about?"

Sabina knew better than thank her father even by a
glance. She turned and rummaged in a chest, and brought
a bundle of papers to the table.

"Sir, in England some of our people are allowed to buy
and sell on board their own ships, aren't they?"

"Yes."

"But there's also a place in London called the German
Steelyard. I've heard that it's a walled-in area—with many
dwellings and warehouses and a weighing office."

"I've never been there but I've heard of it."

"Then why"—her voice unhurried, Sabina came to the
point—"why, sir, must we go on buying English wool
through Antwerp? You have ships of your own, sir."

"Because Master Loeb of Antwerp has always done it for
us," Conrad told her.

"Does he buy direct from England?"

"No, he has a very good agent in London."

"And do we buy silks from Italy in the same way?"

"Of course we don't, and you've always known it. You've
met many clients from Florence and Venice—"

"I suppose Master Loeb has to pay his London agent?"

Conrad nodded a little impatiently.

"And we pay Master Loeb a fair commission, don't we?"

"I suppose it is fair. He's always been satisfied."

Sabina made a small gesture as though the matter of
Master Loeb's satisfaction were of no concern to her.

"So really we pay more than double on every bale of
wool we get shipped from England?"

"Well, there are the freight charges."

"I know, sir, but if we had someone of our own in London, we would certainly pay him and pay the freight charges too, but we wouldn't have to pay Master Loeb's commission. I've looked into it all carefully, sir. There are merchants who have their own agents in London, and they pay less than we do. Here, I've got some figures ready for you."

But Conrad shook his head.

"That would be very awkward. Why, my father used to deal with that house at Antwerp."

"And there's another thing," Sabina went on. "Wouldn't it be better to have the wool shipped to one of our own ports? Why should it always go to the Low Countries?"

"Because such has always been the custom."

Sabina forbade herself to smile.

"A good custom may sometimes turn into a bad habit, sir. You've said so yourself."

"And there's nobody I know in London," Conrad said stubbornly.

"And there was nobody at Antwerp until my grandfather found Master Loeb's house, and their commission is much too high, sir. The first thing to do is to try and get them to bring it down. The recent increase in weavers' wages might be a good excuse. Please, sir, let me write to Antwerp—"

"They'd take no notice of a letter from a woman."

"But could you not sign it?" asked Sabina.

"And if I were to break with Master Loeb, what would I do in London?"

"Have a man of your own. Pay him a wage. That will answer far better, sir. Middlemen are often necessary—we must have them at Genoa and at Famagusta on Cyprus because we have not enough ships to send to the East, but is there any need for a middleman between our house and the English wool-market?"

"I can think of no man I could send to London."

"But I can," Sabina offered, "and he's in the city. I hear that the Council think of finding employment for him. He is Richard of Troyes."

She had quite expected her father to bang his fist on the table, and the gesture did not startle her.

"I shall never employ him."

Sabina waited an instant and then leant forward a little.

"Sir, you've trained me very well and you've always taught me that home matters belong to Stephen's Light and business matters to the counting-house. We are not in the parlour now. That very sad affair is more than two years old. Your fellow councillors would approve of it. The man has travelled, and he is known to speak English."

"I shall never employ him. And it's hardly fitting that you should ask me to do so. Where's your pride, girl? Why, I had once thought that you loved him."

"My pride is beyond hurting," Sabina said quietly. "As to the other matter," she shrugged, "there's my work and there's Stephen's Light, and that's enough. There'll be no need for me ever to meet him, and it is evident that he has tried to make up for the wrong he did."

"Never—"

"But, sir, all of you sitting in council have agreed upon it. I know it. And it would be far better for him to leave the city." Sabina hesitated and then decided to say no more.

For several minutes Conrad sat silently. Then he rose.

"After dinner, you may draft a letter to Master Loeb—
but I promise nothing further."

Sabina stood up and watched him move to the door. He
walked slowly as though the long violet gown, trimmed
with the broad band of grey fur, were too heavy for him. All
his years were in that slow gait, and sunlight caught at the
silver flecking his brown hair. Sabina watched and suddenly found herself brushing a few tears off her eyes.

She had feared and obeyed him all her life. Lately, she
had learned to respect him. That day she knew that she
loved him even though she might never permit herself to
express her feelings by the least caress. He had stood silent
in the parlour, and now Sabina saw his silence in terms of
an affirmation of all the vehemence shaped by her lips. She
would never hear him praise her, that she knew, and she
also knew that she needed no words from him. In telling
her to draft that letter to Antwerp, Conrad had once more
approved her.

[5]

"But why should Master Conrad do it?" asked Richard.

"I have had no instructions about his motives," Master
Albert, the wall-eyed lawyer, spoke coldly. "I am here to
make the formal offer. Lodgings shall be found for you at
the German Steelyard in London, and it is Master Conrad's
wish that you travel through France." The occasion un-
luckily did not permit Master Albert to plunge into the
reminiscences of his own stay in Paris but a gentle sigh
might here surely be allowed him. "I'm also instructed to

tell you that if your work is not satisfactory, there is a six months' notice, to be operable mutually, and it's Master Conrad's wish that you make your report once a year—at St. Pirim's Wharf."

"Which is a good distance from Stephen's Light," remarked Richard, and the lawyer said nothing.

A small oak table stood between them with a dish of fruit and a stone jar of wine. Richard, partly to hide his confusion, partly to gain time for his answer, moved the jar a little nearer to Master Albert. But the lawyer did not even shake his head: he merely ignored the wine. He had not wanted to be sent on such a mission at all but, his reluctance overcome by Conrad's abrupt persuasion, Master Albert had gone to the guildhall. He sat in the chair, his shoulders erect and his eyes cold. It was a dry, windy day, with clouds of grey-yellow dust swirling about in the streets. Master Albert felt thirsty but he would not drink. Let the gentlemen of the Council pet and cosset that young rascal as much as it pleased them all because he had come back pretending to be ready to pay the fines. Master Albert could never forget the injury by him inflicted. Let Sabina's father make a fool of himself in offering employment to such a man! That was of no concern to Master Albert. Dissuade his old friend he could not. Approve of the plan he would not. He sat there as a lawyer, and the articles of that agreement began and ended the matter for him. He cleared his throat and hoped he would soon get home, be rid of his heavy formal gown, and have good old Rhenish brought him by his wife.

"Well," said Richard at last, "it's true that I've been to England on some occasions—but I'm still puzzled and you sit here and tell me nothing at all." He paused, hoping for some communication from Master Albert and, none coming, Richard shrugged. "Lodgings in London, did you say? But I wouldn't be in London all the time. There's York and Lincoln and Stamford, too—"

"I know nothing of that country. Your lodgings are to be in London. Are those places in its neighbourhood?"

"Indeed, no," said Richard, and again Master Albert wished the young man would stop pushing the stone jar towards him.

"And the wool you buy is to be shipped direct to Hamburg."

"Yes, I understand."

Master Albert's yellow stumpy fingers tapped on the papers.

"The articles are all set out clearly. There's one condition, however, which is necessarily left out of the agreement. As I have told you, the annual report will be taken to St. Pirim's Wharf. You are not to appear at Stephen's Light."

"And need that be turned into a formal condition?" asked Richard almost too calmly.

"I can't answer such a question. These are my instructions. Your report is to be made round about St. John's Day."

"When do you want my answer?"

"Now," Master Albert told him.

"And did—er—Master Conrad expect me to accept his offer?"

"You don't suppose a lawyer is likely to discuss his clients with you, do you?"

Richard said nothing. He got up and, hands behind him, strolled to the little window. It offered him no other landscape than that of a narrow cobbled yard with a man in a faded blue doublet sponging a horse in the corner. In less than a minute Richard came back to the table.

"All right. Please let me sign the paper."

"But you haven't read it—"

"You've told me all about the conditions, haven't you?"

"That's not enough," protested Master Albert, his training gaining over his loathing of Richard. "Young man, who but a fool would sign a paper without reading it?"

"But I am a fool," said Richard, picking up a quill, "and you'll forgive me, Master Albert, but you're another because you wouldn't have come here otherwise, and Master Conrad's foolishness—"

"Stop! I can't allow you to speak of him in such terms."

Richard shrugged.

"But you've rather forced my candour, Master Albert. Now let me sign at once."

He dipped the quill, he wrote his name, and had the paper sanded in less time than it took the lawyer to realize his difficult mission was ended. He hurried away—to a cup of wine he thought he had deserved, and Richard took to pacing the room up and down.

The affair rather suggested a hem of indifferent cloth being tacked on to a gown of rich velvet. He had come back by virtue of a compulsion he could not account for. However, unconsciously, Richard had staked everything on a single turn of pitch and toss, and he had won. The city fathers had interpreted his intention in letters of silver and gold. Richard could not say if they were right or wrong because he had no very clear idea of his own intention. He had heard of Lady Augusta's threatening letters but he knew well that no head of a religious house could ride a high horse in an independent town. He had also heard that some burghers in the city were thinking of offering him permanent employment. He knew now that he would never have accepted any work in the city. He had toyed with some vague plans of his own. The fines, duly paid, had certainly depleted what resources of his there had been at the bankers at Lübeck, and work of a kind he must have. He had thought of approaching King Vladislaz in Bohemia, or the Margrave of Bradenburg. Richard had, after all, met merchants of note in parts of Asia Minor, and such connections carried much value.

But Richard had never expected any offer to come to him from Conrad the mercer. The two men had met but once at a distance enabling them to forego the exchange of glance or word. Richard certainly knew of Conrad's refusal to accept any part of the fine paid into the city funds. He also knew of Sabina's position at Stephen's Light. So far, he had not met her. The offer, its origins to him unknown, inevitably humiliated him in that he was forbidden all future access to Stephen's Light. None the less, the same compulsion which had made Richard return to the city from Genoa, now made him pledge his acceptance to Master Albert.

Left alone in the room, Richard steeled himself to consider nothing except the purely business side of the offer. England would certainly be better than any place in Asia Minor. He had been there; he spoke the language not too badly, and he liked the people. There was a dynastical war going on but that would hardly affect a foreigner. Sheep must be sheared, wool clipped, weighed and sold even if the House of Lancaster fought the House of York. And he had paid one or two fleeting visits to the Steelyard in London, and had a few faint memories of Yorkshire. Much of it all would be new to him and the mere idea of the newness was enough to hearten him—always so long as he considered it all in severely business terms.

But here, inconsequentially, Richard remembered the little lute left behind in Genoa. Once, he had loved to play it. And he also remembered a light French song by him sung one evening at Stephen's Light and Sabina's face as she sat, deep in listening.

He left the house hurriedly and plunged down a narrow shadowy street leading down to the river bank. He hoped he might find a boat to hire there, and he also hoped he would find the bank deserted. So it was—except for a few women so busily gossiping—as they thumped their linen, that they had no leisure to spare for a stranger. Richard must wait for his boat a little. He sat down on the warm stubbly grass, the women's shrill voices beating against his consciousness.

"It's said in their books somewhere that lard is to be eaten on Sundays only, and they guzzle it every day, I know. My husband's niece works in the kitchens on the Island. She doesn't see lard every day, not she!"

"Lard's nothing! They get finest wheaten bread and egg soup for breakfast, too. They'd a great lady to stay there, and they all had roast pheasants and a great pike in plum jelly for dinner! Ah yes, go on licking your lips, dears! Not

for the likes of us to serve God and the Holy Lady! What
will you?"

"Nothing for us but to swallow our pottage and be thankful for the sour ale when we get it! And that's not often
either—but then we're not in religion."

At last, a boat was free to hire and Richard, flinging a
coin at the boatman, rowed a little way down towards the
meadows owned by the monks of St. Eugene. There he
moored the boat, leapt ashore and, coming to a clump of
juniper trees half-way up the meadow, he threw himself
down. The meadow rose upwards to the orchards of Stephen's Light. He could see the rose-red flutings of its several chimneys. He stared, his chin propped in both hands.
He had no idea what had compelled him to leave his room
for the meadow. He stared at the chimneys and the trees
planted by Sabina's grandfather. Under that same roof he,
Richard, had lied so easily and pleasantly. There, too, he
had plighted his troth but to break it without a moment's
reflection.

Suddenly he guessed that it was Sabina who had urged
her father to offer him, Richard, the post in London. The
mordantly expressed terms of his employment were now
clear to him. They would use him as a tool—and no more.

"I must refuse it," Richard thought, at brush with anger,
bitterness and a sharp-fanged sense of humiliation. "I was
a fool not to say so to Master Albert."

And here he remembered his hurried signature sprawled
at the foot of the agreement. He had once dishonoured a
far more binding promise. There seemed no reason why he
should hesitate to dishonour a much less compelling agree-

ment, but he did so hesitate. Presently, he saw a figure appear at the little gate at the very top of the meadow. The distance was so great that Richard could see little more than a faint rose drift of a gown, but instantly he leapt to his feet and ran back to the boat.

Within a week he left the city by the west gate for Strasburg and Paris.

PART VII

"Your Heart in My Heart..."

A FEW months had passed. The mission to Stephen's Light was now little more than an uncomfortably coloured memory to Dame Lucia and Dame Blanche. They had brought an accurate enough report to Lady Augusta. They had held a chapter and agreed unanimously—with Dame Elizabeth's dissenting opinion cleverly silenced by Dame Cosima—that the affront to the dignity of the house far outweighed the appalling sentiments expressed by Sabina. Alone, Dame Elizabeth was later heard to say that she had not expected any different outcome. The matter was settled by sending a letter to Rome, its wording carefully shorn of the least ambiguity: Sabina, daughter of Conrad the mercer, on being invited to enter the House of Our Lady and St. Matthias, the Apostle, had refused to do so. What she had said, argued Lady Augusta, was of no concern to anyone, and she reminded the ladies that an accusation of heresy might all too easily involve them in fresh difficulties with the burghers.

Moreover, her own hands were full. She was still pursuing the difficult matter of Dame Adela's dowry, and her temper might have been trying beyond all endurance were it not for the happy news from Brunswick which announced the death of a distant cousin together with the bestowal of an ample legacy to the house.

About that time, Rowena, the head cook, decided that she had reached the end of her forbearance with Minnie, who had forgotten to stir the larded milk so that the carefully prepared mixture had curdled and must be thrown away. Rowena immediately remembered all the mislaid skillets, dented cauldrons and broken spoons which liberally signposted the years of Minnie's servitude in the kitchens.

"Let the wench go and work elsewhere, Madam," Rowena begged Dame Anna. "She gives me the shivers every time I look at her. The Holy Lady knows that I've tried to be kind to her after a fashion, but nothing's been any good. She looks at you as though she were a damned soul and you were answerable for it, if you know what I mean, Madam."

Dame Anna certainly did not know. Nor was she sure if she would recognize Minnie at sight. None the less, Dame Anna agreed politely. Dame Lucia and Dame Blanche at once decided that there was no need to trouble Lady Augusta about such an insignificant matter. Let the girl be sent to work in the kitchen gardens, they told Dame Anna.

Minnie heard and could not believe her ears. This surely was freedom! And more! This was a foretaste of the golden-floored paradise! To be sent away from the smoky, greasy kitchens with their troubling drifts of spices she might not eat, their deafening clatter of iron against iron, their steam and heat! To be sent away from roofs and walls into a world where she could breathe, away from the perpetual hostility of people, where she could stay happy with pigs rootling under old apple trees, and near beehives, with the good air smelling of earth and dung and rain! There would, of course, be men at work, but the kitchen gardens were spacious, and Minnie realized that—at least, she would have God's free skies overhead instead of the dark imprisoning menace of the raftered ceilings in the kitchens.

The very first morning she came on a linnet with a wounded wing, and tried to nurse it. Yet it died between her palms. The hoe flung aside, Minnie began scrabbling in the ground at the foot of an old plum tree. Here she would bury the small thing and mark the place with a stone. Scrabbling, she came on an oblong red-rose stone about the size of a filbert kernel. Squatting with her back to the path, Minnie rubbed the moist earth off the stone. It seemed a pretty enough bauble to her. She turned it about and about, and loved the sun playing on it. She had found it, and therefore, as she thought, it belonged to her pretty much in the same fashion as her own fingers and toes. She knelt, cupping the stone in both hands, and thus did Dame Griselda find her.

Nobody ever thought Dame Griselda to be of the least importance. Her birth certainly answered all the requirements but her dowry had been rather negligible, to say the very least. She had in consequence never been given any office on the Island. Lady Isabella would snap at her. Lady Augusta ignored her, and the other ladies always managed to escape listening to her complaints about the food, the weather, and a mysterious pain in her left knee. She had been a shadow and a cipher, but it fell to her to find Minnie that morning.

"What have you got there?"

Minnie screamed and tightened her clasp. Dame Griselda stooped, slapped her face, and wrenched open the small, grubby hands.

"Ah," she said in a deeply satisfied voice, "you must have stolen it, of course. You were just about to bury it under that tree, weren't you? And have you ever heard what can be done to thieves?" She smiled pleasantly and added a ghoulish detail or two, and Minnie screamed again. Dame Griselda rubbed the stone with the edge of her veil, looked, breathed on the stone a little, and rubbed still harder. It took to shining so fiercely that Minnie's heart ached for the sheer beauty of it. Dame Griselda called to one of the men to keep Minnie in rigorous custody, carefully placed the stone in her pouch, and made straight for the abbess's lodgings only to be told that Lady Augusta was engaged.

"But she must see me. It's most important. Indeed, it concerns the whole house."

Lady Augusta was examining the details of the legacy from Brunswick. She frowned.

"What's the matter? Take care not to disturb me with a foolish story. If your shoulder still pains you, go to the infirmary."

"It's my left knee, my lady," said Dame Griselda incautiously, and Lady Augusta stamped her foot.

"Well, what is the matter?"

Miraculously wise for once, Dame Griselda said nothing. She curtseyed for the second time and laid the jewel on the table. Lady Augusta's fingers dropped the quill.

"Gracious, wherever did you find it? It must be the great rose ruby given by the Emperor Sigismund to Lady Theodora. I heard about it being lost from my Aunt, Dame

Louisa, but, of course, you would know nothing about that. I was only a novice then. It was supposed to have been stolen, now I come to think of it, not lost. . . ."

Her hands meekly folded, Dame Griselda told the story. Three or four ladies, standing in the doorway, heard it excitedly. None chose to remember that the Emperor Sigismund had been dead for more than forty years and that Lady Theodora had ended her abbacy—to the intense relief of the house—fully fifteen years before Minnie came to the Island. To all the ladies it was evident that the girl had stolen it and that she had meant to hide it. Dame Griselda, coming down the abbess's stairway, smiled, conscious of her great hour. Not a lady but had ample leisure to listen to her repeated recital of the brief scene in the kitchen gardens, and after dinner Dame Anna even shared her private hoard of comfits with Dame Griselda. Meanwhile, two women from the farmyard were directed to give a hard beating to Minnie, whose ultimate fate was to be decided at Lady Augusta's pleasure.

When evening fell, Minnie, bruised and bleeding, hungry and dumb with misery, was pushed into a barn behind the stables. It took her some time to notice a hole in a wall, and by dint of superhuman efforts she scrambled through the hole. In the dark, she made for the lake shore. She had no plans and no urges. All she longed for was to escape from the Island, and fortune smiled on her for the first time in her life. Minnie stumbled on a little boat.

She never remembered rowing across to the mainland and leaping ashore. Misery and panic driving her on and on, Minnie stumbled up a steep thick wood and presently struck a road. With no sense of any bearings in her, she tramped on and on until sheer exhaustion gained over the terror, and she tumbled to sleep among a clump of gorse bushes. She woke early enough and at once plodded on. Dawn had long broken when she saw the city gates at what seemed an incredible distance but somehow Minnie succeeded in covering it. Cloudily aware of a huddle of hovels nestling close to the city walls, she exercised a daring which had been dormant all her days, and knocked at the first door to beg for some water and a crust.

Meanwhile, Dame Griselda's triumph ended in a disaster. The two farm women came to the barn, unlocked the door, and at once remarked the hole in the wall. They were busily and volubly accusing each other of negligence when a gardener, passing, caught the drift of the trouble and ran to tell the story to the portress. Everybody at leisure, including the forty-five ladies, made for the lake shore, and it was at first thought that Minnie had drowned herself in the lake, and the ladies remembered that they were not allowed to pray for suicides. But that same afternoon, a bailiff, returning from the mainland, had a hurried interview with Dame Lucia. At supper, Dame Cosima was able to say to Dame Hildegard:

"Really, Madam, Dame Griselda should have been more certain of her facts. What did anything matter so long as the Emperor's ruby was restored to the Island? And now I fear that the wretched girl may do us harm—for all she is an idiot."

The bailiff's story had certainly disturbed some among the ladies. None the less, it seemed pleasant to cold-shoulder Dame Griselda once again.

Minnie had knocked at the very first door along her way. The hovel belonged to Luke the weaver. By the evening, the low-ceiled room at the Silver Fish was crowded with weavers and others, and the full glory of the hour belonged to Luke. Matted hair falling over his forehead, his long thin arms gesturing, Luke repeated the story over and over again. The girl was but a poor half-witted bastard—but what did that matter in the face of Christian justice?

"They all but murdered her on the Island! Why, neighbours, you couldn't count the welts on her shoulders, and the smock all but falling off her back! The wife found a lump of cold porridge for her, and you'd have thought the wench had never seen food for weeks! She's skin and bone, and yet my wife's niece says that some of those stiff-necked bitches on the Island are that fat they can hardly get through a doorway!"

Tautened, angry voices rang up and down the smoky room:

"Yes, it's time they were taught a good sharp lesson, those ladies on the Island! And we must get the masters to join with us, neighbours! None among the masters has much use for those women seeing how they insulted one of their own kind!"

"Yes, indeed, Conrad the mercer's daughter not good enough for the likes of them!"

"Not a burgher ever invited over there, and the poor dole wasn't fit for a pig to eat!"

"Clear the lake of the vermin, I say! We've had more than enough of them!"

"That abbess of theirs once threatened us with the Emperor, didn't she? And isn't she a cousin of his? You see, folks, if she doesn't try and get the imperial rabble to take our liberties away!"

"Well, neighbours," Luke raised his voice above the hubub. "Talk is talk, but what do we do?"

"Get the Archbishop to tell those black witches to leave the Island—"

"Don't be a fool, neighbour! He's got nothing to do with them."

"Rubbish! He's hand in glove with that abbess."

"No, he isn't. They say he'd such a poor dinner there that he'll never go again."

"Still," Luke broke in, "he is archbishop, and all the church scum stand together in a manner of speaking—unless they happen to fall out among themselves over taxes and lawsuits. We'll go and tell him that we must have justice done. The girl's no serf for all she's a bastard. So, neighbours, up the hill we march tomorrow, and never mind their falchions and halberds."

From the Silver Fish, the men made for Luke's hovel. Minnie had just woken up, and was being given a plate of cold beans. They all crowded round about her, their eyes hot with anger and sympathy at once. Minnie swallowed the beans. Wiping her mouth, she stared at the people. It was obvious that having shown her kindness, they expected a return. Minnie leant forward and clenched her fists.

"I've seen her," she began huskily. "She's spoken to me. She was so good, and the ladies would have none of her. They meant to have her drowned, and someone came and rescued her—but they say that she died just the same. I

don't rightly know. . . ." Minnie stopped, but the silence
told her they were waiting for more.

"I suppose she's dead. . . . Yes, she's dead, and she
was good. I've seen her together with the Holy Lady, but
she's still so unhappy."

The men shuffled their feet. Their women stared fear-
fully. Luke cleared his throat. "Who are you talking about?"

Minnie's eyes went furtive.

"You won't beat me if I tell you—"

"Thunder strike us if we were to touch a hair on your
head."

"It was that young lady," Minnie mumbled. "The one
who they say ran away with somebody. She was so good.
She smiled at me. She was so unhappy, and they would
have none of her."

Pleased with their evident attention, her stomach incredibly satisfied and her fears allayed, Minnie mumbled
on and on. The men kept nodding their matted heads. The
women gasped and crossed themselves from time to time.
It was as clear as noontide that the young woman who had
run away from the Island was a saint and that the ladies
had all but murdered her.

At last Luke spoke slowly:

"Now I see why that young man came back into the city.
He never did break his betrothal, folks. He merely rescued
a saint, a good Christian that he is, and then she went and
died of the sickness, and, of course, he must come and explain it all to the Council. Little wonder that those witches
have been at his throat! Why, I've heard it said they want
to see him burnt alive."

By the next morning, not a citizen but was convinced
that the Island, having been privileged to harbour a saint,
had most callously and cruelly rejected her. Luke's little
hovel was constantly crowded with insatiably curious visitors, and Minnie, treated kindly, given ample food and
drink, sat on the floor and talked on and on. In her own
mind, at least, Dame Adela had long been an honestly
haloed saint.

[2]

They had just finished breakfast at Stephen's Light
when Conrad, about to rise, clutched at the arms of his
chair and fell, face forward, in among the broken meats
scattered on the table. Anna screamed and Sabina shouted
for help. Instantly, Hilda, Hugo and a few of the kitchen
women rushed into the room. There was no question of
carrying Conrad up the steep, narrow stairway. Hugo and
the women had him moved to a settle, and there he lay,
his face turned blotchily purple, his lower jaw fallen, and
his finger-tips gone a dull blue.

Anna sobbed. To Sabina it seemed as though the end of
the world had broken over Stephen's Light, and for some
moments the power to think and to act was gone from her
so entirely that it fell to Hilda to do what was necessary.
Sabina, turned to stone and ice, knelt by the settle, half-
aware of the whispers and the bustle going on in the room.
They tried to revive Conrad by cold water and burnt feathers. They tickled his armpits and the soles of his feet, but

consciousness would not come back to him. Presently, a tall, grey-faced monk of St. Eugene hurried in. Conrad was bled, coloured unguents were rubbed over his chest, and a potion forced between his lips, but it looked as though none of the remedies could reach the heart of the infirmity, and Sabina heard the monk whisper to Hilda, who at once tip-toed out of the room.

Now the place was informed by little more than the heavy breathing from the settle, Anna's smothered sob-bing, and the cloying scent of the unguents. Everybody kept still, and when Sabina saw old Canon Bruno in the doorway, she remembered that the monk from St. Eugene was not a priest, and she understood. At once her heart went pounding as though she found herself falling from a great height. She saw her mother kiss the chased silver lid of a reliquary brought by the canon. She knew that she must rise from her knees, move forward, pay her own homage, and pray, pray, pray, and she also knew she could do none of those things. She stared at the frighteningly twisted, beloved face on the settle, and she wondered if he had already gone from the room and from them. She thought of all he had meant to her, and she knew that her mind could not begin to encompass the thought of his death. She could not imagine the counting-house without him, indeed, she could not think of Stephen's Light and not hear his footfall about the rooms.

But she steeled herself to be aware and to listen. The harsh, saw-like breathing still came from the body sprawled on the settle, and a feather-light finger of hope brushed against Sabina's heart.

"Now I must pray," she said to herself, her unseeing eyes upon the spirals of dust weaving a golden tapestry in the air, and then she heard the Canon's clear voice:

". . . *Suscipiat te Christus qui vocavit te, et in sinum Abrahae Angeli deducant te. . . . Requiem aeternam dona ei, Domine, et lux perpetua luceat ei.*"

"But how does he know? How does he know?" Sabina wondered within the silence fallen upon the room.

She never knew how long she knelt there. At last she rose from her knees and touched her mother's hand.

"Madam" she whispered, and then again more urgently, "Madam!"

But Anna heard nothing. Anna had gone beyond the comfort of voice or touch. The coif slipped to the back of her head, Anna knelt by the settle, her hands clutching at the hem of Conrad's crimson gown. She had ceased sobbing, and her upturned face seemed stony and still as though she would never cry or speak again. Sabina stayed by her.

At last, Anna released her clasp, and with the thumb and forefinger of her left hand removed a piece of broiled fish from Conrad's fur-edged cuff. The fragment between her fingers, she looked about helplessly, and Sabina stooped to take the little piece from her.

"Madam," she said for the third time, and this once Anna heard her. Slowly she turned away from the settle and seized Sabina's hands in hers so hard that it hurt.

"Child, child! And he couldn't even receive the Host—"

"All is surely well with him," said Sabina, and briefly wondered at the temerity of such an assumption but she would not unsay it.

Much later, Hilda came into the room, and Sabina went into the counting-house. The long table, littered with papers, ledgers, samples of multicoloured stuffs, the high-backed chair, the indifferent sun slanting across the deeply cradled floor, all helped to unlock the door which would not open whilst Sabina stayed in the parlour of Stephen's Light. Now she cried bitterly and loudly, and the tears eased and also enabled her so that she remembered that now—with the first, sharply blended moments behind her—it was her duty, and not Hilda's to arrange for the day's sad necessities. She rang the handbell, and when Martin answered it, Sabina disciplined herself to speak steadily:

"Ask Master Albert to come to the house. Go to the rector of St. Agnes' and bespeak thirty masses, and see to it that the candles used are of the very finest wax. Hilda will tell you about the funeral feast. Then get Grabo to choose three bolts of the best black cloth we have in stock and to send it to the house, and tell Maria the semptress to be here after sundown. That's all. Now go."

When a little later Sabina left the counting-house, Stephen's Light stood dark against the summer sunlight, all its shutters closed and the heavy leather curtain over the front door secured by an iron bar across it in token that no customers could be received that day. In candlelight and in the scent of spices the women's whispers rang hollow:

"Get the box of mastic from the storeroom."

"Fetch the lavender oil and mind you don't spill it."

"Get me another towel and more warm water—"

"Bring the candle nearer—"

"Fetch a comb somebody—"

"Sweet Mary, where is the head-cloth?"

Sabina went up the stairway, found Anna in her room, and clasped both hands round her mother's knees.

"He was not old," Anna sobbed. "Not old at all. How could the saints have allowed it?"

"They tell me that blood rushed into his heart and head, Madam."

"But they bled him. They bled him twice, and there was the relic of the True Cross. That saved Master Luke's wife when she had a bad fever and they all despaired of her."

Here a servant came to say that Master Albert was in the house. Anna shook her head. Sabina hesitated.

"We must see him, Madam," she said at last.

"Why should I see him or anyone? It's your business now to attend to callers even though I can't understand how it ever could be a woman's business. Still, I suppose your father would have wished it to be so. Go and see Master Albert."

And Sabina went.

So it began and so it continued. In between crying, telling her beads and watching by the coffin, Anna kept saying that everything was now Sabina's concern, and added:

"Your father would have wished it to be so."

A few days after the funeral, Master Albert brought Conrad's will to Stephen's Light. Anna, a long black veil over her face, went into the parlour most reluctantly and kept so still that they all wondered if she heard a single clause of the lengthy paper read so sonorously and slowly by Master Albert.

The will certainly surprised Sabina and the entire household at Stephen's Light. It astonished the city, and in due time it would astonish Conrad's numerous friends and acquaintance scattered all over the Empire. But it did not seem to surprise Anna. Motionless in her corner, she offered no comment except that she felt certain those were her dear husband's true wishes.

Conrad left his soul to the Blessed Trinity, the Lady Mary, St. Sturm, and all the saints; he bequeathed a sum to the rector of St. Agnes' and another to the cathedral for twelve requiem masses to be said every year in perpetuity, and there was money set aside for the charities of his gild. His great silver cup was to go to his cousin at Würzburg and his turquoise buckles to Martin. There was something for Hilda and smaller remembrances for every member of the household, but not a single ducat was left to any religious house, not even to the monks of St. Eugene, whose lands adjoined his own. Stephen's Light, the warehouses and the wharves, the mills, the monies to his credit at various banking houses, and the shares in the salt mine at Lüneburg, all was left to " 'my daughter, Sabina, to whose care I commend my wife. Should my said daughter die unmarried, all the aforesaid messuages, tenements, etc., etc., to be left to the mercers' gild in this city. . . .' "

Sabina, her eyes wide, almost forgot to order food and wine for Master Albert's refreshment.

"When did my father have the will drawn up?" she asked.

He told her, and Sabina remembered that it was just about that time when she had dared to make her first independent suggestion in what concerned the stocks of English frieze and kersey. For all her hesitation and daring, it had then seemed such a very unimportant matter. Now she knew that Conrad must have looked upon it as a landmark, and the will once again confirmed his belief in her. She raised a hand and found that her eyes were moist. She sat, unashamed of her tears. She felt surprised, a little frightened, and too deeply moved to say anything about it.

And at that moment she heard Master Albert say to Anna:

"You wouldn't have heard about it, Madam, but there's been a bit of trouble in the city—all on account of some servant-girl. A weaver's befriended her, and a crowd marched up the hill and beleaguered the palace for a day and a night though nobody could say what they wanted of the Archbishop. They were nearly all drunk, I heard, and it was hard to make out what they were shouting about. However, it's all come to nothing at the end." Master Albert sipped his wine appreciatively. "The workers are such difficult people. Why, I still remember when I was in Paris—"

"I wish you would tell us something more about the march up the hill," said Sabina hurriedly, but it appeared that Master Albert had nothing to add, and the story of the journey to Paris must again be heard at Stephen's Light.

[3]

The city seemed quiet enough, and Sabina, engrossed in the business at the counting-house, had heard nothing about Minnie's escape from the Island and the daily gatherings at the house of Luke the weaver. Stephen's Light, having buried its master, had the doors of a great barn opened wide, and crowds of tattered men, women and children trooped in to eat spiced beef and drink buttered ale in Conrad's memory. At the end, each guest was given a small coin and a candle, and prayers for Conrad's soul were asked by Hilda on behalf of his family. In the parlour, Anna's friends and neighbours sat and murmured condolences. Mulled wine and the traditional saffron cakes were offered to them. They all wept a little as they kissed Anna, but it was obvious that Conrad's will engaged their curiosity to the exclusion of all interest in cakes and wine. Some of them asked brief, cautious questions, but others displayed an eagerness which, as Hilda said, would have been more fitting at a market than in a house of grief.

"There was that fat Mistress Barbara, my pet," Hilda reported to Sabina, "and she said, 'surely, things are all upside down in the world when a girl is allowed to run her father's business. My own daughter would never be permitted to do so,' she said, and it was all I could do, my sweet, not to tell her that her daughter couldn't tell a ledger from a sucking-pig with the brain she's got. And there'll be many tongues wagging in that silly fashion, and never you mind their chatter! The master always knew best, God rest his soul."

"Have you heard any more about that trouble in the city?" Sabina wanted to know, and Hilda shrugged.

"It isn't as though I've had much leisure to get out and about, my chick. Oh yes, the weavers shouted a lot and all the rest of it. I suppose it's all calmed down now that they've got a bit more money to spend on ale at the Silver Fish, but I don't really know much about it."

Yet a few nights later Sabina was wakened by St. Agnes'

great bell ringing to muster. She slipped on her shift and ran out. Behind her, she heard Anna scream in alarm, and from below came Martin's voice:

"It's all right, Madam. I've got every man out of the warehouses, and the walls are well guarded, and there's enough boiling pitch for any rascal who'd try to poke his head in here—"

"Stay with my mother," Sabina flung at Hilda and came down the stairway. In the wildly flickering light of orange-red torches and rushlights, she saw Martin, his hair tousled, his leather jerkin flung across his shoulders.

"What's happened?"

He spoke in a lower key:

"I didn't want to upset the mistress, Madam. Folks say it's the men rising against the Island, but it's such a bedlam in the streets that I've had every gate barred and the wall corners manned."

"The Island?"

"So I've heard." Martin shuffled his feet. "It's just a bunch of weavers got together, Madam, and Hugo heard them shouting down the street that they'll muster and cross over at dawn. By all accounts, they're all drunk, and nobody can tell what mischief they'll be up to."

"But what has the Island got to do with them?"

Martin shrugged.

"Nobody knows for certain except that they know the Lady's been threatening them all on account of that old trouble." He halted, suddenly conscious of drawing near very thin ice. "You know, Madam, nobody could reason with the rabble."

"What about the city guard?"

"It isn't the city guard ringing St. Agnes' bell, Madam."

"I didn't ask about the bell. Where are the city guard?"

"Well, I've heard it said that the Island's none of their business. I'd say myself that the ladies have got enough men of their own, but I thought I'd better have Stephen's Light guarded through the night just in case the rabble came down our street."

"Yes, guard the house, and tell Hugo to saddle a horse for me, and I'd better have two of the men with me."

"Madam—"

"Yes," said Sabina. "You say the Island's no concern for the city guard, but it should be someone's concern. I mean to make it mine. Tell them to hurry with the horses," and she turned to get her cloak and her pattens, to reassure her mother, to say a few words to Hilda. She felt neither excited nor frightened: she had an odd sense of a heightened clarity in her thoughts. She must get across and she must warn the ladies.

Two men behind her, Sabina rode down past St. Eugene's meadows and made a wide detour to reach the lake at a point not too near the usual landing-place. They rode in silence, the men pinning their faith on the chance of finding a casually moored boat by the shore. Leaving the hamlet well to their right, they began picking their way through the wood which sloped right down to the lip of the lake. Once, long, long ago, that wood used to belong to the Island, and there still lingered thin echoes of a story about a young bride perished in the lake and her husband ending his days on the Island. He was supposed to have written a great Christian poem before his death, *Veni, Sancte Spiritus.* . . . Now the man's very name was forgotten, yet there remained some fragrance about the legend, and here Sabina remembered Dame Elizabeth telling her about a room in the north-west cloister which formed part of the ancient buildings and was supposed to be the very same room where the young poet had worked and died. On Sabina asking if the place was haunted, Dame Elizabeth had smiled.

"Not quite in the way you mean, my dear."

But now they reached the shore, and Sabina forgot the unknown young poet. She thought about Richard, now in her service, and she realized that he would soon be returning to the city to make his report at St. Pirim's Wharf, and she knew that she remembered it because she had not been to the Island since he left it.

They were fortunate to find a small flat-bottomed craft. One of the men stayed behind with the horses. The other, steadying the boat with an oar, helped Sabina to jump down, and they were off. Presently, in spite of the dark, she thought she could make out the distant outline of roofs and towers which should have been her home.

"At some such hour, they left together, and now she is dead, and he's dead to me." Sabina freed one arm from the folds of her cloak and dropped her hand over the gunwale, and the cold silken water almost burned her fingers. She heard the soft, measured plashing of the water against the keel, and she felt very much alone in a cold dark world informed with little more than a few sable-coloured memories of another crossing in the dark, a crossing she had not witnessed and which she could imagine so vividly. Why, that crossing might have been made in the very same boat which was now carrying her over to the Island. It was certainly the same water and the same skies, and Sabina shivered as though she, too, were involved in the shame, the futility, and the bitter dark beauty of it all.

Soon the man was shipping the oars. Sabina got up slowly.

"It must be long past the Nocturne time," she thought, and said aloud: "I may have to wait, Peter. Stay with the boat. I shall find my own way to the lodge."

[4]

Sir Hugo, the chaplain, who lived in the room above the gateway, had been in his dotage for some time. He never forgot, however, to amble along to the church and there to vest himself—with Dame Blanche's help—and he was still able to get through a mass and an occasional liturgical Office. Sometimes he provided entertainment for the ladies as, for instance, one Easter, when his very sonorous *Ecce, Terram Sanctam vidi,* instead of the customary *Vidi Aquam* inevitably reminded the ladies of his descent from valiant crusading ancestors. Sir Hugo had never travelled further than Augsburg, but that did not prevent him from imagining himself deeply familiar with every hallowed reach of the Holy Land. Lady Isabella, careless about his clothes and furniture, had indulged his dearest passion by lavishing books on him. Lady Augusta, duly remembering the serge for cassocks and the leather for sandals, had also built him a bath-house. That, as the ladies thought, should have been enough hint for anyone, but apparently it was not enough for Sir Hugo. He was pleased with the bathhouse because it yielded more space for his library, but his body and the water, frequently poured into a great wooden tub, never touched each other.

Now that he was so old, he slept but little and always fitfully. That night, on hearing the Nocturne bell, he got up, not for Office, but for the pleasure of an hour's browsing among his books. He turned to Wittelweiler's "Ring" and reached the passage where the lover ties a stone to a love letter, flings it up at his beloved's window, and badly bruises her head. Just at that moment something hit his own case- ment very hard. Sir Hugo thought that Henry von Wittel- weiler, dead these twenty years and more, probably needed a prayer for the repose of his evidently unquiet soul. Sir Hugo, a brief prayer muttered, picked up Albert the Great's *Liber Cosmographicus*, when the casement rattled once again and even more forcibly.

Then he decided to brave the danger and to poke his head out.

"Please open the gate to me," said a woman's urgent voice.

Sir Hugo frowned. It was much too early for mass, and no woman had any business to be standing outside the gate. Moreover, he longed to get back to Albert's book. He ab- horred interruptions, and he disliked the idea that his little casement might well have been smashed by a stranger. Still, it was a woman and not a ghost, and good breeding in- sisted that he should say something. He said it at great length.

"I am chaplain to this abbey, Madam, and you can't be one of the inmates because you wouldn't be standing out- side the gate. The head is the abbess who is probably asleep at this hour. There's also the sacrist to give out candles, and she always wears gloves when washing the altar plate, and I'm sure she finds it most uncomfortable. There's also the chambress whose office means that she must interfere with everything. And there's the portress. And they're all asleep. And I'm not a gate-keeper. In fact, I doubt if I have the key. Have you come for breakfast? It's much too early, but I've got some bread and a piece of bacon."

He drew his breath at last, and Sabina said as patiently as she could:

"Sir Hugo, I've come from the mainland. My name is Sabina. I was taught my letters here. You may remember me."

He did not, and he said so—but not too briefly.

"Please," Sabina broke in, "I must see the Lady."

"She will be asleep for some time yet. She hears mass in her private chapel, and that not very often. I know because I say it for her, and I can't remember receiving any summons for today. If you wish to see her, you'll have to wait. There's a little door to the left of the gate, and you can come up my stairs if you like."

Sabina considered the skies. Still slate-grey and sullen in the west, they were already brushed with faint pink to the east. Presently, a bell would ring and Sir Hugo go to say mass in the church. She thought she might just as well wait in his lodgings.

But she had almost to struggle for breath when she came in. Sir Hugo had opened his casement on hearing her voice outside. Otherwise, thought Sabina, no fresh air had found its way in for untold seasons. Books littered the floor, and layers of comfortably undisturbed dust spoke of Sir Hugo's obduracy in not allowing entry to any woman armed with a broom. The low ceiling, once prettily painted in red and blue, now afforded habitation to so many spiders that Sabina could not see either wood or paint for the cobwebs. A corner of the table had been cleared for the trencher but both bread and bacon had fallen on the floor, there to neighbour a particularly dusty folio and a piece of cloth which might once have been a towel.

The place was horrible. None the less, Sir Hugo's bow reminded Sabina all she had once heard of his exalted beginnings. He could not remember her, he certainly had not expected her, but she might have been an empress for the courtesy he paid her.

Sabina having politely refused both the bread and the bacon, he began entertaining her with a story from Mandeville about the earthly paradise where every well smelt of rare spices.

"But that, of course, is a mere fable. I prefer to think of the Holy Land, where is kept the lance made of the wood of the Cross. It shines at night like the sun at high noon. Seen it? Of course I've seen it. I go on my voyage there so very often. Somebody's written a book about a beautiful island somewhere, once discovered, then lost, and never found again. How very foolish that is! You can never lose what you've found. The real Holy Place is here, Madam, between you and me, in this very room. Indeed, I'd say that it was everywhere. It's all so very simple because the Lord came down for everybody, and you know it was so still that night that not even a blade of grass moved in any field, so holy was His coming down to us."

Expecting the bell about to chime, Sabina glanced at the

old man. Everybody said he was not altogether right in his mind. Now Sabina wondered if that could at all be true: he spoke so sensibly, and what he said was true though few people in her world cared to talk much of those things. He caught her glance and patted her cold hand.

"In hunger, cold and dark, in war and pestilence, in loss and all sorrow, the Holy Places abide with us. For that He came to be among us."

Here, however, the bell began chiming. Sabina murmured her thanks. In the grey light she hurried through the familiar gate. Presently, she found herself in the garth, and, unfortunately, the first lady to see her was Dame Griselda.

"*In nomine Patris . . .*" she began primly, but Sabina interrupted the pious preamble.

"I've come to see the Lady, Madam. Please——"

Dame Griselda looked aghast.

"I'm afraid I couldn't go and take the message to her. She's very likely asleep. Do you know what happened about that ruby? It was I who found it, and yet they've blamed me for everything since then. You are Sabina, aren't you? And I believe you were supposed to come here, and then you wouldn't. It's all rather sad——"

"Please, Madam," Sabina's eyes went almost wild, "it's most urgent——"

"But, dear child, you couldn't possibly see the Lady so early. What's happened?"

"It's so urgent——"

"Is it a fire? An earthquake? St. Ursula, defend us! Can it be that the Turk is threatening the city?"

"No, no," cried Sabina, at brush with despair and then she caught sight of Dame Elizabeth at the foot of a stairway. Throwing an abrupt apology to Dame Griselda, Sabina flew across the garth.

"Madam, oh, Madam," she panted. "Please send a message to the Lady at once. Now there's no need for me to see her. I've come . . ." and breathlessly she told the story.

Dame Elizabeth heard her out, led her to a bench by the fountain, and hurried off to the abbess's lodgings. Presently she returned.

"Now come and eat, Sabina. You look all spent. You needn't worry—everything shall be done in time, and our bailiffs will see to the barges. But you must have some food, and then the Lady will want to see you and to thank you on our behalf."

"But I must get back to Stephen's Light," said Sabina, "I've left one of our men all alone with the horses on the mainland, and there's no need for any thanks." She paused in the manner of someone searching for apt words. "You see, Madam, I wasn't thinking of any of you in particular when I decided to come. It was merely something to get done. I knew my mother would be safe with all the men about the place."

"Then why did you come?" asked Dame Elizabeth.

They had left the garth and were now sitting in a small vaulted room off the north-west cloister, a very bare room with a little rough furniture, some books, and rushes strewn rather untidily on the stone floor. Sabina had never been there before, but she found it cool and pleasant to sit there for a few moments. She blushed a deep pink at Dame Elizabeth's question.

"Why did I come? Why, Madam, I said it was just something to do. Anyone would have done just the same—"

"I see," said Dame Elizabeth quietly. "Thank you for answering my questions so frankly."

Sabina looked up. It was surely the same Dame Elizabeth whom she had once both feared and loved as her mistress, of whom, however, she had not thought very much since leaving the Island, the same Dame Elizabeth who had never been singled out for any important office, who had gone about her ways nearly always alone, always unremarked. Yet, as Sabina looked at her, seated on a low stool by the latticed window, it seemed to her, Sabina—even though she could never have explained it to herself—that in Dame Elizabeth was the true heart-beat of the Island, something that affirmed and confirmed the deep purposes of the life there led, something that held the key to the secret lying so far beneath many tiresome and trivial surfaces.

"But I didn't really know how to answer your question, Madam," she faltered.

Dame Elizabeth smiled and urged a little more food on her.

[5]

On Sabina's return to Stephen's Light, she found it at first difficult to take in all the varied immediacies of life. She must listen to her mother's inevitable chiding, she spoke to Martin and to Hilda, and she assured everybody that all would go well, but she felt as though she were speaking of matters which did not at all concern the heart of life. Certainly, it lay with the Council to prevent a part of the population from indulging in violent gestures, and it was the business of Lady Augusta's bailiffs to take what precautions they chose to defend the Island. After all, it was fitting that God and St. Matthias should protect their own. But all such considerations were like so many wisps of sacking left about after a bale of cloth had been pulled out of its wrappings. You swept them away. You did not give them any thought. Your business was to examine the quality of the cloth.

So Sabina felt. But when she came to examine that quality, she knew she could not do it. She did indeed reflect —however dimly—on that very odd sense of calm and worthwhileness also that she had felt at the moment of Dame Elizabeth's telling her that a question had been well answered when she, Sabina, had not given any answer at all. The older woman's words had affirmed a friendship Sabina had never imagined to exist. They had also thrown light on a large and satisfying landscape. That was all. It seemed simple. It was also tremendous, and it pleased Sabina to think that she had been able to cross over to the Island.

For about a week Stephen's Light kept its gates barred. Then they heard that the weavers had indeed reached the lake shore, found no craft except one perilously leaking wherry, and in the end a violent thunderstorm had driven them back to the city. They had not reached the Island, but they still had Luke's hovel to go to, and Minnie felt that she had come into her own. Nobody had hit her or even shouted at her since her escape from the Island. There was ample food, too, though Minnie wished they would not keep her indoors so much. She longed for space and for

air, and she escaped outside as often as she could. And the
visitors kept coming, and Minnie duly continued her story:

"Yes, I've seen her—with the Lady Mary and someone
else. They killed her because she was good to me. They're
all so rich on the Island, and they'll have chariots and white
horses to take them to heaven, but they're not kind. It won't
be a poor girl's heaven at all but a place with spices and
roast geese and sweet flowers and no kindness, and there's
no Lady Mary in that heaven." Minnie stopped to drink a
little warm milk and went on mumbling: "I had a little loaf
once baked for me by a kitchen woman, and one of the
ladies saw me carry it away, and I was beaten for daring to
touch a piece of wheaten bread. So they said. But she will
walk again and smile at all the poor. She may be killed
again and again and she'll never be dead. She is in the true
heaven—close to the Lady Mary, where they have wheaten
bread for all the poor, and plenty of wood to warm you on
a cold night."

The women listened, nodding their untidily coifed heads.
At the Silver Fish there was much drinking and shouting
but they all remembered that none among them could swim
and nobody forgot the mysterious absence of all craft at
the landing-stage by the lake shore. It was finally decided
that the devil must have warned the ladies, and it seemed
a less wearying business to listen to Minnie than to run
amok in a wood at night. Little by little, the city stepped
back to its customary rhythm, and pedlars discussed
French girdles and Spanish leather rather than the death
of an unrecognized saint. At Stephen's Light, bars and
shutters came down, the unconcerned poultry clamoured
for their breakfast, and Hilda stood in the back porch argu-

ing with Maria, the sempstress, about a gown of slate-grey say to be made for Anna. In the counting-house Sabina and Martin were discussing the latest consignment of rose and gold damask about to arrive from Florence.

"It's quoted much too high," Sabina said firmly.

"They say freight charges have been put up again—"

"The stuff comes overland," she threw out a sharp reminder, and Martin shrugged.

"I know, Madam. That's just their manner of talking. Look at the people in Lyons! They say the prices are hardening everywhere."

"We must lower the demand," Sabina told him. "What's the stuff used for? Vestments only. A few royal brides might want it for their kirtles. That's all. And I know there's enough in stock. You will cancel that order in Florence."

He hesitated.

"It may well be quoted still higher in a year or so—"

"Not if the demand stops growing," she said. "And that can well be seen to. The price they ask is absurd. Cancel the order." And, having dismissed Martin, Sabina went down into the yard, and there found Hilda folding up the slate-grey say.

"A fine day, my chick. Just the right weather for St. John's Eve."

"Ah yes—"

"And the man's back in the city. They say he's lodging at the Black Eagle."

"You're creasing the say," Sabina told her, and thought, "Martin should have told me. . . ."

She turned towards the orchard where pears were already forming. The world had suddenly become very

noisy, she thought, even the hens were cackling about
Richard's return, and the blackthorns were rustling his
name, and the rusty winch by the well repeated it, the silken
swish of the milk falling into a bucket had the same echo,
and even the piece of say between Hilda's hands whispered
it. All of it was such foolishness, Sabina said to herself, and
she must indeed cease from thinking about it. She was glad
to remember her father's words about business being hard.
Of course, there must be business done at St. Pirim's Wharf.
She knew the man had done well in England. Even Master
Loeb at Antwerp had taken no umbrage, so skilfully had
Richard managed the severance between them. Also Sabina
knew that he had bought the wool at the right price. Yes,
there would be his report, and there was also the matter of
his wages to be seen to by Martin or Grabo, and there was
nothing else.

[6]

In a meagrely furnished room at the Black Eagle, Richard
was waiting for Master Albert to come to him. His pale grey-
blue hosen and the fashionably slashed doublet of green
and yellow were the only colour in the grim dusty place. A
trencher of bread soaked in red wine was before him and a
tall jar filled with the best Rhenish the house could provide. Richard was about to fill his cup when the door
opened.

"Why should you have sent for me?" demanded Master
Albert and, as once before, refused to drink in Richard's
company.

"Because it was from you that I accepted my present employment."

"I offered it to you on my client's instructions, and your acceptance put an end to my part in the affair."

"But I thought it would be proper for you to receive my notice," said Richard, and Master Albert's small eyes turned dark with anger.

"Why?"

"Because I choose to do so, and I thought it would be better to give it to you in person than—"

The lawyer broke in:

"This is outrageous! Have you forgotten the terms of the contract? Six months' notice is binding. You'll have to remain till Christmas. Is that clear?"

"Not at all. I'm within my rights. Six months' notice implies six months' wages. That amount is due me, and I have decided to waive it."

"But what's the matter? A contract, young man, isn't like an egg to be broken for your supper." Here Master Albert's face looked ugly. "But, perhaps, that's your usual method of dealing with contracts. Having dishonoured one, you wouldn't think much of dishonouring another."

If he had hoped to slake his anger by watching Richard's temper, he was soon disillusioned. The colour never mounted into Richard's face. He merely said, his voice as steady as ever:

"There's no question of anything being broken. My six months' wages cover it all."

"But don't you like the job? Or is it the English climate? Have you fallen foul of anyone there?"

"Oh no!"

"So there's no reason at all—"

"There is a reason," and the emphasis Richard put on the last word suggested a key being turned in the lock.

Master Albert rose from his chair and gripped the table with both hands.

"So it is for me to go and tell her, I suppose," he said heavily. "Well, I did warn her father that he'd no business to employ you, and I was right."

"And you should be pleased that you are right," Richard spoke so blandly that all words failed Master Albert. He eased his feelings a little by slamming the door behind him.

Richard ate the bread, wiped his fingers, and leant back in the chair. He had not expected any other reaction from Master Albert. How could anyone explain to a piece of dry leather shaped as a man that there were things which must be resolved at once or not at all? Richard had served Conrad. Sabina he could not serve. He would go and leave his report at St. Pirim's Wharf, stay on at the Black Eagle a little while, and then go out East. All matters were now concluded for him in Europe: he had paid his fines and had served an apprenticeship as difficult for his pride as—so he supposed—it was good for his soul. Conrad was dead, and Sabina stood in his place. Richard had heard much about her. He knew, too, about her crossing over to the Island, a foolhardy and generous gesture which reminded him of much that had best be forgotten. He had often been a knave. Once at least he had been a fool. He would never be a fool again, and he would try and avoid a knave's course in the future. But all of it concerned himself deeply and intimately, and was no business of a fat little lawyer with an inkhorn for a heart and cuttlefish powder for brains.

Sabina had scant leisure for Master Albert that day.

"He wants to leave our service? Of course, he must go if he chooses. Please see to the cancelling of his contract. You say he won't take the wages due him? Well, we couldn't compel him, could we?"

"But what are you going to do for an agent in England?" asked Master Albert.

"One thing at a time used to be my dear father's motto, and I follow it," she told him, and rang the handbell for Martin.

[7]

The man from Famagusta in Cyprus had a large belly, several chins, and a squint in his right eye. His long silken beard was scented, and all the ostlers at the Black Eagle stared at the magnificence of the sky-blue doublet slashed with red, but the man from Famagusta took no notice of the ostlers. He climbed up the stairway with as much alacrity as his shape allowed him, he bowed to Richard, he rubbed his plump dead-white hands, and spoke urgently:

"I was in Lübeck last winter, and in London also. I've heard about you. You're uncommonly sharp, but your sharpness doesn't annoy people. It would be good to have you on Cyprus as our agent. There are folk in Genoa who like you, and a very important person in Damascus might entertain you some day. I believe you speak a little Greek. That would be useful. Now I am on my way to Salzburg to see a friend. When I return here, shall I call on you again?"

"Why should you want me?" asked Richard.

The man from Famagusta twisted a big ruby ring round and round his left forefinger.

"You took away Master Loeb's custom, and yet you never exchanged angry words with him, and he's never wished you ill. You were daring enough to go to England and there you bought English wool—at your own price."

"At the market price."

"You made it the market price, and you managed it so cleverly that nobody really knew—except an odd foreigner or two in London. You left the service of the Hansa in apparent disgrace, and yet they still speak well of you at Lübeck. You must either have a good brain or else a fool's good fortune." Here the man from Famagusta bowed, one fat hand pressed to his stomach. "I prefer to think that you have a good brain. Shall I call here again and discuss it at our leisure? I have a barrel of excellent Hungarian wine in my baggage if that should tempt you."

"Please come again," Richard told him.

He hoped that the stranger from Famagusta would not stay at Salzburg too long.

It was just at that time that Lady Augusta heard from the Archbishop—not about Dame Adela's dowry but about Dame Melburga's revenues. It had all happened under her predecessor, and Lady Augusta had to turn to Dame Lucia's records to refresh her memory. Dame Melburga's father had been outlawed by the Duke of Brunswick and all his estates forfeited. Now, according to the Archbishop's letter, the case was settled very much in favour of the Island, and certain revenues would be sent on the signing of a few papers once Lady Augusta had furnished him with some information about a few legal details. Lady Augusta at once sent a messenger to the Dominican hospice to ask for one night's shelter. Dame Blanche and Dame Lucia were chosen to accompany her. That same day, however, Dame Elizabeth asked for an interview, and Lady Augusta gave it with a good grace. All the ladies agreed that the Island had been protected by virtue of Sabina's warning, and Sabina's visit, Lady Augusta realized, might have borne little fruit—had it not been for Dame Elizabeth's timely intervention and good sense. Indeed, Lady Augusta said to herself that Sabina would never have ventured to come across were it not for the sake of her old mistress. Therefore, Dame Elizabeth must again be given the charge of the library, the pleasure of the abbess's table at supper, and have her place in chapter settled well away from the draughty north-east corner.

"My lady, you are going to the mainland tomorrow?"

"Why yes, Dame Elizabeth. The city is as quiet as a mill-pond, and I hear that the Archbishop has twice sung mass at the cathedral."

"Could you take me with you, my lady?"

"I suppose you would like to call at Stephen's Light? Well, perhaps we should pay them a visit and take a gift with us, of course. A small relic, I think. Let Dame Blanche choose it before Vespers. Indeed, it is a very good idea, Dame Elizabeth. I think I'll have you and Dame Lucia accompany me. There is really no need for Dame Blanche to come with us."

At the Dominican hospice where the three ladies arrived with a bailiff and six outriders, the small fussy prioress ventured to commend Lady Augusta's courage.

"Of course, everything has been perfectly quiet, and that dreadful girl doesn't seem to excite the people by her stories anymore. No doubt you have heard about her?"

"I never listen to gossip, Madam," said Lady Augusta frostily.

Three palfreys for the ladies and seven horses for the men were waiting to take them up the hill to the Archbishop's palace. They reached a waste space close to one of the inns when Dame Elizabeth reined in. Standing at a corner was Minnie, a fairly tidy smock on her body and a beatific smile on her face. She had escaped into the open once again, she felt the wind about her, and the skies were over her head. So she stood smiling.

Dame Elizabeth was the only one among the ladies who recognized her. She turned her head away when Minnie saw the little cavalcade coming towards her. She stared at the gleaming cross on Lady Augusta's bosom, and the smile was at once wiped off Minnie's face. She knew they were coming to take her away, she must have talked far too much, and they were coming after her, to beat her, perhaps, to kill her. Minnie, the knowledge darkening her thought, screamed.

"St. Ursula, bless us," said Lady Augusta. "What a shriek! Is someone being killed?"

"No, no, my lady, it's only a girl," Dame Elizabeth said hurriedly, praying that they might pass on when Minnie screamed again just as the palfreys were drawing level with her, and Dame Lucia shook her fist at Minnie.

"Stop making such a noise, girl!"

That was enough. At once Minnie became articulate in a different manner. She had but one idea in her mind and Dame Lucia's angry gesture made her hasten to have that idea expressed in a single word. "Murder," shouted Minnie, straining her lungs to their utmost and, almost before the ladies knew what was happening, they were surrounded by a crowd of furious men and howling women. They turned —but the bailiff and the six men were already separated by the crowd.

What followed was a hideous nightmare. The three ladies were dragged off their palfreys, their veils and wimples torn off, their faces and necks clawed and scratched. The entire world became mud, dust and blood, and a frenzied inhuman chorus:

"Down with the Island!"

"Down with the nuns!"

"Give it them, every black bitch of them!"

"Down with them!"

A savage kick sent Dame Lucia sprawling on the ground. Dame Elizabeth, blood trickling from a gash on her forehead, swayed under a vicious blow yet held her own, but it was Lady Augusta who stepped back into the hardy and valiant centuries that had bred her people. She fought and she fought like a lioness. Dame Lucia was calling on the entire heavenly hierarchy to come to their rescue. Lady Augusta preserved her breath for the struggle. Grim, dishevelled, the veil torn off her head, her face and neck streaked with mud and blood, she gave blow for blow, kick for kick, punch for punch. But she stood alone against an enraged crowd. A stone aimed at her head missed and hit a window of the inn behind them, but another nearly blinded her. She swayed and spoke through clenched teeth.

"Keep on your feet, Dame Elizabeth. No matter what happens, keep on your feet. Nobody should fall till they are dead."

But here she felt that the world was growing very black and still except for the clatter of hoofs from a distance. She then heard Dame Lucia's agonized wail:

"It's the devil, my lady, it's the devil himself."

Lady Augusta swayed again and more violently, but she schooled herself to open her eyes. She could see but dimly for the blood running down her face. But she recognized the young man who had once, wearing an elegant yellow doublet, come to the Island.

"Fool," Lady Augusta said succinctly to Dame Lucia. "St. Augustine's always right! The happy fault. . . . The happy fault. . . ."

[8]

The three ladies had meant to pay a call at Stephen's Light. Now they must be half-carried across the forecourt. They knew little about it. They barely heard the heavy, nail-studded gate slam to behind them. They hardly heard the angry and hungry shouts of the rabble chasing them on foot down the narrow street. When they were more or less recovered, they found themselves in an inner parlour of Stephen's Light, Anna and the servants bustling in and out with salves and cordials, with towels, wine and warm water. Presently, their wounds were bathed, anointed and bound, and veils and clean gowns were brought in by Hilda. At last, Lady Augusta was able to move her swollen lips.

"I must apologize for such a disturbance," she turned to Anna. "We had indeed meant to pay you a call but never in such a manner."

"What apologies are needed, my lady? It's such an honour—"

"I would call it a very odd honour. I'm most grateful for all the help. I fear that my gold cross and the topaz beads must have got lost in that skirmish. However, I believe that Dame Elizabeth and myself gave them nearly as good as we got, and let's thank Our Lady and all the saints for such a timely rescue—"

"But it was surely the devil who rescued us, my lady," quavered Dame Lucia.

"Is it beyond the power of an omnipotent God to use the devil on occasions?" demanded Lady Augusta, and the theological rapier silenced Dame Lucia for the rest of the day.

Alone, in the heart of that inevitable bustle, Dame Elizabeth remained quiet. Anna had bathed the wound across her forehead and put a little salve on it, but Dame Elizabeth tidied her sorrily tattered condition with her own hands. That done, she offered to help the women but Anna insisted that she should stay quiet, and kept telling the maids:

"A cushion for the Lady's back, Gerti, and fetch the blue say coverlet for the Lady's knees. Fill Dame Lucia's cup with wine, Mathilda. Oh and another little saffron cake for Dame Elizabeth. Oh dear goodness, there is not enough fruit in the dish. Gerti, Gerti!"

"She's gone to fetch a coverlet for my knees, Madam," said Lady Augusta, "but I'm sure I don't need it."

"Oh but, my lady, the best in this house would hardly be good enough for you. What a calamity and what an honour!"

"And where is Sabina?" asked Dame Elizabeth.

She was leaning against the door-post. She had hurried out with the rest of the household, she had duly kissed the Lady's hand and curtseyed to the others; she had heard the terrible story, had bustled, fetched and carried with the other women. Now, in spite of her mother's noisy chatter, she thought that there seemed to be an island of quiet in the room, and it felt good, Sabina thought, to have the ladies accept sanctuary at Stephen's Light. It seemed all of a piece with so many other things, and here she glanced at Dame Elizabeth, and shy little smiles were exchanged between them.

Yes, they were all safe at Stephen's Light. Its stout gates would stand firm against any kicks and blows and, presently, she knew, the city guard would come and disperse the rabble, and twenty councillors would gather together to consider the matter. Mere shouting and even a few burned-out barges were all very well but such a violent trespass would not pass unpunished, so Sabina heard Martin say to the other men.

Martin, she knew, was out in the forecourt, and all the other men were there, too. She heard Lady Augusta say to Anna:

"Yes, indeed, it would be fitting for us to sing a *Te Deum* in gratitude for such a deliverance."

"Of course, my lady, and here are some lemon wafers and a little more wine."

To sing a *Te Deum!* Yes, Sabina could well understand it. The ladies had been rescued from a most unpleasant fate. Here she heard Hilda's voice outside the door.

"Ah, my pet, all the wenches have their hands full. Would you mind going to the trough to wash these?" and Sabina did not recoil from a mass of blood-stained cloths. Of course she would take them to the trough. She felt slightly dizzy. She longed for air, and was glad to slip out into the scented summer afternoon. She smelt honey, roses and musk, and stood briefly, idly, and breathed deep. She came to the trough and saw the clear water redden as she tumbled the cloths into it. She took out the wooden plug and watched the water run out into the narrow grooved gutter. Then she replaced the plug and stooped for the iron bucket when it was seized by two roughly bandaged hands. Sabina let go the bucket, took a step back, and felt very cold.

"You'll forgive me, but the bucket looks heavy."

He bent to empty it into the trough, and she stared at his hands, a big rent across his right shoulder, an open gash on the chin, the blood already turned to rusty brown.

"You should have come into the house," she said at last, and bent to rinse the cloths in the clean water.

"One of your men has seen to my hands," Richard said lightly, "and, Madam, I have no business to be even in this forecourt—except that I have now left your service."

Sabina said nothing. Her hands became busy with the cloths. At the other end of the forecourt, Martin and the men sprawled eating bread and sausage and drinking beer out of stone bottles. A pink-breasted pigeon strutted past the trough. The sun was hot upon the broad red-grey flags of the forecourt. From the opened windows came the sounds of voices. The ladies were there, and Dame Elizabeth was one of them. It seemed good to have Dame Elizabeth at Stephen's Light.

Sabina stopped rinsing and again removed the little wooden plug. She knew he was behind her, and she did not turn as she said gravely:

"It was a very wild business—"

"Yes. Fortunately, a few of the Archbishop's men happened to be near. Of course, according to law, they interfered in what didn't concern them. But the city guard were nowhere, and the crowd looked ugly enough. The Archbishop's men risked their lives, Madam."

"And so did you," said Sabina, and turned and looked at him. He would not avoid her eyes but he said nothing beyond remarking that the bucket was empty and he could fetch some more water from the well if she wished it. She did not answer him.

"I hear you lodge at the Black Eagle, so Master Albert tells me."

"Yes," he hesitated briefly, "and I'm soon going to Famagusta in Cyprus." He paused and asked again, "Shall I fetch more water?"

And again Sabina made no reply. Through the opened windows the voices reached her:

"Te Deum laudamus: te Dominum confitemur.
Te aeternum Patrem: omnis terra veneratur:
Tibi omnes Angeli: tibi Caeli et universae Potestates:

Tibi Cherubim et Seraphim: incessabili voce proclamant: Sanctus, Sanctus, Sanctus. . . ."

And, hearing, they both stood still.

Never had Sabina heard the words sung in such a way. She knew that she, too, wanted to thank, and she had no words of her own. Those other, infinitely purer and lovelier words were being chanted in a room at Stephen's Light, and all its stones and timber seemed to echo every accent. Thanksgiving for sunlight and for nightfall, thanksgiving for joy and for sorrow, indeed, thanksgiving for everything because God made all things and only a crippled understanding could not reach to the secret of Him behind a darkened hour and a broken delight. Sabina listened, and then an echo of the words fell into her heart. It fell there, it became a truth, a light, an inward fortress. Her face grave, Sabina looked at Richard.

"But I'd so much rather you did not go to Cyprus," she told him.

E. M. ALMEDINGEN grew up in pre-Revolutionary Russia and now lives outside of Bath, England. Born into a scholarly, aristocratic family, with English and German as well as Russian roots, she attended the University of St. Petersburg and was a member of its history faculty before leaving the country in 1922. She is a distinguished medieval scholar and author of many books on Russian history, as well as a number of books for young people.